Praise for THE RED GARDEN

"A backstage pass to the making of a single town's legends."
—*The New York Times*

"An absorbing portrait of a town, told through its unforgettable
people. . . . masterful."
—*People* magazine, 4 stars and a *People* Pick

"[A] dreamy, fabulist series of connected stories. . . . These tales,
with their tight, soft focus on America, cast their own spell."
—*Washington Post*

"Hoffman succeeds in spinning her usual folkloric magic,
if not more."
—*Elle*

"[A] spellbinding exploration of innocence, devotion, and
experience."
—*Parade Picks*

"Alice Hoffman infuses her trademark magical realism into
gently linked stories. . . . A richly and uniquely detailed history of
family and Americana."
—*Family Circle*

"Evokes the beauty and the wonder of the natural world,
whether wildlife or wildflowers, as a renewing force.
Like all legends, these express poetic truth."
—*Raleigh News & Observer*

"When I need a memorable book to keep me warm on a winter's night, I generally look no further than Alice Hoffman."
—*The Oregonion*

"Hoffman's writing is so beautiful it's almost painful to read. . . . [She] makes the magic she writes about feel so real, as though I could, at any moment, find myself in the town of Blackwell and the mysterious garden that bears only red fruit."
—ELEANOR BROWN, author of *The Weird Sisters* (*The Miami Herald*)

"In gloriously sensuous, suspenseful, mystical, tragic, and redemptive episodes, Hoffman subtly alters her language, from an almost biblical voice to increasingly nuanced and intricate prose reflecting the burgeoning social and psychological complexities her passionate and searching characters face in an ever-changing world."
—*Booklist* (starred review)

"Hoffman has done it again, crafting a poignant, compelling collection of fairy tales suffused with pathos and brightened by flashes of magic. Her fans, as well as those of magical realism in general, will be enchanted."
—*Library Journal* (starred review)

"Alice Hoffman, herself a shining star among American novelists, possesses the stunning ability to express the numinous in the most prosaic language. . . . One secret of her ongoing appeal, year after year, book after book, is her keen perception. And in *The Red Garden,* Hoffman delivers a body of stories that explores the depths of reality as well as its enduring quirkiness."
—*BookPage*

The
RED GARDEN

The
RED GARDEN

Alice Hoffman

Broadway Paperbacks
New York

BROADWAY

Copyright © 2011 by Alice Hoffman

All rights reserved.
Published in the United States by Broadway Paperbacks, an imprint of the Crown Publishing Group, a division of Random House, Inc., New York.
www.crownpublishing.com

Some sections of *The Red Garden* have previously been published in *Kenyon Review, Five Points, Boulevard, Southwest Review, Harvard Review, Prairie Schooner,* and *The Yale Review.*

Broadway Paperbacks and its logo, a letter B bisected on the diagonal, are trademarks of Random House, Inc.

Originally published in hardcover in the United States by Crown Publishers, an imprint of the Crown Publishing Group, a division of Random House, Inc., New York, in 2011.

Library of Congress Cataloging-in-Publication Data

Hoffman, Alice.
The Red Garden / Alice Hoffman
p. cm
1. City and town life—Massachusetts—Fiction.
2. Massachusetts—Fiction. I. Title.
PS3558O3447R43   2010
813´.54—dc22   2010006246

ISBN 978-0-307-40597-5
eISBN 978-0-307-72083-2

Printed in the United States of America

Book design by Lauren Dong
Cover design by Laura Duffy
Cover photography © Fabio Panichi/Trigger Images

9 10

First Paperback Edition

In memory of Albert J. Guerard,

the great critic, writer, and teacher,

who in his fifty years at Harvard and Stanford universities

changed the voice of American fiction and

also changed my life

Contents

The
RED GARDEN

THE BEAR'S HOUSE

THE TOWN OF BLACKWELL, MASSACHUSETTS, changed its name in 1786. It had been called Bearsville when it was founded in 1750, but it quickly became apparent that a name such as that did little to encourage new settlers. True, there were nearly as many black bears in the woods then as there were pine trees, but there were also more eel in the river than there were ferns sprouting on the banks. You could stick your hand into the murky green shallows and catch half a dozen of the creatures without using bait. If you ventured in waist-high you'd be surrounded in moments. Yet no one considered calling the village Eelsville, even though people ate eel pie on a regular basis and many of the men in town wore eelskin belts and boots. They said wearing eel made them lucky at cards, but when it came to the rest of life, love for instance, or business acumen, they had no luck at all.

The town's original name was always discussed and remembered in August, a dry yellow month when the grass was tall and bears ate their fill of blueberries on Hightop Mountain, a craggy Berkshire County landmark that separated Blackwell from the rest of the world. August was the time when the festival to commemorate Hallie Brady was held, but those who thought she'd been born in that month were mistaken. In fact, she had been born in Birmingham, England, on the sixteenth of March into unhappy circumstances. An orphan, long on her own, she'd been forced to find employment at a hatmaker's at the age of eleven. It was an unsavory situation that included more than merely fashioning hatbands out of black ribbon. The factory owner lurked close by, running his hands over Hallie's pale, freckled skin as though he owned her. She bided her time. She was the sort of person ready to face the wilderness, a young woman certain she had nothing more to lose. When compared to her childhood, all the hardships of the Berkshires added up to heaven, despite the deep, nearly endless winters.

Even in the heat of summer, when there were mosquitoes skimming over the surface of the river and bees bumped against windowpanes, people looked out at Hightop and shivered. Not everyone was as brave as Hallie Brady, and the local people who followed the founders knew how killing the darkest months in these parts could be. They wondered how the first settlers had managed to survive that initial winter, when there were bears in every tree and the snowdrifts were said to be as tall as a man. Before Hallie and the settlers arrived, the far side of Hightop was unpopulated. The native people who camped nearby vowed that no man would ever find happiness west of the mountain. Hunters never crossed into that territory even though the woods were filled with wolves and fox. There were red-tailed hawks, deer, squirrels, and more bears than anyone could count. Still they stayed away. They believed some places were forbidden, and that men were no more the kings of all things than the bees that swarmed over the mountain in midsummer.

William Brady headed the first expedition. He decided that he needed a wife before he set into the wild, western parts of Massachusetts, a ready partner to help carry the weight of the journey. He met Hallie in Boston a month after her arrival, and before another month had passed they said *I do* and started out west. Hallie had been fending for herself ever since leaving England. William was the first man to ask her for her hand, and she quickly agreed. She didn't believe in romance, but she did have faith in her own future. He was forty, she was seventeen. He had already failed at everything he had tried; she hadn't yet begun to live. Hallie had the impression that the marriage was a mistake on their wedding night, spent at a raucous inn near Boston harbor. William had done his husbandly business, then had dropped into a deep, twitchy sleep. He hadn't uttered a single word during their lovemaking. Soon Hallie would realize she should have been grateful for that, but on that night she seemed absurdly alone, considering she was a newly married woman.

William had a single virtue. He was an excellent salesman. He had sold Hallie on the notion of their marriage, and soon afterward he managed to convince three other families to travel with them out west. There was safety in numbers, especially when heading across the mountains. The Motts and the Starrs signed on, along with the Partridges, who had a young son named Harry. Hallie quickly began to suspect she had married a confidence man. In fact, William Brady was running from debtor's prison and a long list of failed projects that included bilking people of their earnings. He convinced the three other families to pay for everything they'd need to set out: the horses, the mules, the dried meat, the flour, the cornmeal. In exchange, William would lead the way. He said he had experience, but in fact he had never been farther west than Concord. He led them in circles for the full month of October, a foolish time to start out across uncharted land, fumbling through the wilderness until an early blinding snowstorm stopped their progress. They had just scrambled over Hightop Mountain when the bad weather overtook them. Where they hunkered down, in the valley below, marked the beginning of Bearsville.

The first person who spotted a bear was six-year-old Harry Partridge. Winter had still not fully arrived, yet there was already snow on the ground. They had been living like gypsies as the men tried their best to build a real shelter. Harry shouted for them to leave their work on the rickety log house and had them run down to the meadow to see. The men laughed when they spied a leafy squirrel's nest up in the tree, which might have easily looked like a vicious beast to a boy from Boston.

From then on, that spot was known as Harry's Bear.

Go right past Harry's Bear and you'll find the stack of wood, they would say to each other after that. *Make a left at Harry's Bear and head for the creek.*

Such unconscionable teasing always made Harry's face flush. But he was not the only one who feared bears. The women— Rachel Mott, Elizabeth Starr, and Susanna Partridge, Harry's mother—were nervous when darkness fell. Food had been stolen from the wooden storehouse. They'd heard things rustling in the woods when they went to collect chokeberries, the last of the season's, barely enough to keep them alive. They saw footprints that were monstrously large in the muck near the river. No wonder they had trouble sleeping at night, even after they moved into the poorly built shelter where they could never stay warm. An ashy fire was kept burning day and night, airing through a hole in the roof. Smoke turned their faces and feet black, and several times they almost froze to death. They woke in the mornings with crusts of ice in their hair and on their clothes. They might have starved as well, despairing over everything that had happened in their lives since they'd had the misfortune to meet William Brady, if Hallie hadn't made her way down to the river one day, driven by hunger and fury. She could not believe how helpless her stranded group was. None of the men were skilled hunters. They knew little about survival. She felt they had all been bewitched by the mountain, ready to lie down on their straw pallets, close their eyes, and give up the one life on earth they'd been granted.

Hallie went out on her own. She tramped over the frozen marshes, ignoring the patches of briars. When she got to the riverside, she took a rock and smashed through the skim of ice over the water. Then with her bare hands she reached into the blackness and collected a potful of eels for a stew. They wriggled and fought, the way eels do, but because of the cold they were in a half sleep and Hallie easily won the fight. She had come all the way from England and she didn't intend to die her first winter out, not on the western side of this high dark mountain. After that, she built traps out of twigs and rope and, with Harry beside her, began to catch rabbits in the meadow. It was November by then, and above the mountain the sky turned a luminous blue late in the day, like ink spilling out on a page. Hallie and Harry could see their breath puffing into the air as they traipsed through the woods. They could hear the rabbits scrambling underneath the traps when they were caught. It was true; rabbits cried. They sounded like children, shivering and lost.

Harry felt sorry for the rabbits and wanted to keep them as pets, but Hallie patiently explained that a pet was of no use to a dead person. Without food, they would all be lost. She made her point when she firmly broke the rabbits' necks. She next concocted a net out of a satin skirt she'd bought in Birmingham, an article of clothing she had done terrible things in order to afford. That was the way she had earned her fare to Boston as well. That man who had lingered beside her had been willing to pay just to touch her. When he had, she would think about the world she was about to find, a wilderness where tall trees sheltered you, where heaven was so close by you could see its vast reaches.

William Brady laughed at her when she set off. He said women weren't hunters and that she'd freeze her fingers off in the cold, but she went out into the snow, the poorly made door wobbling on its nailed hinges as it slammed shut behind her. She was patient enough to catch trout in the creek that she had decided to call Dead Husband's Creek. It was just a wishful thought on Hallie's part, and it always made her and Harry laugh as they fished together. *How many dead husbands could you fit in the river? Oh, one would be just enough.* When the trout were fried in a black cast-iron pan they were delicious, even though there was no salt or rosemary to use for flavoring.

At night Hallie slept next to Harry. She suggested that the child might need the heat of her body to warm him or he would freeze to death. That was most likely true—Harry was a somewhat delicate child—but this excuse was a way to avoid her husband, and it did the trick. William Brady was so exhausted from the never-ending work in their settlement he didn't bother to argue and claim his wife for himself.

IN THE DEAD of winter, the drifts were eight feet high. There was very little wood to keep the fire burning. The women on the expedition stopped talking. They had nothing to say. They were starving to death. Elizabeth Starr's hair turned white, even though she was still a young woman. Susanna Partridge, Harry's mother, had a ghostly look in her eye. The men could no longer remember how on earth William Brady had talked them into leaving Boston in the first place. He'd said something about owning all the land they wanted, everything for as far as the eye could see, but that didn't seem so appealing anymore. What they saw was the country of their own demise. Two of the horses and one of the mules had died, then had been eaten, by wolves, it appeared. The last two horses, one black and one roan, were kept inside with the families, in a dark, fenced-off section of the shelter. Once, Hallie thought she heard them crying, even though she knew that was impossible; horses weren't like foolish rabbits. But in the morning the roan was dead.

Hallie took that as a message from their savior: Those who didn't move forward were condemned to their miserable fates. That morning Hallie put on all of the clothes she owned. She slipped on William's high boots. She wore mittens and a shawl that the hatmaker's wife had given her when she'd left England. That man who had thought Hallie belonged to him had been wrong, and his wife must have prayed that the same had been true for herself. She'd whispered that she wished she was going to Boston as well.

"Those are my boots," William Brady said when he saw his wife ready to go into the woods.

Hallie already knew her husband was not a generous man. "What's the difference?" she countered. "You're not going anywhere, are you?"

William Brady was in a fog of regret due to his bad choices. He'd rather be sitting in debtor's prison than be trapped beneath the western slope of Hightop Mountain. He wasn't about to pull on his boots and go in search of his own cold death.

"No." Hallie nodded when he backed off. "I thought not. You'll just sit here and die."

She took a rifle from the shelf. When the other women told her she was mad to go—surely she'd freeze before she reached the meadow—she said she didn't care. She would rather die trying to live than simply give up like the rest of them. It was still snowing and the wind made a creaking sound. Yes, it was cold, but as soon as she left the shelter Hallie felt better. Being alone was a huge relief. She couldn't stand the people who'd come here to the Berkshires. They were fearful and small, ready to leap into their own graves. It was a while before Hallie realized that Harry had sneaked out, following in her wake, leaping from the pressed-down snow of one of her boot steps to the next.

"Go back," Hallie told him.

Harry shook his head. He kept thinking of those rabbits they'd found, broken and boiled in the big cast-iron pot, and how, when he closed his eyes and pretended they weren't rabbits, they had tasted delicious.

"Fine," Hallie allowed. "But you'd better keep up."

They went through the meadow and into the woods. It was easier to walk in the wilderness. Much of the snow had caught in the boughs of the pine trees. They took a path through the brambles, where the drifts weren't as high. The world was white and peaceful and quiet. A squirrel ran up a tree. Hallie aimed and fired, but she missed it. A bundle of snow dropped from the tree she had hit.

By dusk they were lost. It was the hour when the ink began to spread across the sky, only the dark was dotted with white flecks as snow speckled down. Hallie wrapped her shawl around Harry's head so that he looked like a little old woman rather than a frightened six-year-old. Hallie gazed at the falling snow and the endless woods. She was not yet eighteen. She thought that when she made it back she would name this area Dead Husband's Woods. She didn't think she would laugh at a name like that. She would think herself lucky to get out alive.

A star shone and flickered. Impossible since it wasn't yet fully dark. Hallie picked up the boy and carried him toward the flickering. She thought about the way the Israelites were led out of the desert. She decided she would simply put one foot in front of the other in her husband's heavy too-big boots. Because of this she was led to Hightop Mountain where the jagged cliffs were riddled with shimmery mica. Each bit of mica was like a shining star. Salvation was mysterious, wasn't that always true? There was a cave at the base of the mountain. Hallie thought about manna, how you had to be ready to receive what you were given. She went in without any fears of possible dangers. She had made her choice. Despite everything she did not wish to be back in the hat shop in Birmingham, plucking feathers from the corpses of peacocks and doves, fending off the attentions of the owner.

Harry was exhausted and freezing. He'd fallen asleep on her shoulder. That was lucky for him. He didn't see the bear in the cave. Hallie stopped. Her breathing was quick. Her choice was to go back out into the snow and die with Harry, or lie down beside the slumbering bear to warm their nearly frozen bodies. She chose the latter. The big bear seemed dead even though it snuffled. It didn't move and its eyes were closed. Alongside were two cubs, one dead, the other alive and nursing.

Hallie rested Harry Partridge up against the big bear and urged him to drink its milk. In a half sleep he did as he was told, still caught up in his dreams. The little bear who nursed along-side him mewled and pushed at the interloper, then concentrated on feeding. Later, Hallie, too, drank from the bear. She had never tasted anything so rich and delicious as its milk. She felt warmed to her soul. While Harry and the bears slept she stood at the mouth of the cave looking out. The snow was falling lightly and the world seemed a fairyland. Hallie felt enchanted. She felt as though anything could happen.

She brought the little dead bear home, dragging the frozen carcass through the snow. It was difficult going because she had to carry the sleeping Harry as well, hoisted upon her shoulder. She was stronger than she looked in many ways. But she refused to assist when they skinned the little bear and readied the meat. Instead she stood outside and gazed at the mountain. She hated the house and those people. She hated their weakness and their hunger. Harry woke from his dreams and came to stand by her.

He didn't remember much of what had happened, only that they had been lost and then had found their way home.

The next time she went to the cave, Hallie made certain to leave Harry at home. She cared for him as if he were her own, but she didn't want him accidentally telling the others where she'd gone. She brought along a bucket for the milk. She would lie to the members of the expedition, insist she had found a cow wandering the forest. They would be hungry enough to believe whatever she said. She didn't want those fool men setting out to kill a slumbering mother bear and her cub.

Now when she took the gun no one said anything about a woman not being able to hunt. On the way through the woods she heard a crunching sound in the snow. She thought about wolves. Her throat tightened, then she saw clearly and her fear abided. It was a man making camp, setting up a tent, whistling to himself. Hallie had dealt with his species before. She held up the rifle and cocked it. The stranger turned when he heard the sight click. He was a trapper. He threw up his hands and shouted to her in French, a language she recognized but didn't understand. He reached down to a stone circle he'd made in the snow where he kept his belongings, then held up some skinned rabbits, offering her several. *Pour vous,* he said. *Ici.* As if she knew what that meant. But she knew what she saw. The rabbits would keep them fed for days. Hallie approached. She felt like an animal herself, drawn to the scent of blood. Her shawl fell off her head. That was when the trapper realized she was a woman.

Hallie took the rabbits. She didn't believe in something for nothing. In return she gave the man her wedding ring. She'd lost so much weight it was slipping off her finger anyway.

"Go on," she said when the trapper seemed puzzled. "Take

it. It's real gold. Now go away." She slapped her hands together in an attempt to make him understand. She felt a wave of protectiveness, not for the people in the cold wooden house, but for the bears in their den. "Go back where you came from. You can't camp here."

The man nodded. His name was Flynn. He'd only spoken French because most of the trappers in these mountains were down from Canada and he'd assumed this woman belonged to them. He himself was from Albany and clearly understood every word Hallie said.

He pretended to leave, but instead hid behind some pine trees. Sheltered by their branches, he watched Hallie go inside the cave, then come out later with the bucket of milk. He thought it was curious. And yet he was enthralled despite the cold and the strangeness of the day. He felt the sort of desire for her that a man might feel for a creature he had never before sighted.

Hallie told her husband that her ring must have fallen off when she was milking the cow she swore she had found loose in the woods. In fact, Flynn was just then studying her ring, biting on it to see what it was made of as he stood beside the ravine near the frozen waterfall Hallie called Dead Husband's Falls. It was definitely gold.

The next time the trapper spied Hallie, he followed her. When she turned to see him and asked him what he thought he was doing, he looped his arms around her, pulling her close. He forgot his life in Albany. Hallie was not like any other woman. She was tempted, lonely. But before he could have her, she made him promise he would never shoot a bear. He laughed but she insisted. She had already come inside his tent and was slipping off her coat, so what could he do? It was a foolish request, and like a fool he agreed. He slid his hands inside her clothes, his body into hers. As soon as they were done, and he had turned his back, Hallie left him. She was quiet as she took the path up to the mountain. The mother bear was sleeping in the cave. The cub came to curl up beside Hallie. He recognized her and had waited for her. She petted him and sang to him, and for a time she could forget everything that had happened to her and everything that would happen to her still. No wonder Flynn found he was jealous when she left him. When he'd turned to find her gone, he'd wondered who it was she truly loved.

HALLIE BRADY SAVED her neighbors from starvation that winter. But instead of being grateful, they seemed to grow afraid of her, as if they were mere humans and she was something more. The women stopped speaking when she came near. The men made certain to avoid her, including her own husband. She didn't complain or seem put out. She took every chance to escape their company. Her life had veered off into the mountainside. She had found the place where she was sheltered, where the reaches of the next kingdom seemed close enough to touch. Soon she could find her way to the mountain in the dark.

When Harry turned seven, Hallie made him a little cake out of cornmeal and bear's milk. It was almost spring. The snow had begun to melt and where it did there was swamp cabbage that was edible if you boiled it for hours and held your nose when you took a bite. There were baby eels gathering under the melting ice, tender when cooked in their own skins. The first stalks of wild asparagus appeared in the marshland that Hallie told Harry was called Dead Husband's Swamp.

One day Flynn was waiting for her just beyond the clearing. He had never before come so near to where they lived. All winter they had lain together and each time she had run off afterward, leaving him wondering about her true nature. On this day he told her it was the season when the bears were waking. That meant it was time for him to go back to Albany, where, he now admitted to Hallie, he had a wife. He had loved Hallie, truly, but the mountain was only a place to hunt, there was no life for him there. Flynn wouldn't be back and she knew it. Albany was far, and there were other, better places for a trapper to spend the winter. Hallie didn't look at him when he said his good-byes. She already knew something was different inside her. And why would she beg him to stay? When she thought back to the winter they'd spent together, what she would miss most of all was the bear.

That night Hallie got under the blankets with her husband. He was surprised, but he didn't turn her down. She hoped Harry over in the corner wouldn't hear him grunting, but she was glad that William was loud enough to cause Elizabeth Starr to hush them from the loft where the Starrs slept. Hallie prayed this one time would be enough so when the baby came, everyone would be convinced it belonged to William Brady.

HALLIE WENT BACK to the cave once more. She saw footprints and pools of blood. She sat down and wept. The mother bear had been killed and skinned right there at the mouth of her den. There were bits of bone on the ground. Hallie felt that her heart had been broken. Like a fool she'd trusted Flynn's promise. He was a liar, like most men. She had worked so hard all winter to survive, but now she wished winter had never ended. As she was leaving, Hallie saw the footprints leading away from the cave, those of a small bear wandering off alone. She sank to her knees, grateful that the cub was out there somewhere, still alive.

She threw herself into work in the hopes that she would stop mourning the bear. The settlers began to follow her lead and became equally industrious. They snapped out of their gloom and worked hard all through the summer. Soon all had blood blisters on their hands. Tom Partridge chopped off half his thumb while swinging an ax, but even that didn't stop him. People were renewed by the simple fact that they were still alive. They were mindful of the many ways in which they'd been blessed each morning when they saw the first glimmer of daylight.

By November, when the babies were born—twins, a boy and a girl—the families each had their own houses. The new homes were built in a circle around a wild grassy area that Hallie and Harry had dubbed Dead Husband's Park. Hallie's baby girl was very beautiful, with eggshell-blue eyes and skin that shone with good health, but the boy was too small. He couldn't seem to breathe. He didn't open his eyes. That was when Hallie knew he wouldn't last. He lived for only one week. Hallie insisted on burying him behind the house, in the place where she'd begun a garden in the summer, to ensure he wouldn't be too far away. After the burial she sat down in the weeds. She didn't get up again. No one could urge her back to her house, not even Harry. She wouldn't hold her baby girl or even drink a sip of water. She wrapped herself in the shawl that the hatmaker's wife had given her when she left England. She wore her husband's leather boots, the ones she'd had on when she tramped through the forest that first time, when she'd found her way the way pilgrims do, following nothing more than her own faith.

During the day she was silent, but at night they could hear her crying. Susanna Partridge covered Harry's ears so he wouldn't have to listen, because every time he did, he cried as well. Rachel Mott had not long ago had a baby herself and she took in the Bradys' little girl and nursed her. She gave her a name as well, since no one else had bothered, calling her Josephine, after her own mother.

ONE NIGHT HARRY Partridge looked out to see Hallie in what should have been the garden but was now a graveyard. She wasn't alone. There was a bear out there with her. Harry rubbed his eyes. It was late, after all, and very dark. The night was pitch, the wind was rising. He thought about the time he'd been so certain there was a bear up in a tree in the meadow and it had only been a squirrel's nest. He remembered how all the men had laughed at him, including his father. Harry hadn't liked that one bit. He blamed himself for the name the men had given their town. Every time someone passing through said *Bearsville* he thought they were making a mockery of him. He wished the town was called anything else, even New Boston, a name that would not remind him of what a fool he'd once been.

Harry often thought about the time when he'd nearly frozen to death, when he hadn't had solid food for three days, and he'd run after Hallie Brady because she was the only one who seemed sure there was a future waiting. He'd had a dream about a bear then, too. That bear had saved him and sang to him and told him to hush. That bear had promised that everything would soon be set right.

In the Partridges' house Harry's bed was downstairs by the fire while his parents slept up in the loft. He thought what he saw in the garden of the Bradys' house was most likely a dream, so it was best that he creep back to his mattress, which was stuffed with late-summer straw. Still he worried about Hallie Brady out in the dark with a bear. If the truth be told, he wished Hallie were his mother. His own mother was distant and afraid of things such as thunderstorms and blizzards and bears. Hallie, he knew, wasn't frightened of much in this world.

When he woke the next morning, Harry wondered if there really had been a bear out behind the Bradys' house. Perhaps he should have rescued Hallie, or at the very least, called out. He was terrified to think he might peer through the window only to see blood and bones. But when he gazed outside there was only the patch of tall grass that marked the little burial ground. Hallie Brady wasn't there anymore, however. She'd recovered her strength. She had gone to Rachel Mott's house and taken back her baby girl, whom she renamed Beatrice, the name of her baby sister who had died at birth, even though everyone else continued to call the child Josephine.

THAT NIGHT HARRY Partridge sneaked out of his house. His mother had told him never to go out alone after dark, but he went anyway. It was growing cold. The sky was blue-black and still. All the brilliant leaves had dropped from the trees; only a few brown ones remained. Ice was forming on Eel River and skimming the pond Harry and Hallie called Dead Husband's

Lake. There were squirrels nesting high in the trees, the mark of a hard winter to come.

Harry knocked and when Hallie called for him to come in, he did so. She was in a chair rocking the baby, engrossed in the little girl's lovely face. William Brady was already up in the loft, asleep. The past year had taken a toll. It had done that to them all.

"She looks like a nice baby," Harry said in his most polite voice. He didn't really know how children were supposed to behave because he was never around them. When he thought of himself, he envisioned a small, fully grown individual, only one without the privileges of a man. His mother refused to let him have a gun, for instance. She wouldn't let him ride the horse, either.

"She is a nice baby," Hallie said. "Her name is Beatrice."

"I thought it was Josephine." Harry was confused. He always felt that way when he was with Hallie. As if anything could happen. He liked that feeling, but he was afraid of it too.

"It's Beatrice," Hallie said firmly.

Harry sat down on the floor even though there was some new furniture a peddler from Lenox had sold the Bradys. William was no longer poor. He'd been the first to craft expensive items out of eelskin—belts, then wallets, now boots. They were beautiful and waterproof and highly valued. The other men had followed suit, just as they'd followed him into the unknown Massachusetts wilderness. Peddlers from Lenox and Albany and Stockbridge were more than happy to trade for the fine leather goods, which they then resold in Boston at a higher cost.

Because of the eels in the river the Partridges had been able to buy a cow, the Motts some chickens and goats, and the Starrs could afford some sheep and a brand-new barn.

"I dream about bears sometimes," Harry said, offhand. He gazed up, curious for Hallie's reaction.

"That sounds like a nice dream," she replied.

"Does it?"

"A lovely dream."

Hallie put the baby in the cradle that Jonathan Mott had made for the infant. The Motts had been led to believe they would be raising the baby, since Hallie hadn't seemed the least bit interested after the other twin's death. They had actually seemed a little put out when Hallie came to fetch her own child. "Don't come by my house," Hallie had protested when Rachel Mott tried to stop her from taking the child. "Don't you even try."

The baby was dozing, so Hallie went to the cold box for a serving of the Indian pudding she'd made for Harry. It tasted of molasses and honey. It was so delicious Harry felt he could eat a hundred bowlsful. But before he was even half done with his serving, he heard his mother calling. She must have woken to find he wasn't in his place by the fire. She would most probably not let him go hunting with his father in the morning. She would say he was a bad, irresponsible boy.

Harry took another forkful of the corn pudding. Hallie was humming a little song. Her face was plain and pretty at the same time. In the firelight her eyes looked bright.

There was Harry's mother right outside, knocking at the door. He would have to go home now.

"Did you ever wish you had a different life?" Harry asked.

Hallie Brady nodded. She was looking right at him. "All the time."

❧

SIXTEEN YEARS LATER there were ten more families living in Bearsville, mostly from Boston, although a pastor from New York had settled in, along with a couple named Collier who'd been lost in a snowstorm, just as the original settlers had been all those years before. The Kellys stayed with the Mott family, then decided to build a house near the creek since Clement Kelly was a fisherman by trade. A well was dug in what became the town center, surrounded by black mica stones, and people liked to meet there and gossip. It still wasn't much of a town. When William Brady died, after a fever that left him unable to move or to eat, thirty-seven people attended his funeral, and that included everyone in town. The pastor, John Jacob, gave the epistle, and although Hallie declined to speak, Josephine Brady read a poem she had written about her father. She was a dreamy girl of sixteen who hadn't inherited her mother's instincts for survival. In fact, she seemed a target for the cruelty of the world. She was often stung by bees, for they were drawn to her because she was so sweet, her mother told her. She was also extremely bright, the only one in town who could write a poem. There was hardly a dry eye at the service by the time she was through, even though William Brady wasn't particularly well liked. He was a taciturn man who preferred to be left alone with his eelskins and his tools.

There was a proper burying ground now. The Motts' third son had died in a fall, and a traveling peddler had frozen to death before anyone had known he'd come to town and holed up in the meetinghouse, which was so cold ice formed on the floor. The Starrs had experienced the greatest portion of sorrow. Byron and Elizabeth had buried two of their six children—Constant, Patience, Fear, and Love had survived, but Consider had come down with fever when he was two, and Wrestling had taken four days to be born, his spirit having already flown before his body arrived on this earth.

A burying ground was the true mark of an established town. Theirs was at the far end of the meadow. It was a spring day when they buried William Brady. Larks and swallows flitted through the grass. There were tufts of white pollen drifting beneath the budding branches in the woods. Josephine Brady followed the wagon that carried her father's pine coffin. Her mother walked along behind her, with Josephine's intended, Harry Partridge.

"Now it truly is Dead Husband's Meadow," Hallie murmured to the young man who would soon be her son-in-law.

"I suppose so." They exchanged an amused look. Harry often dreamed about the year when they'd first come here, when there were so many things that needed naming.

Josephine turned around when she heard them chatting. "What are you two talking about?"

"Nothing, Bee," Harry assured her. It was the nickname Josephine's mother and her beloved used for her. Josephine thought it was because she'd been stung so often. She had no memory of her name being Beatrice; no one in town ever used that name, although her mother had called her Bee for as long as Josephine could remember. People thought Josephine was young and innocent, just a loose-limbed girl with long blond hair, but she knew more than people gave her credit for. She knew, for instance, that Harry Partridge was by far the best man west of Hightop, just as she'd known that her parents hadn't the kind of love she wanted for herself. In the winters her mother often went off to the mountain. Sometimes she didn't return for days.

"Don't ask her where she's going, because she'll never tell you the truth," Josephine's father said when he was alive, and so she never did. Her mother was an unusual person, quiet and self-assured and very private. She was able to take care of herself in the wilderness, for once upon a time the wilderness was all she had. She assured Josephine she was fine on her own, even up on the mountain. The strangest thing about her was the way she gazed out the window, as if there was someplace she wanted to be, some other life that was more worth living.

IN THE SEASON after William Brady's death, Hallie stayed away for several weeks, even longer than usual. When she came back, Josephine was already halfway through trimming her wedding dress. Mrs. Mott, who'd never had daughters of her own, had been helping with the stitchery. If a daughter's wedding was a glorious time, Josephine wondered why it was that her mother had looked happy until she walked through the door and was home once more.

The wedding was held in the garden. The body of Josephine's twin was still there. Hallie refused to have his remains moved to the burying ground, and she still spent a good deal of time in that garden. She bought seeds from peddlers for flowers and herbs whenever they passed through. Once she went to Albany herself and came back with three rosebush seedlings that had been brought all the way from England. She favored plants that she'd spied in the gardens of fine houses in Birmingham, the ones she used to pass by on the way to the hatmaker's when she was a girl. But she also liked local varieties that she found on the mountain: trout lilies, wood violet, ferns. Anything wild would do.

Josephine wore a garland made of daisies that complemented the white dress she and Mrs. Mott had sewn by hand. She was the first and most beautiful bride in the village. Harry moved into the Bradys' house afterward. He had always preferred it to his own and had been working all year to add a room for himself and his new wife. There were tended fields outside town now, and Harry and his father, Tom, grew corn and wheat and beans. They carted the surplus to Lenox and Amherst. They marked off their acreage with stone walls, carrying the boulders down from the ridgetop until their backs nearly gave out, proud of all they'd created out of the wilderness. It was a different place than it had been all those years ago, when there was little to shelter a man but the tall pine trees. Still Harry dreamed sometimes about that first year, and in his dreams there wasn't any hunger or cold. The woods stretched on forever and everything was white.

IT HAPPENED IN August, when the fields were dry and hot. The month was halfway done and there hadn't been rain for weeks. It was so hot that people went swimming in the river despite the eels and the dangerous currents. So hot Harry Partridge couldn't sleep. One evening he went to the back door to try to catch a cool breeze. That's when he saw them in the garden. Hallie Brady and the bear. By then the bear was old. From a distance Hallie Brady looked the way she had all those years ago, when they were naming waterfalls and creeks, when everything was a mystery and a revelation, and every river and meadow and snowdrift was something to be tamed.

Harry wasn't dreaming or imagining anything. He ran for the rifle that was kept above the fireplace, then charged outside and fired. He did it without thinking, with a hero's response, but in the end he was anything but. Afterward, when he dreamed, he dreamed about the look on her face, the tenderness there, the terrible sorrow. In that instant he saw everything there was to know about love. It terrified and humbled him and made him realize how little he knew.

By the time the neighbors heard the shot and came running, Hallie Brady was gone. She'd run off to the woods, her dress covered with blood. Although the neighbors sent out a search party, choosing men who knew the woods around Hightop, they didn't find her. Afterward, they wanted to skin the bear, make good use of the meat and the pelt, but Harry forbade it. He himself dug the grave in the garden. He worked so hard his hands bled. He had been attached to Hallie from the time he was a child, so of course he would be upset and want the job of the burial for himself. People closed their windows, and went to bed, and didn't think about it anymore. All the same, they could hear him sobbing. When at last he came inside, Harry removed the hammer from the rifle he'd used. He would never take up a gun again.

It was days before Josephine realized her mother wouldn't be coming back. Weeks before she stopped looking out over Hightop Mountain. She never asked her husband why he'd killed the bear or why her mother had run off. She never asked why years later, when they had been married for many years and had raised two daughters, Harry suddenly decided to run for mayor. The first resolution he passed was to change the name of the town. The second was to sign an edict for a yearly celebration honoring Hallie Brady in the middle of August. Some people believed it to be the founder's birthday, but it was only the mark of blueberry season, the time when people who knew the territory avoided Hightop Mountain, leaving it to the bears.

EIGHT NIGHTS OF LOVE

1792

THE TREE OF LIFE WAS PLANTED IN THE center of Blackwell. People said that when it bloomed, anyone standing beneath its boughs could ask for mercy for his sins. For decades a town bylaw forbade defacing the tree, but at night people took cuttings. They secretly planted saplings in their yards, wrapping the tender bark in burlap to ward off the cold. Such thievery was meant to protect the future of the town, which people said would flourish as long as the Tree of Life did. Should the original tree ever be struck by lightning or consumed by beetles, the cuttings ensured there would be others to take its place. In time the apples that came from these trees, the same fruit that had tempted Adam and Eve, came to be called the Blackwell Look-No-Further. Once you'd come to Blackwell and tasted these apples, you would never need go anywhere else. If the whole world beckoned, you'd still be happy enough to spend your life in this small valley in Massachusetts.

THERE WEREN'T MANY people who saw the man who planted the original tree on the day he arrived in Blackwell. He was John Chapman, who came to town with his half brother, Nathaniel. John was eighteen and Nathaniel only eleven. They were quiet and serious, and both seemed older than their age. They'd left home to sleep in meadows, under the stars. John had worked as an apprentice in an apple orchard, and as far as he was concerned his employment there had been a part of God's plan. He had a philosophy about freedom, one that had come to him in a dream, then had filtered into his waking life. He eschewed things made by man and yearned for a more godly and natural state. He believed that every creature belonged to God equally, a product of divine love and wisdom. Man and beast, insect and tree, all of it reflected the face of the Maker. John had been reading pamphlets written by Swedenborg, the Christian mystic, and the sentiment of charity as divine spoke deeply to him. He felt swept up in something far bigger than himself.

In Leominster, where John had been born, the streets were filthy. His neighbors had sickened and fought among each other. Many had died young. As a child he'd seen a man gun down his wife in the road. He'd seen dogs tied up and left to starve, children set out to fend for themselves. He ached to sleep in the grass with the sound of buzzing all around him. He dreamed of a time when there were trees everywhere instead of houses. Every tree was perfect, unlike human beings, especially the variety of tree that brought forth what John believed to be manna—the apple. When turned into cider and fermented, the juice of the apple was nearly holy in nature. The drink could transport a man out of himself, into a world much closer to God. Not drunkenness—that was not the goal—but an ecstatic state.

John and Nathaniel made their way easily across Hightop Mountain. They were young and strong, buoyed by faith. Each carried a sack on his back and a staff of apple wood from the oldest tree in their town, which had been cut down so that the main road could be expanded. That was the day John decided to head west. As he watched the gnarled branches of that old tree in his hometown destroyed, something inside made him veer radically from the path of other men. He had a yearning for heaven on earth, and that surely wasn't Leominster. When he walked out the door, his half brother was right behind him.

It was the season when the bears woke, when snow was melting and the air was bracing. Just sleeping in those mountains, waking to hear the rushing echo of the streams that formed the Eel River down in the valley, could induce near ecstasy. From a perch on the mica-lined crag it was possible to spy the town of Blackwell below them. It was the kind of village that needed manna.

John Chapman was tall and thin and didn't need much sleep. He had long dark hair, which he vowed he would never again cut. His face was angular and beautiful, but in his opinion an ant was more beautiful than he would ever be, a black snake more wondrous. When he first set off for the West, he decided he would have as little as possible to do with anything that had been man-made. The divine was in every human, as it was in him. The closer he was to the natural world, the closer to heaven.

He wore homespun clothes and no shoes. As he tramped through the countryside his excitement increased. For some reason he didn't feel the cold, perhaps because he was burning up with ideas.

He crouched down next to his brother and shook him awake. They had their breakfast, some tea boiled from mint and bearberry, along with a few handfuls of fiddlehead ferns cooked over the fire in the one pan they carried with them. John had vowed never to eat another living creature or to cause pain to any being. He liked the light-headed feeling that eating so little gave him. He was steady enough, sure of himself as he led Nathaniel down the mountain, then across the plain that people in these parts called Husband's Meadow, a field that in summer filled with pitcher plants and black-eyed Susans.

It was a small town. The sky was still dark, with bands of pearly gray breaking through. The men from the Starr family were already at work in the pastures on the far side of the Eel River, Harry Partridge was off fishing, the Motts were chopping down trees to expand the small meetinghouse. The only one to see the Chapman boys come into town was Minette Jacob, who had gone out to hang herself from the big oak tree in the meadow, a length of strong rope trailing from her hands.

The meadow grass swished under her boots and around her long skirt. Minette was pale with a cloud of dark hair. She resembled the Partridge side of her family, rather than the Bradys, who tended to be redheads with independent temperaments. She had little in common with the pious Jacobs, the family she had married into, only that their son had been her husband.

Minette had planned this dreadful undertaking carefully, well aware of the hour when she would at last be alone in Husband's

Meadow and could finally end her life on earth. She stopped when she saw the strangers striding toward her. Her heart sank. She knew that self-harm was an abomination, but she was beyond caring. She had lost her husband, William, to measles, and their newborn child, Josie, as well. Two weeks later, her dear sister, Lucy Ann Partridge, only sixteen, had passed on. Minette had no reason to be in the world. She was nineteen and a lost soul. She had not slept for five nights or had a bite of food. Daily life had become a blur, but now her vision cleared. She watched the boy and the man walking through the tall grass, and all at once she knew they were angels who'd been sent to her. She dropped to her knees right there.

They found her like that, whispering a prayer under her breath, eyes closed, prepared to meet and be undone by a fiery celestial sword.

"What's this all about?" Nathaniel whispered to his older brother. The world was a strange, open place to them both now that they'd left Leominster. Nathaniel was still young enough to believe that there was an explanation for everything, and John's explanation was that the Lord was everywhere. The sunshine was bright that day. There were blackflies in the air, flitting around them, and the sound of bumblebees droned in the tall grass.

"It's about mercy," John replied. He gazed down at the woman before him with the rope in her hands and knew that this was a divine moment that would forever change both their lives.

He dropped to his knees beside her, then took her hands in his. The rope fell into the grass, coiled like a snake. Minette looked up, shocked. She had expected to be burned alive. Now she gazed into John Chapman's kind, soulful eyes.

"You have no idea what's inside of you," he said to her. He was younger than she, but he spoke with authority. Minette had indeed believed there was nothing inside of her, so it was as though he had answered her unspoken prayer. There was some sort of spark between them that had to do with questions and answers. But there was also something more. Minette felt as if she were opening, as if what was bruised inside her was in his hands. She wondered if this is what an angel did to you.

Minette stayed on her knees while John Chapman planted the Tree of Life, right there in the meadow. He had hundreds of seeds in his knapsack, taken from the orchard where he'd worked and from the cider mills he'd passed, but he also had a few saplings that were wrapped in cloth and twine, one of which he presented to the town of Blackwell.

After he was done, they sat in the grass and watched meadow-larks and drank some of the hard cider John carried with him in a metal flask. When the cider went down, it burned. The burning spread out into Minette's chest in an arc and then in a circle. She laughed at the feeling, and at the larks, and at the fact that she was still alive when she hadn't meant to be.

"You forgot that the world was this beautiful," John said to her then, and she knew she'd been right in her first impression, that he was indeed an angel, and that he'd been sent to her, and that while she had believed she had come out on this morning to finish her life, there had been a different plan meant for her all along.

MINETTE TOOK THE Chapman brothers back to the cottage William Jacob had built for her in the acre behind her father's house. The bigger house had belonged to her grandmother Hallie Brady, who had founded the town, and had been added on to piecemeal as more children came along. Minette's father seemed to have grown old all at once after his wife and younger daughter and grandchild had died. He didn't seem to notice Minette and her losses. There was no one to whom she could confide her sorrows, but somehow this man John understood them without her needing to voice a single one aloud. "We have one Father," he told her. "And He knows our pain and our salvation."

Minette offered the Chapmans an extra pallet in front of the fireplace in her cottage, but they said they preferred to sleep outside, under the stars. She fixed them dinner, and although they accepted bread and honey, they would not take more. "There's no need for us to have more than our share," John explained. "We take our lessons from the bees, who work for the glory of our Maker."

On that first night Minette looked out the window and watched them. The boy was in a blanket roll, but John slept with nothing covering him other than the night air. It was so early in the spring, there were patches of ice in the shady sections of the yard. The bears in the forest still slumbered in their dens. As she sat there, Minette felt her milk come in, even though her baby had been gone for weeks.

In the morning everyone in town knew the Chapmans were there. They had made their camp in the patch of garden behind the house that had a peculiar red soil. People noticed the brothers down at the well in the center of town, pouring buckets of water to wash the soil from their bare feet, stained red from the dirt. Someone said only the devil had red feet. That sort of gossip traveled quickly. Minette's father, Harry Partridge, came to her cottage soon after. Minette was baking a maple sugar pie. Her father took note of the knapsacks and blankets set against the garden gate.

"You're letting strangers into your house? Do you think that's wise?"

"They sleep outside."

Minette knew that the Chapmans were planting an orchard down in the meadow. They'd gone off early in the morning dark and were at work when most people were in their beds. They planned to do this all across the country so that the land would be a sea of apples, manna from heaven in a line leading west.

"They're just boys," she told her father, who was hardly comforted by her words.

That night Minette fed the Chapmans pie for supper, outside in the garden. The brothers had worked all day. They had walked past the burying ground in the meadow and had seen the stones for Minette's husband and child and sister and mother. Before supper, they held hands and said a prayer for those no longer in the living world. As John spoke about meeting with angels in the world above their own, Minette cried for the first time since her sister's passing. That night she slept with the window open. She slept better than she had in a month.

The Jacobs began it, taking up the idle gossip, insisting that the devils with red feet were now at work in the meadow and needed to be stopped. Soon the town was in an uproar. The men joined together at the meetinghouse and decided to take action. But when they came for the boys, they found Minette outside with the brothers, meaning to sleep in the open air with the strangers. The Chapmans were given ten minutes to get out of

William Jacob's widow's yard and twenty-four hours to leave Blackwell.

The boys went as far as the meadow, where they set up their camp in the grass. It was a cool, dewy night, and the foxes in the hollow nearby bolted, surprised by the sudden intrusion. It made no difference to the Chapmans where they slept. It was Minette who cared. She packed a bag and followed them. She felt headstrong and light. She'd heard stories to the effect that her grandmother had disappeared one August night, and she wondered if she had felt the way Minette herself did now, not caring if she ever saw anyone in town ever again.

Minette wore her old black skirt, one she didn't mind ruining if burrs caught in the fabric. She had on a pair of her husband's old boots. The brothers weren't surprised to see her. They accepted all they were offered and considered every moment a blessing. They had their supper in the meadow that night. Fresh asparagus, fiddlehead ferns, the last of the maple sugar pie. That was the night Minette realized that John Chapman didn't sleep. When she startled awake, surprised to find herself where she was, beneath the stars, she saw that he hadn't yet lain down. He was hunched in the grass, on fire with ideas. He said he didn't need sleep. It was a waste of time and he had too much to accomplish. Minette stayed beside him. They studied the sky, and she listened attentively when he told her that every set of stars told a story. There was a spider, there was a crab, there was the lion of the night.

Her father came out to the meadow the next day to find that Minette was laboring with the men, planting seeds. There was soil on her hands and on her face. Her black skirt was hiked up out of the mud.

"You should come home." Harry Partridge would have been firmer but he knew that if you tugged too hard on someone who was beginning to wander, they might just bolt and run.

Minette shook her head. She loved her father, but she couldn't go back.

That night she and John went for a walk after Nathaniel was asleep. There was a blanket of clouds over the stars, like a carpet, a thin veil separating the world from the sky. They went as far as the start of the mountain, where the caves were. They knew that spring had fully arrived when they saw signs of bear: pawprints, shrubs trampled. She kissed him then, in a way she had never kissed her husband. She leapt forward into the shining light. When she'd been married she had been too busy to notice that the world was beautiful. Or perhaps she'd known and had forgotten.

The next day the men in town came to the meadow with a document they had drawn up that evicted the Chapmans from town. John Chapman stood to face his accusers. He was far taller than any of the other men. He said that someday they would understand his motives and would be grateful that he had lingered in their town. He had divine work to finish before he moved on.

When would that be? the men wanted to know. They were edgy facing him. If they'd had a jail, they would have thrown him into it. Their eviction notice was only as good as its effects.

"Three days," John told them. "But what I've done here will stay with you forever."

They didn't know if they liked the sound of that or not, but they backed off and allowed him the time he'd asked for.

That night John and Minette went back into the woods and lay together. John had never been with a woman before, and everything about Minette was a miracle to him. Once she laughed out loud because of the way he was studying her. "It's because you're perfect and wonderful," he said solemnly.

He watched while she slipped out of her clothes, something her husband would have never done. She felt as if she was a constellation or a blade of grass.

They planted till noon the next day. Then she insisted the brothers must see the Eel River, which was rushing with melted snow, its current so loud they had to shout. They took off their clothes right there on the riverbank, all three of them, though Nathaniel was shy at first, then plunged into the water. John was careful not to step on any of the eels that lived in the shallows. He lifted one up to examine for a moment. "Brother eel," he said before replacing the creature into the waters from which it had come.

Minette felt cold and hot at the same time. She had lost nearly everyone but she was standing in the Eel River, the deep water rushing past, the sunlight beating down on her slim shoulders. She felt the eels swimming along, ancient mysterious creatures that managed to survive the terribly cold winters in Blackwell beneath a cover of ice.

HARRY PARTRIDGE CAME to see them at suppertime. They had a fire burning, and sparks drifted into the sky. Minette's father had brought a loaf of bread, gratefully accepted, and a pot of stew, which he alone ate. He ignored the fact that John didn't wear shoes and that his hair was so long. The air was thick with mosquitoes. Bats swooped across the meadow, feeding upon them. It was a beautiful spring night.

After supper Harry asked John Chapman what his intentions were.

"I intend to make this country a garden of trees," John said solemnly.

"I mean Minette. Your intentions toward her."

John nodded. "I intend to remind her that she's alive."

It was all Harry could do not to punch him. "And then?" he managed to ask.

"Then on to the West," John said.

Afterward, Harry took Minette aside. He realized she was just a girl. He had expected too much from her and had been so consumed with his own sorrows he had never noticed hers. "Do you hear what he's saying?" Harry asked his daughter. "Do you understand? He's not staying here. He's not the man for you."

Minette laughed and hugged her father. He couldn't begin to know what had been revealed to her. He had no idea that the universe could be found in a single instant, a drop of water, a blade of grass, a leaf of an apple tree.

That night Minette slept in John's arms, warmed by his strange heat. There were burrs on her skirt and in her hair. The scent of the river clung to her skin. She thought about her father sitting at home, worrying about her, and of her own little house, empty. In the morning, the Chapmans got ready to go. There was a light rain falling that John said would be good for the seeds they planted. In a hundred years there would be a hundred trees and each one would bear fruit. Minette waited, but he didn't ask her to go. She was not especially surprised. Nathaniel shook her hand and wished her well and said if he ever came back this way he would surely stop and visit. John Chapman was singing to himself the way he sometimes did. The rain didn't bother him. He was already moving forward, thinking about stories he'd heard about the West, how the land was so endless and untouched it was indeed like heaven.

The larks were swooping through the rain. The river was running so fast they could hear it in this meadow. Minette kissed him good-bye in a way she had never kissed her husband, and John kissed her back as if she was perfect and wondrous and alive.

IN THE MIDDLE of the next winter one of the Starr boys came running into town. The tree John Chapman had planted in Husband's Meadow had bloomed. Everyone went to see, tromping through the snow. It was twilight and the snow was still falling. Indeed, one bough of the young tree was covered with apple blossoms. This was an impossibility, a miracle, not unlike Minette Jacob's baby being born ten months after her husband's death. It was the reason the apples from this wonderful tree were called Look-No-Furthers. It was why Minette's father, Harry Partridge—who was so close to his grandson that the boy took his last name when he came of age—vowed he would never eat apples again.

THE YEAR THERE WAS NO SUMMER

1816

THERE WAS FROST IN THE GARDEN IN JUNE. Clothes set out on the line froze, their wrinkles set in place. Bedsheets turned hard as stone. The wind from Hightop Mountain gusted across the meadows, sifting through cracks below windows and doors, chilling residents to the bone. Horses in their barns grew skittish when the sky pooled into black puddles in the middle of the day. The spring had been unnaturally cold and dry, and now the weather took a turn for the worse. Throughout the Commonwealth, cornfields were ruined and vegetables were covered with slick coatings of ice. There was talk of a famine to come. People were preoccupied, panicked. Perhaps that was why no one noticed when Rebecca and Ernest Starr's daughter Amy disappeared.

The Starrs lived in the house local people called the Museum. Ernest Starr was a collector. He searched out rocks, seeds, minerals, animal skeletons. On his mantel there was a moose jaw and a rust-colored fox's pelt. In his cabinet he kept a strange piece of rock that was always hot to the touch and another in which there was a hole caused by a four-inch piece of hail that Ernest himself had witnessed before the ice melted into a wash of greenish water there in his hands. He had specimens preserved in jars of salt and liked nothing more than to study the desiccated bodies of bats and birds. He was enthralled by the wonders of nature and took special delight in amassing information no one else had. Over the years he'd gathered a library of atlases, maps, and scientific books that were so rare, professors from Harvard College had come to view them.

The Starrs were an old family in town, with ancestors who were part of the founding expedition. Ernest had inherited the wheat fields beyond Band's Meadow, as well as the leatherworks. He was a man in his forties, distracted, intelligent, the father of five. He employed several men to work at the farm and had only weeks earlier hired a new woman to come in to help with the laundry and meals. The housemaid lived among the ragtag settlement of horse traders from Virginia who had recently set up camp on the far side of the Eel River, but Ernest didn't hold that against her. He was a fair and liberal man. The Starrs' house was bustling, and Ernest had trained himself to read and study in the midst of extreme chaos. Doors slammed, children argued and laughed—none of that stopped him. When his wife, Rebecca, called everyone to lunch, he often ignored her. Rebecca would then have a tray brought to his study so he could go on working through meals. He was currently fascinated by moths and had been searching the mountains for elusive varieties. Set upon his desk there were glass bell jars and a small bottle of spirits that was used to stun the moths, which he could then pin and study.

On the day his daughter disappeared there was stew and molasses bread for lunch, with lemon sponge cake for dessert. He remembered that because he wrote it down in his dietary book, in which he recorded all of his meals. He thought such a diary might be of interest if he were ever diagnosed with an illness that might be related to diet. He worked all that morning in his study on the day of the storm, as the temperature outside dipped. It was the coldest June ever recorded, not just in the Commonwealth but all up and down the Atlantic Coast, as far west as Pennsylvania. There were no birds that year, for their eggs had frozen in their shells. Foxes and wolves had come down from the mountains, searching for food, drawing ever nearer to town. The eels in the river were sleepy because of the frigid water and were therefore easy to catch. Since many in town made their living from fashioning eelskin wallets and belts and shoes, and were employed at the Starrs' leatherworks, there was a mob of fishermen down on the banks. People wore high boots and gloves as they rushed into the brackish water with their nets and hooks. It was a sea of eel flesh, the water roiling. Black thunderhead clouds were moving in from the west, a sign of worse weather to come.

No one realized Amy Starr was missing until it began to snow. Rebecca thought the drifting white drops fluttering into the yard were blossoms from the apple trees, then she remembered that the leaves on the fruit trees had been stunted from the spring drought. Apple blossoms had never formed. The little girl in question was six years old, a quiet, well-behaved child. She was the last to follow the birth of her brothers and sisters: Henry was ten; Olive, twelve; William, thirteen; and the eldest was sixteen-year-old Mary. By dinnertime the sky was black as coal. The falling snow was gaining muster, nearly six inches on the ground already when Amy's absence became known. She didn't show up at the table for dinner, even though she was usually the first to scramble onto her chair, her folded napkin neatly placed in her lap. No one could remember seeing her all day. Had she been at lunch? Had she been at play?

Rebecca rose from the table and looked through the rooms, growing increasingly worried. She called and called, but there was no reply. When she reached Ernest's study, up on the third floor, her neck was flushed even though she was shivering. It had gotten progressively colder as she'd gone from room to room, and she took that as a bad sign. The hired woman, Sonia, had read her fortune that morning, using a pack of cards she kept tied up with a silk scarf. They had sat in the kitchen engrossed in the future while they were supposed to be paying attention to the preserved pears simmering in the kettle. Sonia had laid out her mistress's fortune on the pine trestle table. One card was for love, another for luck. Sonia had put down a third card, then had quickly snatched it up again. "That one's a mistake," she said. But Rebecca had seen it. The card was death.

ERNEST AND THE boys got on their coats and boots and gloves and went to search outside the house in places where the child was likely to be found. Amy often played in the barn, or in the garden, or in the orchard of apple trees that this year hadn't bloomed. She liked to pretend she was a horse, or a fine lady, or a man who planted trees. As the youngest, she was used to entertaining herself and going off on her own. Ernest and his sons came back after a while, ashen, huffing and puffing from the cold. The snow was now more than ten inches high. When they admitted they hadn't seen a sign of Amy, Rebecca burst into tears. Ernest told his wife not to worry, he would search again. He went out once more with Henry and William. He told his boys to keep looking while he himself ran to the pastor's house. When Reverend Smith heard Ernest's story, he, too, put on his coat. The men went on to the meetinghouse, where they raced up the steps and rang the bell. Four peals meant an emergency.

In the parlor at home, Olive stayed with her mother, who was nearly faint with nerves, but Mary drew on her coat and hat and slipped outside. The whole town of Blackwell was covered with mounds of snow. Nearly a foot in some places. The world seemed enchanted and strange. Mary could hear the cows in the meadows lowing as she went on to the meetinghouse. Some girls had a fear of the dark and of being out alone, but Mary wasn't one of those. She had long red hair and a wide mouth and an especially curious nature. She was a voracious reader and secretly borrowed her father's books, even the ones about anatomy. She was bright enough to have frightened her mother with her ideas. On more than one occasion, Rebecca had taken her eldest daughter aside to ask, "What good can ever come from a girl with so much knowledge?"

When Mary entered the meetinghouse, the men were forming into search parties. Lanterns were brought around, for although the snow made the night quite brilliant, there were dark places they would need to look into, vegetable cellars and sheds, for instance, out-of-the-way spots where a child might have hidden in order to wait out a storm.

Mary's uncle, Tom Partridge, joined with her father and brothers in the search. There were eight other groups. Every house in Blackwell was gone through. Barns were examined, and porches, and gardens. Tom Partridge even climbed down the well in the town center, a rope tied round his middle. Nothing was found. At midnight they all gathered back at the meetinghouse. The searchers were spent and exhausted. Most people's fingers and toes were half frozen. Mary noticed that her brother Henry, who was only a boy, the youngest of the searchers, looked blue. His teeth were chattering, and he bit down on his lip, trying to control his shivering. All the same, the townspeople would not stop their searching and only fanned out farther. The men got their walking sticks, refilled their lanterns with oil, then set forth in a large group. People didn't say out loud what they feared. They stared straight ahead.

Mary walked at the rear. Her brother William came up to her.

"You shouldn't be here," he said. "Go home."

"I'll be where I like," Mary replied. She took Will's hand in hers. They had been allies in all things, and they were once again on this baffling night.

"We'll find her," William said, but he was thirteen and he didn't sound sure of himself. Mary had a lump in her throat. She hadn't thought before her brother had spoken that they might not.

WHEN THEY GOT to Band's Meadow they stopped. The wayfarers from Virginia had wagons there; the horses were quiet in the deep snowfall in their corral. Six wagons were set around in a circle. The trees were thick with snow, and the boughs, already leafing, were breaking under the weight. The snow looked green when Mary gazed upward through the frozen leaves.

The travelers had cleared a place for their bonfire, and several people sat around it, as if the falling snow was indeed apple blossom petals and nothing more. It seemed odd that the outsiders would be awake so late at night; there were even children playing in the snow, riveted by the firelight. The men in the search party huddled closer together, their wariness apparent. Mary had snow on her eyelashes. She'd never before noticed there could be color in the dark. The bonfire was red and orange and looked like a sunset when she narrowed her eyes. The group from town stood there, shifting uneasily, until some dogs from the campground noticed them. The dogs barked and ran over yapping, and the spell, or whatever it had been, that had kept the men motionless was broken. The search party went forward, and the men from the encampment came to meet the local men in the meadow. Mary lagged behind. She was afraid of dogs, and one collie shadowed her. A tall young man whistled through his teeth and the collie went trotting off.

Perhaps people began to be suspicious when they came upon the outsiders in their camp, or perhaps that anxiety had already begun the moment the child disappeared, a whisper of doubt that had grown as the men from town walked through the fields of snow. Now it was suggested out loud that it was a strange coincidence for the child to be missing so soon after the horse traders had appeared. The wayfarers agreed to have their wagons searched. The men from Blackwell were not as careful as they'd been when looking through their own neighbors' homes. Blankets, clothes, pots and pans, sleeping pallets stuffed with hay, all of it was tossed into heaps in the snow. The horse traders stood together, speaking in a language no one else understood. The women and children were quiet around the bonfire; even the sleepy babies had been brought out. Mary saw Sonia, who came to their house every day to clean and cook. Three children held on to Sonia's legs. Mary was surprised. She hadn't thought about Sonia having children. She went to sit beside Sonia on a bench that had been fashioned from an oak tree. There were two or three dogs around and some puppies in a crate, nesting in some old clothes.

"I'm sorry about your sister," Sonia said. "But they won't find her with us."

When Mary glanced over to the wagons, the young man with the dog was staring at her.

"That's my brother," Sonia told her. "He can help you."

His name was Yaron, and his dog could find anything and anyone. All the collie needed was a scrap of the missing person's clothing. Once the dog picked up a scent there was no stopping him.

"Should we tell them?" Mary nodded to the men from town.

"Would they believe us?" Sonia shrugged.

They decided to search on their own. Sonia left the children with another woman and accompanied Mary and Yaron through the field with the dog, whose name was Birdie. The collie was sable and cream colored with flowing hair and a long sensitive nose. He and his owner looked alike, except that Yaron's hair was dark. They both seemed standoffish, as though they had other things on their mind. Yaron had his chin lifted, as if expecting to be engaged in a fight at any time. No one spoke as they walked along, the dog trotting before them. Mary was shivering so badly she'd begun to shake. The snowy June, the dark sky, the outsiders beside her—all of it made her feel disoriented, even though they had soon enough reached town, and then her street, and then the house where she had lived her whole life long. Every lamp was glowing and the Museum loomed hugely. For some reason Mary was embarrassed in front of Sonia and Yaron to have been granted so much. She wanted to say, *None of it means anything to me. Only the people inside matter.* Instead she asked if those were Birdie's puppies in the box in the settlement.

Sonia and Yaron exchanged an amused look. Yaron looked a little less cross. He said something to his sister that Mary didn't understand.

"He said he hopes so," Sonia told Mary. "Since Birdie is the only male dog in the camp."

They left the collie in the yard, stomped the snow from their boots, then went inside. Rebecca Starr and Mary's sister Olive were in the parlor, by the fire. When they heard footsteps, they leapt up.

"Where is she?" Rebecca said.

"They haven't found her yet," Mary told her mother. "But this man's dog can find her."

When the dog's talent was explained, Olive ran for one of Amy's dresses.

"Do you have the cards?" Rebecca asked her housemaid. She'd become obsessed with knowing the future, and she begged for another reading.

Sonia looked at her brother, who shook his head and said,

"Na." Sonia laid out the cards for Rebecca. She was a mother herself and understood the need for a glimmer of hope. She turned over the first card. The Queen of Hearts.

"Your daughter," Sonia said.

She turned over another. The Queen of Diamonds. Sonia stopped.

"And that one?" Rebecca wanted to know.

Sonia paused. "Your other daughter," she told Rebecca.

They all turned to Mary.

"That means I'll find her," Mary said.

Olive had returned with Amy's best dress, blue muslin with ribbon smocking. Mary took it and nodded to Yaron and they turned to go.

"Kaj dajas?" Sonia called to her brother, but he didn't bother to call back an answer and Sonia didn't need one. She knew they were going to try to find the little girl; she wouldn't have expected less, even though it would probably be wiser for the travelers to pack up and leave before they were blamed for whatever happened. Mary and Yaron went through the kitchen, outside to where the dog was waiting. Yaron got on one knee and let the dog smell the dress. The dog did so, then barked excitedly.

"He has her scent," Yaron said. "It's a good sign."

Birdie went through the yard and they followed the dog across the green, past the old Brady house, the first one built in Blackwell when the town was settled, where young Tom Partridge lived now. It looked different in the night, like a house she'd never been to before. They went round the yard, into the rear garden, the one that was never planted, for it had once been a burying ground. The dog stopped. Yaron knelt down again. He dug through the snow. The soil was red here, and there were climbing roses, frozen, buried inside a tall drift. Yaron accidentally pricked himself on some thorns and his blood dripped into the snow. Mary felt her heart leap. She wanted to move forward. Instead she backed away. The dog barked again, and Yaron scooped more snow. There was a scrap of fabric. Mary came to kneel beside him. She was trembling, but she forced herself to be steady. Yaron glanced at her, then quickly looked away.

"Oh," Mary breathed. It was Amy's poppet doll that they had sewn together only weeks ago. Amy was never without it. Mary sat back on her heels as though she'd been struck. The dog was headed toward the far end of the property.

Yaron stood and reached out his hand to Mary. She suddenly felt too young to be where she was, in the red garden on a cold, black night with a man she didn't know. Freckles of snow were still falling. Later the wind would be fierce, but for now everything was silent. They could hear the dog trotting through the drifts.

"I don't know," Mary said softly. She wasn't sure what she meant by her own remark. Did she mean she didn't know if she could go on or where they should look? Or did she mean that she didn't know what to think or feel?

"You don't have to," Yaron assured her. "The dog knows. All we have to do is follow."

Mary took Yaron's hand, and he helped her to her feet.

"Where are you from?" she asked as they trudged through the snow.

"We came here from Virginia. We'll go west when we leave."

The drifts were even taller here, so Yaron kept Mary's hand in his to help her navigate the snow. His touch was so hot it was burning. They had come to the oldest apple tree in Blackwell. It was the only tree that had bloomed this season, despite the weather.

"Amy liked to play here," Mary said. Then she fell quiet. She didn't like the way she was talking, as if she already knew something it was impossible to know.

Yaron reached to snap a frozen branch from the apple tree and put it in his jacket pocket. "For my horse," he said. "I'll plant it where we go next."

The dog ran back to them and bumped against Yaron's legs. Yaron reached to pet Birdie, but the collie was already running ahead. They followed him for a long way, past the marshy acreage no one bothered with since it was of no use for pastureland or farming. Usually it was possible to hear the Eel River rushing at this time of year, but in the storm much of the river had been covered with a thin crust of ice. Tonight it was quiet.

Mary drew closer to Yaron. He was twenty-two or -three, a man of the world, whereas Mary had never been as far as Lenox. She'd never been outside of Blackwell, except for the times when her father had taken her on expeditions to Hightop Mountain, to look for insects and ferns and the scat of wild creatures that would reveal their diet. She felt like a stranger in a strange land, one of the people the pastor spoke of in his sermons, someone who had wandered very far from home.

The dog was padding back and forth along the riverbank, yelping. Then he stood in one place. Mary went to follow, but Yaron stopped her.

"Let me go," he said.

Mary, who was unafraid of the dark, found she was now frightened. She watched Yaron lope over to his dog. He knelt down to pet the collie, speaking to him softly. Mary wanted to know what he was saying, she wanted to kneel there beside him. Yaron got up and threw a look behind him that troubled her. Then he plunged into the river.

It shocked her to see him disappear beneath the ice. Mary made a gasping noise even though she wasn't the one who'd gone under. She felt that her heart had stopped. The dog raced back and forth on the bank, barking, beside himself at the disappearance of his master. Mary stood there for a second, then she raced to the river. Everything was going fast, the way clouds flew past in a storm, the way snow fell in a blizzard. Yaron was gone, with broken ice flowing in a circle in the place where he had dived in.

Mary stood at the edge of the river, her boots wet. She went deeper still, up to her knees. The water froze her to her bones. She could feel herself sinking into the mud. Through the ice she thought she saw an enormous blue fish. It was like the fish in a dream, the sort you can never catch. Then there was a shadow and the ice broke. Yaron surfaced holding the fish, which was her sister, dripping with water, blue in his arms.

They stood together in the shallows of the river, the little girl's sopping body between them, their breath hot and fast while Mary sobbed and Yaron did his best to comfort her. The dog was quiet now, down on his haunches, his eyes never leaving the child he'd been sent to find. Amy's clothes were frozen stiff, and she was heavy as a block of ice. They laid her down on the riverbank. Mary covered her sister's body with her own and breathed into the little girl's tiny cold mouth. She'd read that it was sometimes possible to bring the dead back by doing so. But it did no good.

"They'll think I did it because I found her," Yaron said.

"No." The snow was oddly bright. Amy looked like a fallen star, shining beside them.

Yaron shook his head. His dark hair was wet. "They always think that."

The clothes he wore were frozen now, too, and there was snow in his hair. Mary thought about the way she'd felt when he'd disappeared into the river. She recalled the look on his face before he dove in. She felt something inside her that was unexpected as Yaron leaned to tenderly close her sister's eyes.

In the morning the search party found the child on the bank of the Eel River, the blue dress covering her. The snow had hardened overnight, and it made a crunching noise beneath their boots. Ernest Starr had to be restrained. He was in a state of grief so immense he vowed he would never let his daughter go. He claimed he would find a way to preserve Amy's body in salt or brandy and she would be with him still, but Rebecca wouldn't hear of it. She insisted her child be taken to the burying ground outside of town, with the service held under the one tree that had managed to bloom in that cold season, the one people called the Tree of Life, which was true enough, for its fruit kept people in town from starving during the coming winter's famine. Rebecca Starr demanded that the coffin be opened so she could take off her child's boots and Amy could walk into the kingdom of heaven in her bare feet. No one was about to deny Rebecca anything. They let her do as she pleased. She had lost two daughters in a single day, for Mary had disappeared. No one dared question Rebecca when she kept the horse traders' pup that had been left on her doorstep. She walked with the collie every day, along the river and through the meadow, where there were still ruts in the earth the following summer when the weather was warm once more and the sky was at last cloudless and clear.

OWL AND MOUSE

1848

EMILY WENT FOR A WALK ON HER LAST DAY at school. Her family was taking her out of Mount Holyoke Seminary; she was needed at home and she hadn't been happy at the school. Her views were her own, and educators did not always appreciate free thought. It was time to leave. But before she went back to the family house and everyone else's demands, she wanted to go somewhere she'd never been. She longed for the woods and for great distances. She'd often gone rambling as a child, collecting nearly six hundred species of wildflowers, some never seen before. She liked to disappear, even when she was in the same room as other people. It was a talent, as it was a curse. There was something that came between Emily and other people, a white linen curtain, hazy. It made the world quieter and farther away, although occasionally she could see through to the other side. She had the feeling that if she went home, she might never get away. She thought of birds caught in nets. There was something inside her, beating against her ribs, urging her to do things she might not otherwise attempt. She had the strongest desire to get lost.

She passed the boundary of the school grounds and kept on. She had always been a walker, and being alone was her natural state. Once she was in the woods, she was a shadow. She recognized wildflowers the way someone else might recognize old friends: velvet-leaf, live forever, lad's love. She stooped to pick a sprig of lad's love and slipped it in her shoe. Local people said it was a charm that would lead you to your true love. She did feel charmed. She went on, hour after hour. She spied red lily, wood lily, trout lily. She crossed two roads, then went into even deeper woods. The forest here was dark and green. The world had become topsy-turvy. Day was night and night was day, and no one on earth knew where she was. She had a wild, careless feeling that made her limbs feel loose and free. There was bloodroot in among the carpet of moss and leaves, hyacinth and squill. She had reached Hightop Mountain without knowing it. At last, she was visiting a place she'd never been to before. She had been walking for almost ten hours, and for most of that time she'd been caught up in a dream. There were black bears up here that could run faster than any man and weighed up to six hundred pounds. Emily had read that injured bears sobbed like human beings, and that gave her some comfort. They were not so unalike.

She slept beneath a tree that night, sitting upright. She imagined she would have been scared for her life out in the open, for she was often terrified in her own room at home, even after double-locking the windows and covering the glass with quilts. Instead, she felt an odd calm spirit here in the wilderness. Was this the way people felt at the instant they leapt into rivers and streams? Was it like this when you fell in love, stood on the train tracks, went to a country where no one spoke your language? That was the country she was in most of the time, a place where people heard what she said but not what she meant. She wanted to be known, but no one knew her.

It was cold in the morning when Emily awoke. She was shivering. Now that it was daylight she realized she had reached the top of the mountain. She made her way down, to the village below. There were brambles, thorn trees, yellow jacket nests, poison oak. She had never walked quite so far and was thrilled and terrified by her own bravery. Her hair was knotted. Her hands were raw. There was dew on her shoes.

Soon the sun warmed the air. Emily went on, past an abandoned house on the outskirts of town. There were rabbits in the yard. They too cried like human beings when trapped. The house at the edge of the woods was old with a thatched roof. What if she lived there? If her brother and father searched for her, they would walk right past, not guessing she was inside. She could will herself to be invisible. Her family would give up hope and stop their search and here she'd be, safe and alone and free. She could make her clothes out of tablecloths, sleep on a pallet of straw, keep the windows open, leaving behind the overriding fear she carried so close to her bones.

She went on, past meadows, through an orchard. There was a canopy of apple blossoms and the air was fragrant. When she gazed up through the haze of white she could imagine there was snow, that heaven had opened, that the world was hers alone. It was a small town she'd stumbled upon, and no one noticed her until she went past the Brady homestead, the oldest house in town. There was a man out in the yard, sitting in a chair in the sunlight. He was in his thirties, handsome, with a dark beard. He was looking up at the sky, but somehow he knew she was there.

"Were you going to pass without saying good morning?" He had a slight accent, a charming manner.

"Good morning," Emily managed to say. She felt as if she had swallowed bees. Perhaps she'd been stung. Later, a red welt would rise on her wrist, one she hadn't noticed as she stood at the gate. She was in a town she'd never been to, conversing with a man who had the nerve to address her as though he knew her, when no one on earth knew her. Likely no one in heaven did either.

"You're not from here," the man said. He knew that much.

"I was in the woods. Looking for wildflowers." It was something of the truth. Enough.

"You're not afraid of bears?" the man teased.

"I fear myself more than I fear any bear," Emily blurted. It was the way she'd felt in her aloneness, the comfort she took in being on the mountain. What might she do next?

"So you're fierce?" He didn't laugh at the notion but asked in all honesty. He sat forward, shifted his gaze.

"I'm a mouse," Emily said, suddenly shamed.

"I doubt that. Have breakfast with me," the man requested. He had a napkin tied around his neck. "I'm desperate to talk to someone interesting." The dark-haired man wore a white shirt and a light-colored suit. He was casual, the way too-handsome men often were. He bordered on rude, but he did have a tray of delicious-looking food set out before him. There were muffins, honey butter, apple slices, along with a plate of bacon. Emily realized she was starving. Still, she hesitated.

"Sir," she said, "I don't even know you."

"I'm Charles Straw," the man said. "My friends call me Carlo."

Emily felt the bird in her chest, trapped in a net.

"Don't say no," this man Charles urged. "How many times does a beautiful woman walk by this old house?"

That was when Emily understood he was blind. She nearly laughed out loud. No one who could see would ever think she was anything but plain. She came in through the gate to take the chair that faced him.

He felt her shadow graze his skin, and he knew he'd drawn her in. He smiled. "So you're not so fierce as you pretend."

"It was you who suggested I was anything other than a mouse," Emily protested. "What happened to your eyes?" she asked when she noticed they were without a gleam. They were the most unusual color—a flat, deep blue. If she had to describe them on a page, she would say a lake, a door to heaven.

"You're very blunt." Charles laughed. "Or is it rude?"

"If you think I'm rude, I can leave." Emily's hands were folded on her lap. She had no intention of going.

Her remark made him smile. He found her charming, unlike most people. "You're very observant. It's called river blindness. Contracted in South America. The cause is a form of worm too tiny for the human eye to see. I swam across a lake in Venezuela that was so deep local people said it reached to the far side of heaven. Unfortunately, it turned out to be hell for me.

That was when the world grew blurry. Though I can see you quite clearly."

Emily let out a short laugh. She held up five fingers in front of his face. As she suspected, he didn't seem to notice. "You can't."

"It's true."

"Impossible," Emily declared. "I'm invisible."

"Not for me. I see inside. One of the benefits of my tragedy."

"Then perhaps it's not a tragedy."

"Life is a tragedy," Charles said pleasantly.

Emily felt the sprig of lad's love in her shoe prick through her stocking. She had said the very same thing to her sister only weeks ago.

"Shall I prove that I can see what no one else can?" Charles asked.

Emily nodded. "Please. Do."

They sat there and nothing happened and Emily didn't know what to think. Then Charles suddenly reached down.

"Did you catch a shadow?" Emily asked, intrigued.

Charles signaled for her to put her hand out. When she did, he placed his hand atop hers and opened it. There was a tiny field mouse. Emily laughed, delighted. "You're like an owl," she declared. "You see in the dark." And from then on, although others might call him Charles or Carlo, she thought of him as her owl.

"He's yours," Charles Straw said. "He's at your mercy."

WHEN CHARLES'S COUSIN Olive Starr Partridge came to fetch the tray, she was surprised to find a young woman deep in conversation with her cousin, and even more startled to see a field mouse in one of the good Spode teacups. Introductions were made, and Charles immediately asked Olive to give Emily a tour of the house and of the garden that had been planted more than a hundred years earlier.

"Don't be silly," Olive said. "I'm sure she has no interest in that old garden."

"She's a botanist," Charles said.

"Amateur," Emily added.

"And don't forget to introduce her to the dog."

"How do you know our Carlo?" Olive asked as she took Emily up to the garden. There were granite steps and a white picket fence. The earth was a funny, reddish color, as if raw pigment had been added to the soil.

"Our paths happened to cross one day," Emily said. She wondered if dreamers knew they were in a dream while it was happening, or if they had no idea that everything around them was purely imagined until the dream had gone.

"Which day was that?" Olive was a nurse and quite protective of her cousin. Her husband and grown sons had traveled to Boston, but she had stayed to care for Carlo. He was terribly ill, yet he insisted he must return to his travels. He had never been one to stay in one place. His steamer trunks were packed and waiting on the porch.

"Today," Emily admitted.

They had reached the garden, ignored for many years. It was a wild tangle filled mostly with thistle. A clutch of larks and sparrows took flight when the women approached.

"It must have been lovely," Emily said.

There was still some scarlet amaranth and a stray crimson larkspur, nearly six feet tall, the likes of which Emily had never seen. There was a scraggly row of ruby lettuce and some bright radishes that Olive had put in, which she now pulled from the ground to have with their dinner. The family lore insisted that only red plants would grow in this stretch of ground. Even those blooms that went in as white or pink or blue turned in a matter of weeks. Emily took a bite of a small, muddy radish. The juice in her mouth was red.

"It's a shame poor Charles can't see any of his old hometown before he leaves again. He's going back."

"To South America?"

"He insists. The Berkshires aren't big enough for him. He says our mountains are hills."

As a boy Charles had spent hours in the library reading journals by James Cook and Lewis and Clark, concocting an imaginary travel journal for himself. While the other boys in town were sledding and ice fishing, Charles was teaching himself Spanish and Arabic in the old abandoned house Emily had passed by. He had always been daring, a naturalist at heart. When he was twelve, he was out with the family dog, a young collie, when a fisher attacked. Fisher cats were large weasels so powerful and fierce they were the only creatures known to kill and eat porcupines, including the quills. Charles and the fisher had fought wildly over the dog. The fisher hissed and growled, arching its back, burying its teeth in the collie's neck. Charles kept his hands around the fisher's throat, choking off its breathing passage. It turned and bit him on the arm, but he managed to strangle it before the fight was through.

When Charles carried the dead collie up to his father's house in the meadow, he was crying, but his face was set. Three years later he left town. He went to Harvard, which didn't interest him, then on to New York, and finally to South America, where he worked as a liaison for American companies. He liked jungle living, the heat, the brackish rivers filled with fish that had pointed teeth. He began to dream in Spanish. He didn't miss a single thing about Massachusetts, not the snow or the people or the proper homes, although there were times when he found himself thinking about Hightop Mountain and walking there with his dog.

Charles didn't know his father had died until six months after the fact. His vision had already begun to fail by then. It might have been partially salvaged if he'd thought to come home. Now that he was back to pay his final respects all he could see were shadows, but even they had begun to fade. Emily's presence had been faint, a mere breeze blowing across his face. Soon there wouldn't even be that. That was why he was leaving while he still could.

During his time with his cousin Olive, Charles had been training a dog to take back to South America, as a companion and helpmate. He was tied up behind the house. When Emily saw him on her way back from the garden, she marveled, delighted. "Is it a bear?" she cried. "An ox?"

She crouched down and petted the huge, gentle creature.

"It's a Newfoundland. My cousin thinks the dog will guide him along the Amazon. It will probably die of heat prostration. Or Carlo will."

Charles had already hired a local boy to travel with him to New York and help with the luggage. Then Charles and the dog would embark a ship bound for Venezuela. Emily stayed for dinner and was glad she did. Charles told her about otters that were as big as tigers, and tiny wild pigs with long tusks, and spotted wildcats that loved their aloneness so well they screamed when they came upon another of their kind. She felt as though she could listen to him all night long, and nearly did. Then it was too late to go. Her excuse for being in Blackwell was simple: She'd gotten lost in the woods. It was partially true and was therefore neither a sin nor a lie. They were happy to take her in as their guest. Before retiring, she went outside with the little box in which she'd kept the field mouse all day. She opened the top and set him free. Charles had said he was at her mercy, and so she did right by the poor thing. But the little mouse stood frozen. "Go on," Emily insisted. She felt the trapped thing inside her and nearly wept when at last the mouse ran away, off into the woods behind the yard, to the owl or hawk that surely was waiting nearby.

THAT NIGHT, SLEEPING in a stranger's house, Emily found herself thinking of a way to keep Charles from leaving. It was a wild, frantic thought. She had no right to it, yet there it was. She rose while it was dark and went outside to sit with the dog. After a while, she took a shovel from a shed, then made her way through the sleeping town. The young Newfoundland followed her, waiting while she crept into the yards of the houses they passed. She found peonies, quince, snowy phlox. She dug up two small rosebushes, one with tea-scented flowers, the other with a scent that reminded her of burned sugar. She pilfered lavender, stargazer lilies, basil, rosemary, sage. She carried her loot back to the house, then went out again, this time to the woods. The dog dutifully waited while she found what she wanted. Four o'clocks, sweet William, lemon mint, swamp pink, tuberose, trillium, marsh clematis, barberry, witch hazel, mallow, honeysuckle, loose-strife. Emily took only scented plants, specimens that announced themselves with their odor. Each flower would be a part of a blind man's garden, a thicket of fragrance in which even the poorest weed might be miraculous.

She worked through the night. The soil in the old garden was indeed red, and by the time Emily was done she looked like something out of a devil's dream. The dog's fur was dusted with soil so that he resembled a creature from another world. Emily took a bucket, filled it at the well, then washed her feet and the dog's paws. She wondered if the mouse had been caught or if he had found his way home. She wondered if her family had realized she was gone, if her brother was searching for her door-to-door, and if Charles would be content with what she'd crafted, a place of beauty he couldn't find anywhere else, even if he searched the whole world over. *Dear Owl,* she would have written if he could have read a note or a letter. *Surely you'll see this. All you have to do is breathe in and there it will be. All you have to do is stay.*

She slept so deeply she didn't hear him leave. She was still muddy, and the sheets she slept on were peppered with specks of red earth. The dog was on the floor beside her bed when she awoke. Charles had left him as a gift. *My dear Mouse, the weather would not have been right for a dog such as this,* he wrote in his note to her. *It would be cruel to take a northern creature there.* She supposed he was right. The deep, relentless heat of the jungle, the fish that bit through flesh with sharp teeth, the worms that could take your sight away.

When she rose from bed, she went to the window. Her

brother was in the yard talking to Olive. He had been searching and had come to take her home. She wondered what she might have said or done if Charles had asked her to leave with him. She wondered if he hesitated as he stood in the garden. Anyone else might have guessed the garden she planted would be white, but Charles had seen it all exactly as she'd crafted it before he went away, the flash of scarlet, the trail of blood, the inside story of who she was.

THE RIVER AT HOME

1863

BLACKWELL, MASSACHUSETTS, WAS REPRE-
sented by the Thirty-fourth Regiment in the War
Between the States, and every able-bodied man, including Tom Partridge's grandsons, who were fourteen and fifteen, had enlisted. The Starrs went and
the Jacobs and the Hildegardes and all the rest.
There was a parade, and people cheered and said the
war would be over in six months. After the parade,
Constant Starr, who had been named for his great-
grandfather and was so handsome half the women in
town were in love with him, kissed his wife, Mattie,
right in front of the meetinghouse. He kissed her
for so long that some other men's wives swooned
just to think of how they might feel in his arms.

When the men and boys left, there were only
women, children, and old men left behind in

Blackwell. The leather factory where eelskin boots and belts had been made for so many years closed down, and the windows looked ghostly in the dim spring light. The bank was vacated and people kept their money piled inside their mattresses, or buried under a stone birdbath, or in a mustard tin in the pantry. The new history museum, opened only months before, was shuttered, and the barn behind it was turned into living quarters and rented out. The women went out to the fields with the horses and mules. With tireless patience they taught their children how to work a plow and tend the apple orchards, the same way they'd instructed them on how to say grace and how to have faith in the future.

Three months later, one of the Partridge boys was sent home with only one leg. His brother had been killed in the field. Two of the Jacobs, father and son, were missing and considered lost. Letters from loved ones could take months to reach home, and so the days were lived hesitantly, and in fear. Constant Starr had fallen in Virginia, but no one in Blackwell knew he had left his earthly life until eight weeks after the fact. A tintype of his body in uniform was eventually sent to his wife, who wore it pinned to her black dress the way another woman might clip on a corsage. People heard Mattie Starr sobbing but there was nothing they could do, no comfort that could offer real solace, although most tried their best to be neighborly. There was little enough in people's pantries and larders, yet neighbors brought pies and stews to Mattie's home, for her and her two children. She didn't open her door, not even for those who knocked and called her name. The food was left out on the porch. Crows pecked at the pies with berry-stained beaks, dogs that roamed through town came and devoured the stews, and all of the Starrs grew thin.

It was a time of great grief, a season unlike any other. When the blackflies came, as they did every spring, folks nearly went mad because of the infestation. They were on the precipice already, reeling from their losses, unable to make sense of how the war could take so much from a single small town. People were reminded of the way life used to be by the appearance of the flowers in May. The reminder was painful, provoking crying fits, despair, and arguments among surviving family members. Spring itself was an affront, and the worst offenders were the fragrant blooms of the lilac saplings brought over from England many years earlier, which had now grown as tall as the rooftops. A group of women went to cut them down one night, axes in hand, tintypes of their beloved sons and husbands and fathers clasped inside the lockets they wore on delicate gold chains at their throats. In the morning the children gathered up purple flowers and danced in circles singing *ashes ashes* until they fell down.

NOT LONG AFTER that, when the trees were in full leaf and the meadows were lush, a young girl in a blue dress began to appear on the banks of the Eel River. Old Mr. Hildegarde was the first to spy her. He was fishing early in the morning when the owls were still soaring across the gunmetal sky, out hunting mice. Hildegarde did not wish to beg from his neighbors, all of whom had little enough, but he and his wife were on the verge of starving as they waited for their garden to bear fruit. Eel stew would have to suffice. The river was high after a snowy winter. Mist was rising from the cold waters into the mild air. Perhaps it was the mist that made Hildegarde stumble and nearly fall into the rushing waters. His boots were wet, and he was out of breath as he steadied himself. And then, quite suddenly, there she was, a little girl standing in the tall grass. Emile Hildegarde had never seen her before and he knew everyone in town, having come from Germany to Massachusetts as a young man. He'd lived in Blackwell the better part of fifty years.

The child he spied couldn't have been more than six, too young to be out alone at this early hour. The river was running so hard she seemed in peril as she scrambled closer to the riverbank. Usually Hildegarde minded his own business, but he started toward the girl, his heart pounding. He cried out, "Be careful," and the emotion in his own voice surprised him. By the time he reached the patch of tall, plumy grass where she'd been standing, there was only a circle of blackflies in the air.

Evan Partridge saw her in the very same place later that week. He had imagined many things since he'd returned from the battle that had taken his leg and his brother's life. He'd come back unable to stop thinking about the surprising darkness of the color of blood and the way sound echoed when men fell to the ground. He thought about doves flushed out of the bushes as the gunfire began and the look of disbelief on his brother's face. Evan managed to get around with a pair of crutches his grandfather Tom made for him. He often came fishing, grateful to be alone at the river, where he watched the high, cold water as if it was a gate to paradise. Each time he was there, he thought about dragging himself over to the banks and throwing himself in. A single step and it would all be out of his hands. He went over the scenario again and again. How cold the river would feel, how fast the water would take him, how pure and deep his last breath would be. He was certain that God would forgive him, considering all he had seen and all he had become at the age of fifteen.

He was thinking about that last cold breath when he saw the girl. She wasn't wearing any shoes. He noticed that. Her dress was blue and it flew out behind her, like a flag. Evan called out something, he didn't know what, a blurted word of warning or surprise. He wondered how he would manage to rescue her should she fall into the water. To his shame he could barely manage to navigate the muddy riverbank. He surely couldn't run. Then she was gone, the way mist disappeared. Evan felt his heart hitting against his ribs as it had in battle when he had embarrassed himself with the intensity of his own fear. He stayed there for a long time waiting for the girl in blue to return. When she didn't, he went home and sat down to dinner with his mother and grandfather. Something hot and strange had settled over him. He felt jarred awake, thrown into the world. He wanted to ask his grandfather if he believed in the afterlife while his mother was at the sink washing the dishes, thinking they couldn't hear her crying. He wanted to ask if in all his years his grandfather had ever received a message from the beyond, and if it had brought him comfort or simply added to his grief.

The next day, Evan went down to the meetinghouse, where the town records were stored. He had kept to himself since his service to the Union and most of his neighbors hadn't seen much of him since his return. Now people nodded a greeting, then looked away politely, not wishing to stare at his single leg. Evan was let into the records room by Mrs. Kelly, who served as the town clerk in her husband's place now that he was in the army. Along the wall there were dark eelskin-covered books recording every birth and death and marriage in Blackwell. Evan sat down at the trestle table and began at the beginning. Soon enough he found the birth of a Mary Starr on April third in the year 1800. No wedding or death date had been listed. Beneath her name was that of Amy Starr, presumably her sister, who had drowned at the age of six. *Hallelujah praise God she will return to us* someone had written in blue ink. The ink looked so fresh it appeared to have been written that day. That was how it seemed to Evan when he thought about the doves rising and his brother falling, as if it had happened that very morning, a mere breath away.

Evan went down to the Starrs' acreage the following morning. They were cousins, but there'd been a falling-out, and the families hadn't seen much of each other. There was Constant's father, William, who seemed an old man, older by far, it seemed, since he'd lost his son. William was sitting on the porch. Lately, that was what he did. He had cloudy blue eyes and white hair and he had on his good tweed jacket, the one he'd worn to the funeral they'd held for Constant in the chapel since no body had been sent home for the burying ground. William Starr didn't say a word when Evan came to sit in a chair beside him, although he was thinking he would give anything to have a son with one leg, on crutches, but alive. Evan spoke of the weather— *Still beautiful*—and Will Starr answered while gazing down the road where the fiddlehead ferns had unfolded—*Indeed.* Then Evan asked about the little girl who had drowned in the year 1816, wondering if the figure in the blue dress on the shore might be William's little sister.

William turned and looked into Evan's open face. In that instant, he understood this boy had seen terrible things.

"My sister drowned one summer," William said evenly. He

didn't mention that his parents had been destroyed by her death, or that his other sister had run away with a horse trader that very night. He didn't say that Amy's favorite dress had been blue. It was the dress she'd been buried in, nearly fifty years earlier.

"I think I saw her by the river." Evan glanced up to see if Mr. Starr would laugh at him, but no, the old man merely shook his head.

"You've been through a war," Will remarked, with more kindness than he imagined he could manage since his beloved son had been taken. "It will take a while before everything you've been through settles down inside you."

"She wasn't wearing any shoes," Evan went on, hoping a further description might jog Mr. Starr's memory.

Little Amy hadn't been wearing shoes when she was found, nor when she was buried. Will's mother had said that in the kingdom of heaven no one wore shoes. She'd made them open the coffin so she could unlace the pair of eelskin boots the women in town had fitted on her daughter when they'd dressed her. Will had glimpsed his sister's pale face. He was terrified that her eyes would be open, but thankfully they were closed.

THE NEXT MORNING they went down to the river together, the old man who didn't care whether he lived and the boy who thought he might already be dead. Since they'd probably have time to spare, they decided to bring their fishing poles. Trout were biting, and in a little over an hour they had both caught two rainbows. Ordinarily they would have spoken out about their good fortune, but not today. They sat on the riverbank and listened to the torrents of water go by. Once Evan thought he saw a flash of blue beyond the willow trees, but it was only a cornflower wavering on a thin green stalk. The next day they came again. Evan had dug worms from the old abandoned garden behind his house where there was red soil that was said to be lucky for fish but unlucky for love, not that he believed in such things. Will had his daughter-in-law fix a lunch for them to bring along. When Mattie Starr overheard what their mission was, and understood that it concerned a messenger from the world to come, her eyes brightened.

"We'll sit there and nothing will happen," her father-in-law assured her. "But at least we'll have a good lunch."

When Will Starr left to meet Evan at the river, Mattie took her children over to Mrs. Kelly's house and asked if her neighbor would mind Glenna, who was only three, and little Will, who would soon be two. Mattie had a wild look in her eyes, and her tone was urgent. Mrs. Kelly agreed to watch the babies, even though she had plenty to care for in her own household, a brood of children and a plot of land to till with the help of a single mule. Mattie didn't take note of Mrs. Kelly's hesitation. She left Will and Glenna and ran off through the meadow in her husband's old fishing boots. She felt light and oddly free, like the seedpods that were carried along in the mild breeze, floating over the fields in wispy gray threads. Mattie had taken to wearing her husband's clothing and had lately been seen tramping through town in britches and Constant's blue jacket. She wore his socks and his undergarments. She slept with the tintype image of Constant inside her nightdress. Sometimes she dreamed he was there with her. She could feel his long thin feet beside hers, his fingers in her hair, his breath on her skin. She woke in the throes of desire, and when she realized she was in the present time and not inside her dream, she didn't want to leave her bed. Sometimes she stayed there until noon, and the children would have gone hungry if their grandfather had not moved in to help care for them.

Mattie hastened through the tall meadow grass, past the oldest apple tree in town, the one people said had long ago saved the population of Blackwell by stubbornly bearing fruit in the year when there was no summer. There was a cloud of white blossoms on the tree. Mattie wondered if there had been apple trees in Virginia when Constant had been there, if the snow had fallen in those meadows in the winter of his death, as it did in Blackwell, so very deep and quiet. She wondered if the soil was as red as it was in the oldest garden in their village, the one behind the Partridge house. *Where blood has fallen, the ground aches but the fruit is sweet*—that's what the old women in town vowed. They thought it would bring her comfort to hear such nonsense, as if her loss could ever be sweetened. No wonder she had stopped talking to most people.

Mattie veered into the woods. There were wild gooseberries here. Just last summer she had brought the children with her to pick some for a pie for Constant's supper. The night before he left she had begged him not to go, knowing as she did so that he wouldn't listen to her pleas. It wasn't like Constant to let the other men down. "It's a war," he told her, as if that would explain everything. "Oh, I don't care," she had answered fiercely. She had pleaded and sat on his lap and kissed him and offered herself to him; she said she would do anything to make him stay, but in the morning he still got up from their bed and packed his bag. He left while he thought she was sleeping. She let him think that. She refused to watch him go.

HALFWAY THROUGH THE woods Mattie could hear the river. The earth was soggier as she went along, dense with moss, thick with fallen leaves and ferns. Mattie's feet kept dry in her husband's boots. Soon enough she saw her father-in-law and the boy who'd come back without a leg. They were watching the river, their backs to Mattie, eating the lunch she'd made them. They didn't hear her walking over the ferns, through the white birch and the pines. Her boots were worn from the steps her husband had taken, and she made little noise; her skirt fluttered around her legs. Mattie was twenty-five and a widow. Everything in her life had already happened to her, the wondrous and terrible both. Her whole world was over; all the rest would only be marking time. She had a sudden deep desire to run. She thought of deer and how they slipped through the woods, invisible, as if they were ghosts themselves. She thought of the river at twilight; she would crouch down onto hands and knees to drink from the cold water, her long pale hair tumbling into the shallows, the ends turned to ice. No one would find her. No one would know where she was. She imagined taking off her clothes, leaving on only the thin undergarments that had belonged to Constant, then stepping into the current, her feet settling between the iron-red rocks, the eels rushing past until they could find a tangle of wild water hyacinth to wrap themselves around, until they had carried her away.

Evan Partridge was finished with his lunch. Bread and butter and some slices of orange cheese. There were fresh wild strawberries, crushed but still good. He closed his eyes against the haze of sunlight falling through the tall trees. For a moment he was back in time, with his brother beside him. He was running home from the schoolhouse, so fast the dust rose behind him in a cloud. He heard the snap of a branch under a boot heel in the woods and caught a faint glimmer from the corner of his eye. He thought of gunfire and doves, and he turned like a shot himself. He saw Mattie Starr, stumbling over a sapling, falling to her knees. He forgot he had only one leg. He galumphed over the forest growth to made sure she hadn't hit her head on a rock. She hadn't even put her hands out to stop herself. It was as though she had just given up and let herself fall.

Mattie's eyes were closed when he reached her. Evan put his arms around her and said, "Wake up." Then he shouted out, and Will Starr came to squat down next to him. In a few moments, Mattie opened her eyes. They were blue. They were like the sky in Virginia, hot and pale, open and endless.

"I saw her," she said. "At the riverside."

The men waited for Mattie to get her bearings, then helped her to her feet. William recognized his son's boots, his socks, the sleeves of his undergarments on Mattie's girlish frame. It should have brought him comfort to know he wasn't alone in his grief, but it caused him only more sorrow. They walked on together to the place where Mattie had seen the little girl. The tall grass was high enough for a child to hide in. They searched around and found nothing. Evan was ashamed to be limping about, hopping around like a frog. Once when he seemed unsteady, Mattie put a hand under his elbow. "You ran fast to come help me," she said to him in gratitude. She was trying to be kind, but Evan bowed his head, even more ashamed of who he had become. From then on when she thought of anguish, Mattie would think of the way he had dipped his head to glance away, as if the world was much too vast and wide, and the only thing contained within it was loneliness.

They sat in a circle in the haunted place, to see if they experienced anything unusual. Will Starr remembered that his little sister used to come here to throw stones in the water. He laughed at her when she told him blue stones could make a wish come true. His sisters Amy and Mary had both been beautiful girls, one lost to the river, the other gone off with a traveling man, leaving behind a family where grief was the only emotion. His other sister, Olive, he had argued with long ago. Will laid his head against a birch tree stump and closed his eyes. The sun was warm and he fell asleep. Soon he was snoring.

"Do you think she has a message for us?" Mattie asked Evan Partridge, referring to the ghost she thought she'd seen. "Maybe she can lead us to the world beyond this one."

Evan didn't know. He wasn't even sure there were such things as spirits and ghosts. "Maybe it's only the way the sunlight comes through the trees. It appears to be a figure, but it's really just a shadow."

"She had a doll with her. I saw it in her hands. Do shadows have dolls?"

Evan smiled. "I suppose not," he said.

"I don't suppose anything," Mattie told him. "Not anymore."

She wondered what it would feel like to drown. How the water would fill your mouth and throat, how you would sink to the stony bottom where the currents were so green and cold, the chilly places the eels like best. You would look up and see the sky through the water and everything would be reversed. Perhaps time itself would go backward, unspooled like thread.

That's what she wanted. This life of hers undone. Mattie went down to the river while her father-in-law slept and the boy stretched out in the grass. She took off the heavy boots and her socks, then unbuttoned her dress and pulled it over her head. Evan sat up straight when she did so, his mouth dry. He'd been seeing things ever since he'd gone to war and perhaps this was simply one more mad vision: the doves flying up, his brother's face, Mattie Starr's nearly naked body, her shoulders, her legs, her back.

She turned and gave him a look. She was real, all right. Evan struggled to his feet. The water was rushing so fast, one step and she would be taken downstream. If he wasn't quick, he would watch mutely while she was swept away, the way he'd watched his world blown to pieces. Evan refused to allow his fate to be this and nothing more, to stand by helplessly while she drowned herself. He would not be defined by his inability to be a man. He raced down to the steep bank. He concentrated and willed himself to run and there he was, his arms around her. She pulled him in with her when she made the jump. They fell slowly, entwined in their strange embrace. There was barely a splash as they went in. It was more of a disappearance. Something invisible, yet there all the same. The river was colder than they would have imagined, ice water from the top of the mountain that had come tumbling down.

They went under to where everything was green. The air bubbles were like clouds. The clouds were like white stones thrown into the far distance. Evan circled one arm around Mattie Starr's waist and with the other he held fast to a log jutting out from the bank. They sputtered and lifted their heads out of the water. They were in a quiet pool set off from the rush of water by stacked logs that served as a dam. The sunlight was falling into the water, spreading out in waves. The air was damp and sweet. Mattie looped her arms around his neck. She kissed him, then pulled away. When she saw the look on Evan's face, she kissed him again. She put her tongue inside his mouth, kissing him more and more deeply. When the undershirt she wore slipped off her shoulders, she didn't grab for it. It floated away, like a white lily. The water was shallow and they could nearly stand up, but it was easier not to. She took his hand and put it between her legs. She let him pull her undergarments down. There were frogs on the banks and tadpoles in the shallows. It was the season of peepers calling all day and all night. She whispered to Evan that it was what she wanted, so he moved himself inside her. He watched her close her eyes, lean her head back. There was no place else and no other time. They weren't going backward or forward. Blackflies spun in a funnel above the current. Evan's head was filled with the sound of water. He thought of the ghost in the grass, her blue dress and bare feet. He thought of the way the doves had flown up into the sky all in a rush, startled by gunfire, and then all he could think was that despite everything that happened, he was alive.

THE TRUTH ABOUT
MY MOTHER

1903

MY MOTHER BEGAN A NEW LIFE HALFWAY through her own. Such things happened often in our town. Blackwell was deep in Berkshire County, where the weather was mysterious and the people were equally unpredictable. Several of the inhabitants were descendants of the founding settlers, families who had intermarried often enough so that many of the women had red hair, with mercurial tempers that suited their coloring. The men were tall and quiet and good at most everything. All of the dogs in town were collies, smart, fast dogs, used to herd cows and sheep; they answered to an individual whistle as if they were birds instead of dogs and understood songs as easily as words.

There were new folks in town as well, people headed out west who were stopped by the mountain on their way to Ohio or Colorado. No one knew how many residents had arrived simply because they were running away from something or someone. My mother, for instance, told everyone she was a schoolteacher and that she'd been born in Manchester, England, and trained in Boston. She said her name was Elinor Book. Because that is what she said, that was what people believed. At that point Blackwell had only a one-room schoolhouse, and my mother taught every age and subject. The town council was happy to hire her when she appeared one day with a small suitcase and no recommendations. She had beautiful handwriting, with full, sensuous letters that betrayed her inner nature. She was given the cottage behind the Brady house, the oldest house in town. When she first arrived, she would stand outside in the garden late at night, when everyone else was in bed. People thought they were hearing coyotes, or one of the dozens of panthers that remained in the woods, but it was my mother, standing in the yard, crying.

It was only Isaac Partridge who lived in the big house. His father, a relation of the town founder, had his leg shot off in the Civil War and when he'd returned, he had married a widow in town with children of her own. They'd all passed on to their greater reward, and Isaac alone was left of the family. He was nearly forty, a bachelor. My mother wasn't yet thirty. It was possible to tell she was beautiful even though she tried her best to hide it. She wore a black coat that covered her figure and tied her hair in a knot so she might look more responsible. But at night when she stood in the garden, she looked young. She looked the way she had when she killed my father in Brooklyn.

$\mathcal{S}\!\!\twoheadleftarrow$

SHE KILLED HIM one April night. We had a house of our own. We were well-off. Money wasn't the problem. My father worked for the new electrical company. He said in time the whole world would be lit up and it would all be his doing and that God would welcome him into a heaven that was lit by electricity. My father wore a suit and a hat when he left in the morning, but when he came home in the evening, he was drunk. My mother and I often hid from him in the vegetable cellar. To me, Brooklyn smelled like the sea and like root cellars. If you went out on our roof, you could see Sheepshead Bay. I didn't like the word *Sheepshead,* but I liked to sit out and watch the blue horizon and listen to our neighbors and the sound of the streetcar. At some point, as twilight was falling, my mother would call my name and we would go down to the cellar the way some people do in towns where there are tornados, except in our house my father was the tornado. It was him we hid from.

Sometimes my father brought home women and we could hear them up in our house, and my mother would put her hands over my ears. Sometimes he'd be sneaky. He'd be so silent that we thought he was in a stupor, sprawled out on the floor, but instead he'd be waiting for us in the parlor. He did things I won't speak about. We try not to remember his name, but it was William Wentworth. He was a vice president at the electric company, and he smelled like smoke. We try not to remember what he did to us, but those are the kinds of things you can't forget. He worked for Edison, whom he called the great man. Electricity was everywhere, like a snake, lighting up the city. In January, it was used to electrocute an elephant in Luna Park in Coney Island. My mother had taken me to see that same elephant the summer before, and we'd fed her peanuts through the bars. Her name was Topsy, a funny name for such an extraordinary creature. She had been noble as she daintily lifted the peanuts from our hands.

Now people said that Topsy was difficult, spooky. She had trampled three of her trainers, at least one of them known to be cruel and abusive. People in the know whispered that he had burned her with cigarettes just for the fun of it, and that there were marks all over her flesh, but none of those reports were in the papers. My father was excited all that week. He was the one in charge. The event would prove that Edison knew more about the dangers of electricity than Westinghouse, whom my father called an upstart. It was a battle of the greats, and in the end a single creature who didn't even belong among us would be proof that Edison's method of electrifying the world was safe, while Westinghouse was a crackpot with liquid lightning that could fry us alive.

Thousands of people came to see Topsy die. My mother thought the desire to view such anguish was a sign of the innate cruelty of human beings. My mother and I weren't like other people. For one thing, we preferred the dark. In the root cellar we saw by candlelight. We had no desire to be part of the audience, clamoring to see the poor creature die. We went because my father insisted. We were among the crush of onlookers who applauded, eager for the show to start, but we didn't holler or clap our hands. It was a horrible sight. The elephant was tied up in ropes, hooked to a platform and a post. Wooden sandals with copper electrodes were attached to her feet. We were in the back of the crowd, but for an instant the elephant looked at me. Her look went right through me. I had to turn away. Later, my mother told me the elephant's last keeper had been sitting on a bench nearby, weeping. She said she wanted a man like that, someone who understood sorrow, not someone who caused it.

After that, things got worse. My mother's true feelings were there in her face. She didn't have to say anything to show how she felt about my father. He reacted as you might imagine he would. Hateful was too small a word. I wondered if the electricity at Luna Park had seeped into his skin, and that was why his meanness grew, like a charge, burning brighter throughout the spring. Fine weather seemed to affect him adversely. But in all honesty he drank whenever there was rain or snow or wind or falling leaves. He drank and burned, and we paid the price. We often kept the lights turned off, though ours had been one of the first houses in Brooklyn to be wired. We kept a lantern beneath my bed.

MY MOTHER KILLED him on the Tuesday after I turned ten. I had come between them when he was beating her, and then he'd suddenly turned on me. He was slapping me and ripping at my clothes. He said words I didn't understand. I knew from the look on my mother's face as she tore me away that something was over and something was begun. My mother and I began to pray, but we prayed for a bad thing, and I wondered if God would welcome us when we stood before him, or if he would turn us out when the time came to face up to who we had been in our lifetimes and what we deserved in the hereafter.

One morning we went out to the fish market. We passed by stands of flounder and piles of mussels dredged from the bay. My mother wasn't there to buy fish. She was thinking about another dish entirely. She turned down an alley where there were factories. The air was acrid. She was so beautiful that men were drawn to her, despite the plain way she dressed. They spoke to my mother and made offers I didn't understand. She didn't answer. She sat me down on a bench and told me not to move. Even if it became night, even if the morning broke through the sky, I was to stay exactly where I was. She gave me a bundle of my clothes and a satchel with some cheese and bread. She said I was to give my name as Sara Book if anyone asked, and to say I was from Manchester, England. That was where her grandmother had been from, and Book had been her grandmother's maiden name. It was still the truth even though the facts were stretched out like the muslin we used for our needlepoint samplers. She said that whatever happened next she would come back for me. She would always be there when I needed her. I believed her. But I was afraid she might be the one who would need me. How would I know if I stayed on the bench? How could I come to her aid?

When she turned to go I followed her.

The streets in Brooklyn were funny and curved. Some of the sidewalks were made of wooden planks that were slippery when it rained. I kept thinking about the elephant. How she had looked at me, begging for something. I should have run to her and cut the ropes that held her, but I stayed and did nothing. Now I saw the elephant whenever I closed my eyes. Her image had been imprinted inside me when the first burst of electricity went through the wires. I couldn't think the word *Topsy* without getting a shiver.

It was beginning to rain, a light spring shower. The air shimmered and the sidewalks were slick. My mother stopped at a shop, then slipped inside. It was a tannery. When I peered in the window, I saw my mother speaking with one of the women who worked there. She took off the pearl brooch my father had given her in their courting days and handed it over. The woman took it between her teeth and bit down to tell if it was real gold. It was. There were boiling vats everywhere, all containing different colors of mixture. The stench of leather was terrible. I covered my mouth and nose with my hand and huffed and puffed in order to breathe. It smelled like death in there and that's what it was.

My mother came out with the packet she had paid dearly for. It was poison. She had on her black coat even though it was a warm evening. She wore it as if it were armor, her shield and her sword. The rain washed away the horrid smell of leather. On my birthday, my mother had made me a chocolate cake with sugar frosting. She told me ten was a special year in a girl's growing up, the year when the direction for all the rest of her life would be set. This is what ten meant to me: I would never sit on a bench and wait for what happened next. I would never look into the crowd, searching for someone to save me.

I FOLLOWED HER, but stayed in the yard when she went into our house. I peeked through the window and watched as she opened the packet and poured it into a glass. My father liked a stiff drink when he came home, to follow the ones he'd already had at whatever tavern he'd chosen that day. I sat under the mustard plant. I liked the bitter scent of mustard leaves. I looked at my legs and wondered if they looked like a woman's legs. It was possible that my father was confused and that was why he had looked at me that way when I'd tried to stop him from hurting my mother. Maybe that was why he'd said the things I knew were bad. My mother had vowed that he couldn't stay away from women, and perhaps he'd forgotten my true age.

I crouched there in the fading twilight. I was in the shadows and I felt safe. For a few moments I forgot about our situation. I watched an anthill where the ants were busy working away, building their house taller and stronger. Some of the first of the season's crickets were calling when he came home. From a distance he looked like a rich man after a day's work. My mother was sitting in a kitchen chair. She didn't run for the root cellar or the closet. She looked calm and beautiful and quiet. That was when I knew she was going to kill him. She'd always run from him before. He went inside. He was a tornado. He did things to my mother I will not speak about, right there in the kitchen. She didn't cry or try to protect herself. He hit her with his belt, which is why she has a line down her face. It's the mark of that day.

When he was done, she offered him the drink.

I sat under the mustard bush until he was finished drinking. I thought there must be another way for men and women to be with each other if people fell in love. I knew I must do as she'd told me. I ran back to the bench where she had left me. She didn't come for me that night. I ate the bread and cheese she'd given me. I didn't answer when men passing by made comments. Early the next morning my mother appeared. She looked tired and she had a suitcase with her. Some people stared because of the mark of the belt on my mother's face, but she said she didn't mind if people stared, as long as they stayed away. We took the ferry to Manhattan, under the shadow of the Williamsburg Bridge, which I had hoped to walk across when it was finished.

We walked to the train station. We went to Albany because it was the next train scheduled. That was how we chose our fate, quickly, ready for whatever happened next. We sat in our seats and didn't speak as we watched the city fade away. I took my mother's hand, and she laced her fingers through mine. We saw green fields, forests, blue skies. We got off in Albany, which wasn't much of a city compared with Brooklyn. We stayed one night in a house where rooms were rented out. We could hear people talking all night in the room right next to ours. I heard a woman laugh, and the sound shone through the darkness, brighter than any light. I was glad we had gotten on that train.

WHEN WE SET out the next day, we did so on foot. The roads were empty and long. Sometimes we went where there were no roads at all. Days passed. Everything in bloom. Birds startled as we went through the grass. I began to like being out in the country, hiking for miles through the fields and on the winding roads. We reached a pretty town called Lenox where everyone was friendly. A woman let us stay in her garden shed. My mother said she was a schoolteacher in search of a job and the woman suggested she try Blackwell, where they were looking for a teacher. My mother told me to stay in Lenox. It was easier for a woman alone to find a position. She would come back for me when everything was settled.

I couldn't help but wonder what might happen if she needed me. When she left, I followed her again. She walked all day and so did I. I ate little berries that grew along the path. My skirt tore on thorn plants, but the air was fresh and warm and bees were everywhere. I was quiet as I went along. No one knew I was there. Even the meadowlarks that slept in their nests among the thistles didn't wake when I ran past.

When we came to a river, my mother took off all her clothes. She washed her hair, then combed it with the tortoise-shell comb she used to pile it atop her head. She walked more slowly now. Soon the town of Blackwell came into view. It was on the other side of a huge apple orchard. The pink and white blooms had not yet unfurled, but the leaves were green. I thought the sea of apple trees was a good sign, there to replace the waters of Sheepshead Bay. I stood outside the meetinghouse while my mother went inside, then traipsed after at a distance when a man took her to see the cottage where the schoolteacher would live. It was right behind the oldest house in the village, the Brady estate, a rambling place with rooms added on, white with black shutters. The owner had donated the cottage for the use of the schoolteacher for the good of the town. Maybe that was why my mother's scar didn't bother the school committee. They thought she'd never find a husband because of it, and that was fine with them. I heard the man who had interviewed my mother say that the town council always hired a single woman to be the teacher because a married woman would think of her own children before she would the children of Blackwell. I imagined the root cellar at home and I missed it for a moment. I missed my mother saying *Don't listen. Close your eyes.*

That night there was heavy rain. I slept in the barn, where there were two horses. The horses were surprised to see me, but when I offered them some hay they quieted down. I wished I had a dog to keep me company. I'd seen several collies in town; a few had gazed at me, but none had barked, and I started to think maybe I was lucky if the dogs took a fancy to me. Maybe

I was in the right place at last. I slept beneath a blanket that smelled like grass. In the morning, a man came in and fed the horses and told them they were good boys. He laughed gently when they butted their heads against him, straining to get close to him. He was older than my father, but he wasn't like a tornado. He was more like the horses. Quiet. He was one of the tall men in Blackwell whose families had known hardship and sorrow, a descendant of the town founders, people who'd lived through blizzards and famine and faced their hardships with the same sure demeanor. It didn't surprise me that after he'd left, the horses whinnied for him to return.

When my mother went to the schoolhouse, I followed her there. My stomach was growling, but I refused to think about my hunger. Twelve children were waiting for her, all dressed in clean clothes, their hands folded in front of them. They all had brought their lunches, and a few had books. At noon, I went back the way I had come. The side door of the big house was open, so I crept inside when I smelled food. I was so hungry I couldn't stop myself when I saw a pie on the counter. I took it, the whole thing. I went out behind the house and sat in the tall grass and ate it all. Afterward I was sick, but I didn't care. I fell asleep right there in the grass until the rain woke me. When I ran into the barn, I felt as though someone was watching me, but when I turned, no one was there.

That night I looked in my mother's window. She was eating supper. The housemaid who worked for Mr. Partridge had brought some stew and a loaf of bread, then she stopped at the barn and left another loaf. That was when I understood that the man who owned the horses knew I was in his barn.

Late that night my mother went into her yard when the

citizens of Blackwell were all in their beds. She wept for all she had lost and all she had done. Gooseflesh rose on my body as I was roused from sleep. The horses became panicky in their stalls when they heard her cries. The man came out of his house. He stopped when he saw my mother. I could see him fall in love with her right then and there in spite of the mark on her face that my father had left. I hadn't understood that love could be visible, as real as the grass or the river. But I understood it now. I saw the man's yearning just as clearly as I saw the horses' desire for hay.

In the morning, after my mother left for the schoolhouse, I went to knock on the door of the big house. The tall man who lived there introduced himself as Isaac Partridge. He wasn't surprised to see me. He invited me in and gave me tea and toast. He told me he was sorry he had no more apple pie to serve me. He said he himself had always preferred pie to cake and could eat one in its entirety at one sitting, just as I had done.

I told him there were three things he had to do to make her love him if that was what he wanted. He seemed interested and amused. He said, "Go on." The first was that he had to give up all drink. He said that was easy enough. He wasn't much of a drinker. The second was that he had to give her his house and take the cottage for his own. That was easy as well. His house was too big for a single man. The third was that he had to give her a daughter. He looked at me then. "I don't know how easy that is," he said. "Easy enough," I assured him.

That night Isaac knocked on my mother's door and said she needed to move into the big house. The cottage was infested with beetles and she had to leave until the infestation was over.

He would live there instead since bugs were no bother to him. My mother looked at him carefully, then agreed. Every night for the next week they had dinner together because the cottage had no kitchen and Isaac had no way to make his meals there. Instead he would knock on the door of the house that he owned—where he was now a visitor—and my mother would welcome him inside. They would sit at the table and eat the meal the housemaid prepared. My mother wore her plain brown dress and her hair pulled up. The mark that separated her face into two halves was red in the candlelight, like a flower. Every morning Mr. Partridge would report to me on the progress of their conversation. I would then tell him more about what my mother liked and what she despised. She hated cruelty, people who made judgments, hash for supper, cigar smoke. She loved roses, fresh fish and mussels, trips by boat, books, children. Mr. Partridge listened carefully and wrote it all down in a notebook.

One evening he invited my mother to the meetinghouse for the council meeting exactly as I suggested. That night he proposed that no liquor be served in the village of Blackwell. Alcohol, he said, was the downfall of many good men and there was no reason for Blackwell to aid in mankind's depravity. My mother gazed at him with surprise as he made this suggestion in his quiet, firm voice. I knew she would be impressed. Since Jack Straw ran the only tavern on his family's land, and it was well outside the town limits, no one disagreed. The bylaw was passed unanimously. My mother walked home beside Mr. Partridge in the dark. She looked at him for a long time as he crossed the yard to the cottage.

We waited until a clear night for the third step. It was the middle of May by then. I knew my mother sat up at nights crying over me. I had seen her writing letters to the address in Lenox where I was supposed to have waited. On the eve of our plan, Mr. and Mrs. Kelly, a well-liked couple in town, went out for a walk along the river as they did every night after their supper. I knew their schedule and had been watching them. They would be our witnesses. Isaac Partridge made certain to be walking there too. When I heard him approach and greet the Kellys, I slipped into the river. I was careful to submerge myself in the exact spot Mr. Partridge had shown me, a pool where the current wouldn't catch me up and carry me downstream. I hung onto a branch and screamed. I thought about Brooklyn and my birthday and the elephant, and soon enough the screams became real in my mouth.

The Kellys watched from the steep bank as Mr. Partridge threw himself in to rescue me, and they helped to revive me. When I came round, I said I couldn't remember what had happened. Only that my parents had drowned and that my name was Sara. I seemed slow-witted, perhaps from my time in the river, but I soon turned out to be a fast learner. People in Blackwell were amazed by how bright I was. Mr. Partridge adopted me and gave me his name that very week. We both signed papers in the meetinghouse and afterward there was a party where mussels and fish that had been brought all the way from Boston were served. Mr. Partridge gave me the two horses in the barn for my very own and, as a special surprise, bought me a pug dog to keep me company. I loved that dog and called him Topsy, allowing him to sleep in my bed atop the feather quilt. In return for all Mr. Partridge had done for me, I gave him the only thing I had. He married my mother on the first of June. As far as he was concerned, she came from Manchester, England, and had been educated in Boston. Just as her contract with the town had stated, she'd never had children of her own, though anyone could see she was partial to me. She was the town schoolteacher and the love of his life. I was the girl who had nearly drowned, but had managed to save myself instead, in the year I turned ten.

THE PRINCIPLES OF DEVOTION

1918

MY SISTER SARA CALLED ME TO HER ROOM on the morning of her death. She was in quarantine in the cottage behind our house, stricken with the Spanish flu, unable to eat or drink, her fever so high she had begun to speak with people who weren't there. In a lucid moment she gathered her strength and wrote a note she then shoved beneath her door. I stood in the yard and read it. It was September and everything was yellow. The bees' nests were high in the trees, which meant a hard winter would follow. Sara wanted me to grant her a last wish. I had never been able to deny her anything. I was ten years old and she was twenty-five, as much a mother to me and my younger sister, Hannah, as our own mother had been. It was an honor to be asked such a favor. If I was afraid of anything, it was only that I would fail her in some way.

Our parents had died the year before, our father first, our mother soon after. They were bound together, people said. They had never spent a night apart and always called each other Mr. and Mrs., as though still delighted and somewhat surprised to find themselves husband and wife. Sara was our father's favorite. He called her his charm and said she brought him luck. Even after she'd married Billy Kelly, who later went to war in France and was now in quarantine himself in the navy yard north of Boston, unable to see his wife as she lay ill, Sara had always come to our father for comfort and advice until his death last winter. Now, perhaps because there was no one else, she'd sent for me.

Mrs. Kelly, Billy's mother, was helping us keep house, but she wouldn't venture inside the cottage for fear of my sister's disease, even though Sara had fallen ill after visiting her son. Each evening, Mrs. Kelly carried a tray across the yard. She fixed a bowl of broth, a plate with some dry rolls, and a pitcher of water. She slid the food through an open window. Even though she had no contact with her daughter-in-law, she wore a mask over her face and hurried back across the yard as if our darling Sara was a venomous snake. I refused to look like a coward to my sister. Sara had told me that a woman who could rescue herself was a woman who would never be in need. But there was no rescue for her now. Her skin was pale, and we could hear her coughing far into the night from across the yard. Our younger sister, Hannah, went to sleep with her hands over her ears so she could blot out our dear Sara's suffering. But I listened. I heard. I sat by my window and wondered what came next, in the world beyond our own.

೬๕

I SLIPPED ON my good blue dress for the visit, even though my black one had been cleaned and pressed and was waiting in the bureau. I didn't wear gloves the way some people did when ministering to the ill. Sara had always been so brave. Perhaps that was why our father favored her. I didn't blame him. She'd been a strong swimmer as a girl and had gained some fame when she crossed from Boston Harbor to Swampscott. A small rowboat had tried to keep pace with her in case she faltered, but they had lost her in the fog. Sara told me that seals had followed her, as if she was one of their own. She was photographed for the newspapers with a garland atop her head, a huge grin across her face, soaking wet in her swimming suit. She was the sort of woman who was more beautiful in difficult times, resolute, ready for action. She had always hiked and fished with our father, and she loved horses. She had a natural affinity with them and said people who used a whip when they rode should be whipped themselves. She was also a painter of some note, and her watercolors were prized not just in Berkshire County, where we lived, but also in Manhattan, where she'd studied. She laughed and insisted that even though she had a New York soul, her heart was in the Berkshires. I had one of her paintings above my bed. It was of Hightop Mountain, which I could see out my window. I preferred my sister's version to the original. When I looked at that painting, I imagined I was Sara, and that for once I could see through her eyes.

Many men had been in love with my sister over the years. Boys in school sent her love notes. Painters asked her to model, but she laughed and told them they should model for her instead. Once a fellow from New York showed up on our doorstep. Our father chased him off by pointing a rifle at him, which was laughable considering my father's kind nature and the fact that the gun hadn't worked for years. My sister's caller stood his ground, and my father invited him in for dinner. He was a wealthy man, bewitched by my sister's talent and her beauty, but in the end Sara chose Billy Kelly, whom she'd known since they were in school. He was steady, she told me, like a rock. I was only a child but I wanted to say a man is not a rock. I myself would have preferred a man who was like a river, changing and quick, always a surprise.

I OPENED THE door of the cottage, eager to do anything my sister asked. There was a scrim of dust in the air, yellow, like the grass in the fields. The parlor was silent, except for the clock on the mantel. I went to the bedroom and knocked. The door opened under my touch. There was Sara, in bed, her dog lying by her side. Our father had bought her that dog, a pug she named Topsy, when she was little more than my age. He was nearly fifteen by now, ancient for his breed. Topsy was her protector and her friend, her only company since she'd taken ill. Now he stood and barked at me, as if he hadn't known me my whole life.

"Topsy." I was startled by how vicious he was. "It's just me."

Sara reached to pet him, and he quieted under her touch. Still he glared at me.

My parents had let my sister name me. Thankfully she hadn't called me something to rhyme with Topsy. I might have been Flopsy if Sara had been a less poetic child. For three weeks I was nameless, a baby in my cradle. At last my sister decided upon Azurine. She said she couldn't find a name beautiful enough for me so she invented one. It was the name of a watercolor paint, a wash of blue-green, mutable, gemlike. Perhaps you belong to anyone who names you. If that was so, then it was surely true of both Topsy and of me. Which of us was more distraught to see my sister in such distress, I couldn't say.

I sat in a chair near the bed and said my sister's name. How extraordinary a word it was, elemental, pure.

"Don't come too close," Sara warned. She held a handkerchief over her mouth. "I've been talking with Mother and Daddy. I speak with them all the time." I shivered to think how close she was to the dead, able to hear their words. "I'm the favorite," she announced, as if she were a little girl and I her proud aunt.

"You're my favorite too," I told her.

She was wasting away, but still beautiful. Because of her fever her hair was wet. She looked the way she had when she was photographed in Boston, standing on the shore.

"I have a wish." Sara's expression was serious and focused. All at once I realized she knew it was the end. I understood I needn't keep that secret from her. For that I was grateful.

I moved my chair closer in order to hear. I had better remember every instant, for it would never come again. There was the tray with last night's supper perched on the sill, untouched. The pitcher of water was filled to the brim. The window was raised and sparrows clustered on the ledge, chattering, pecking at the roll on the plate. I didn't feel that I was ten years old, even though that was the number of my years on earth. Not anymore. I knew more than a girl should know. I saw my sister's sorrow. Maybe I should have been more like Hannah and covered my ears.

"I need you to take care of the one I love. Promise you'll never leave him."

Sara's voice was thick. Speaking was difficult for her. It may have been that she had never before asked anyone for anything and that was difficult as well. In her lifetime she had given far more than she had received. I was speechless when I heard her request. I thought she meant Billy, and for an instant I wondered if she had forgotten I was only a child. I shuddered. Did she expect me to spend my life caring for her husband, perhaps even marrying him the way some surviving sisters did? All the same I gave Sara my promise. My face was wet with tears, but I controlled my voice and managed to sound like a reasonable person, one who had just pledged her life away.

"I'll write to Billy today," I said. "I'll watch over him."

"Billy!" My sister almost smiled. "No. Not Billy. I want you to take Topsy. He'll be yours now."

I was relieved in some ways, saddened in others. It was as though my sister had left the human world behind. And Topsy, who was to be mine, was growling.

"He doesn't like me," I said childishly.

"But I do," Sara countered. "If I didn't trust you more than anyone else, I wouldn't put him in your care."

I took her hand even though you weren't supposed to touch those infected with the flu. The birds at the window had finished with their crumbs. They flew away all at once. The light changed and lengthened. I could hear the wind in the trees. I felt lucky to be there with Sara, to be the one she trusted.

The dog knew before I did. He made a sound that was nearly human, a sob it seemed to me. My sister dropped my hand. I heard something escape from her mouth, her soul perhaps, rushing upward. For one bright moment I thought she might return, but she was gone. I sat there for a while, then went to close the window. When I returned to the bedside, I reached to shut my sister's eyes. Topsy leapt to bite me. There were two drops of blood on my wrist.

No one wanted to prepare the body, so in the end my sister wore the same white nightgown to her funeral she'd worn since falling ill. I brushed her hair, and Topsy watched me. I had smacked his nose after his bite, so he was a little more cautious around me, though he growled again. "Don't you dare," I told him. "You're mine now." He looked at me with his buggy eyes as though I were mad. We were in the same room, mourning my sister. That was all we had in common. It was she who bound us together.

Two laborers from the cemetery brought the coffin into our yard. The men were from Italy and could barely speak English. They came into the cottage, surprised to find only a ten-year-old girl and a little dog tending to the body. They took off their hats as a mark of respect, then carried my sister to the coffin, which rode atop a small wagon they pulled by hand. We followed the wagon, Topsy and I. I saw my sister Hannah through the window of the big house. Mrs. Kelly had insisted it was dangerous to attend the funeral, even though it would be held in the open air. Hannah put up her hand to wave to me, but I went on. The pastor, Johnson Jacob, came and said a prayer. He was a good man, and he waited with me while the laborers dug the grave. He told me that we could not begin to understand the mysteries of our faith, and I wondered why he assumed I had any faith at all. When he left, Topsy and I stayed on, until the earth was replaced. How was it that Sara could be gone? Of all that she might have asked for, how could her wish have been so small?

When it grew dark, I started for the path that led to the cemetery gates. They were beautiful gates, black wrought iron, crafted in France, ordered by a family who had lost their little girl, as if setting out those gates could keep her spirit from wandering. I called for the dog as I started for home, but Topsy stayed where he was. I clapped my hands. He didn't even turn his head. The last of the season's crickets were singing in the grass. Their sound was low and slow. Everything ended. Everything stopped. All at once I realized how alone I was in the graveyard. I felt again that I was only ten years old and that the world was far too much for me. I called and called, but Topsy wouldn't come. The dark was widening and the wind took up. I ran on to the gate. When I looked back, the dog was lying in the grass, like an ugly old cricket.

MRS. KELLY MADE me bathe out in the yard with strong lye soap. I had to burn the clothes I'd worn. I watched as the black dress turned into smoke. When I went up to bed, Hannah slipped in next to me and wept. I comforted her and said Sara was in a better place, but we weren't close after that. I kept to myself, especially after Billy came home. He'd found a new wife while he was in quarantine, a nurse from Boston named Annie. He was a young man and no one expected him to live the rest of his life alone, without a wife and children. They were married in the spring, and Hannah served as a flower girl. I picked the mallows to wind into a garland for her head, but when the day of the wedding came, I said I was ill and stayed away from the church. I went to the cemetery instead. I visited there each afternoon with a bowl of food and a jug of fresh water for Topsy. He had never come away from my sister's grave. All winter he had stayed there, even though it had turned out to be an especially cold season, just as the bees nesting high in the trees had predicted. When snow fell he made a den. I brought him a blanket. There were several nights when I imagined he would freeze to death, but he always was there to greet me the next day. His coat grew thick and rough. His eyes were droopy. He never wagged his tail when he saw me, but he knew me and rose to greet me when I approached.

Now that it was spring, he sprawled out on the grass. It was blackfly season. I set a mesh over a tree branch to form a gauzy tent. I sat there protected from fly bites, but Topsy never came inside, no matter how I might urge him to join me in the tent.

"You're a madman," I said to the dog on the day Billy Kelly married his second wife. "Come sit with me."

Topsy and I were hunkered down in the cemetery, the netting between us. I had brought along a lunch for us to share, but neither of us was hungry and I tossed the crumbs to the birds. Topsy twitched whenever flies circled above his head. He had little marks on his nose and paws from the irritations they caused. Our house was currently decorated with pink ribbons for the wedding supper. Pink was Annie's favorite color. Clove pink, china pink, snow pink. I thought of how when Sara wrapped presents she used string instead of ribbons because she hated waste. "Oh, it's just as good," she would insist when our mother would say her work seemed too homemade. "It's better." My sister hated pink; she preferred the deepest darkest shades of red. Thinking of the roses she had once planted, I sat there in the tent of netting and cried. Maybe Topsy felt some pity for me because later he trotted beside me when I walked to the gate.

By then most people in Blackwell knew that Sara's dog had taken up residence in the cemetery and that he refused to leave. The school had a class trip to visit him, and the pastor came out on Sundays after his sermon and brought biscuits. The grass where Topsy lay was worn away. There was nothing but bare earth. He always went into the woods to do his business, then ran back to his spot. He accepted treats, but only if they were placed directly before him. He ducked his head if anyone tried to pet him. He wasn't interested in their affections. In early fall, when Sara had been gone a year, Annie Kelly had a baby she named Beth Ann. Hannah often minded the baby—she took great pleasure in her—but I wasn't one for children. When the baby reached up to me, I avoided her touch. I said I was clumsy, unable to help out with one so small. I began to take my schoolbooks out to the cemetery so I could read in peace. I was there when an art class from Lenox arrived one afternoon. They set up their easels and made studies of Topsy. The teacher had been an admirer of Sara's work and he gave me one of his drawings on that day. I showed it to Topsy and he gazed at it disdainfully. I laughed and agreed it wasn't a very good likeness. Not so long ago my sister babied him and let him sleep in her bed and Topsy had been as fat as a frog. Now he was skin and bones, even though I brought him his supper each day. There was a white film over his eyes.

I didn't think Topsy would last through another winter, but he did. He always stood to greet me, and when I left, he politely walked me to the gate. Other than those two rituals, he didn't seem to notice my existence. I talked to him sometimes, but he never even tilted his head. He ignored me. I still had the bite mark on my wrist from the day my sister died. The bite had faded, but when I ran my hand over my skin, I could feel it. That following spring I turned twelve. I learned how to make rhubarb pie with a fine crust and how to read Latin. I cut my hair short, and it was a scandal. Everyone was talking about it, but by summer most of the girls in town had followed my lead. Now when I went to the cemetery, Topsy was there by the gate, waiting for me at four o'clock. He could tell time it seemed, and when I was late, he always looked put out. As we walked to my sister's grave I told him what was going on in town, bits of gossip and news. Not that he cared. I told him I couldn't sleep at night, and that I had started swimming in the Eel River, even though I knew I would never be as strong a swimmer as Sara.

One afternoon when there was so much pollen the air itself seemed yellow, Billy Kelly came down the path. I was reading Mary Shelley's *Frankenstein,* which thrilled me, not only the story but the fact that a woman had been daring enough to write it. We had a new library in town and I was there nearly every week, stopping on my way to visit Sara. The librarian had hesitated when I checked out *Frankenstein.* I said, "Don't worry. I'm not afraid of words." Sometimes I read aloud. Now I looked up from my book and there was Billy. He was staring at Topsy. Topsy stared back at him.

"You'd think he'd have died out in the cold," Billy remarked.

As far as I knew Billy had never come out here before. Perhaps his mother had filled his head with some nonsense about disease reaching out from beyond the grave. Perhaps he simply didn't have the heart for such visits.

"He's stubborn," I said. When Topsy gave me a baleful look, I added, "All pugs are. It's the nature of the breed."

"Do you think it's in your best interest to spend so much time out here?" Billy asked me. It was then I realized that people in town were talking about me, thinking I was odd.

"I wasn't thinking about my best interest," I said quietly.

Billy went away, but I stayed until dark. I didn't want to have dinner with the family or speak to anyone, although that night Hannah slipped into my bed the way she used to when she was younger. We were a bit closer, but we were very different. I didn't tell her to leave, but I turned to the wall. I spent more time at the library. I had decided I wanted to further my schooling, perhaps attend Smith College, and Hannah now came to the library with me. There was another baby in the house, and the Kellys seemed to have taken over. It was noisy and hectic even for Hannah. For me, it was like being in a madhouse where I was being driven out of my mind by all the diapers and dinners and laundry and people who meant something to each other but nothing to me.

When you read, the time flies by, and before I knew it I was fifteen, then sixteen, nearly a woman. I was tall, and I kept my hair cut short. People said I looked like Sara, but they were mistaken. Sara had been beautiful. All I had was the name she had given me, and Topsy. He was more than twenty by then, ancient. He had difficulty getting up but he still waited for me every day at four, still walked me back to the edge of the cemetery when I left. He never once set foot outside the gate. Never ventured onto the road. Sometimes the weather prevented me from bringing him his supper. During one bad storm I couldn't get there for several days when the snowdrifts rose higher than our windows and doors. I was certain he'd be gone because of the circumstances, starved or buried alive. But when I finally managed to get out to the cemetery, Topsy was waiting. He'd found a den of sorts in an oak tree and had managed to make it through. He let me pet him now and then, and when I spoke, he turned his head in my direction, though I could tell he couldn't see.

The burial crew found him at Sara's grave one day that summer. Without bothering to ask permission from the town council, they buried him there, beside my sister. Everything was green. For me, this was the most beautiful time of the year in Berkshire County, before the leaves all turned color and dropped away. They say that dogs may dream, and when Topsy was old, his feet would move in his sleep. With his eyes closed he would often make a noise that sounded quite human, as if greeting someone in his dreams. At first it seemed that he believed Sara would return, but as the years went by I understood that his loyalty asked for no reward, and that love comes in unexpected forms. His wish was small, as hers had been—merely to be beside her. As for me, I already knew I would never get what I wanted.

THE FISHERMAN'S WIFE

1935

THE FISHERMAN'S WIFE ARRIVED IN THE spring. She lived in a one-room house in a clearing beside the Eel River. One week the fisherman was gone, and the next he was back with his young beautiful wife, whose black hair was so long she would have stepped on it if she hadn't arranged it atop her head with pins. She didn't speak to anyone in town, or even raise her eyes if someone greeted her. No one knew her name or where she'd come from. In those days, no one asked.

Times were hard, and distractions weren't easy to come by. Perhaps that was why the gossip began. A story can still entrance people even while the world is falling apart. The bank had closed down, and the banker's family had been forced to move into a cottage behind the church; they kept up the grounds in exchange for shelter and food. The leather factory was abandoned, as were many of the mills along the river. In cities everywhere people were starving. In New York, hundreds of shacks had been set up in Central Park. In Albany, riots broke out when people grew hungry. The citizens of Blackwell, Massachusetts, were luckier than most. Many had their own gardens. They stitched their own clothes, owned their properties outright. Still, the disaster of the stock market crash had sifted down from the mighty to the everyday man. Everyone had been damaged: a bank account frozen or emptied, an order for apples canceled, a roof falling down, a son or daughter unable to finish school. Every day people could hear the low whistle of trains that passed through with carloads of orphans sent out west. The trains didn't stop at Blackwell—only in Amherst and Albany—but stray individuals occasionally leapt from passenger cars when they spied a place where they imagined they might find welcome, even if it was only a stretch of woods or a meadow where they could set up camp. Soon there were so many outsiders that a resident of Blackwell no longer knew everyone for miles around. The pastor began to advise that people use caution when coming upon strangers. He suggested they lock their doors.

That was when people began to amuse themselves with tales of the fisherman and his wife. They did so over coffee and when coffee became too dear, over liberty tea, a cheap brew made of loosestrife. The fisherman's wife wasn't much more than twenty—on that everyone agreed—while the fisherman, Horace Kelly, was seventy at least, a man so cantankerous he'd fallen out with his own family and kept to himself. People speculated that the young woman had been desperate, somehow provoked into marrying the old man. Perhaps she'd been a servant or a motherless child. Perhaps Horace had rescued or kidnapped her. According to the most optimistic among them, the fisherman had saved her from some dreadful economic plight—her father had jumped from a ledge in New York City, as so many had done, or she'd come from the Midwest, where farms were failing daily. The doom-sayers said it wouldn't last.

Horace Kelly fished for rainbow trout and salmon that were often seventeen inches long, as much as three pounds, but he was mostly known as one of the best eel-men in the county. It was said that in his lifetime he'd caught over a million eels, setting off at twilight, wrestling his catch into burlap bags since eels often clung to a man's arm in a battle of muscle and slime. Because of Kelly there were far fewer eels in the river than there'd been in the old days, back when the spring thaw meant thousands of them roiling in the water, turning the river black.

The fisherman's wife went door-to-door selling fish that was smoked in a stone oven. She wore a smock over her dress, a black scarf, laced-up boots. She nodded when asked a question, or shrugged if the answer was unknown. She had the price for fish written down on little cards, but if a customer didn't have enough money, she took what they had and made do. On smoke-days the scent of fish lingered over town. There were wisps of dove-colored clouds rising up from the oven, and occasionally a rain of black scales drifted across the yards. Because people's savings had been lost in the bank run and cash was short, they soon began to trade whatever they had in exchange for fish—a basket of apples, fresh strawberries, a clutch of brown eggs from the henhouse. When times grew even worse, they offered whatever treasures they had: silver teaspoons, a turquoise brooch, even a leather-bound copy of *Great Expectations,* which Horace Kelly threw into the smokehouse fire as kindling.

A year went by and circumstances worsened. There was a flurry of crime. Clothes were stolen off washing lines. Gardens were raided. Someone broke into the shuttered Blackwell History Museum and pilfered whatever they thought could be sold for quick cash. The Jack Straw Tavern, closed during Prohibition, reopened, but some passing tramps set a fire and there was serious damage. People began to feel that anything might happen. The futures they had expected had been rewritten by some greater hand, and no one had the slightest idea of what fate might bring next.

The stories about the fisherman and his wife grew stranger. In June, two young women saw the fisherman's wife crouched down at the riverbank. When they looked more closely, they noticed she was feeding bread to an eel that ate from her hand like one of the collie dogs in town. The eel, the women reported, was unusually large. The fisherman's wife had laughed as she fed him, which disproved some people's theory that she was a deaf-mute. She had rested her hand on the eel's back, in a motion so intimate it startled both young women, who glanced away.

Soon afterward some boys in town, forced to fish on a regular basis to put food on their families' tables, spied the fisherman's wife in another strange situation, waist-deep in the river. At first they thought she was a log, or, in the case of the banker's son, Calen Jacob, who was fanciful and bookish, a mermaid. The fisherman's wife bolted when she realized the boys were there, swimming like a fish herself, head underwater, long black hair tumbling down her naked back. Several of the boys had dreams about her after that, and a few dreamt about her their whole lives long, returning to that moment at the river even when they were old men who hadn't caught a fish in decades. After that, the fisherman's wife was often sighted at the river late at night, wading in the water. People went to look for her the way they'd scan the sky when there was the promise of shooting stars. On more than one occasion she'd been caught talking to the eels the way another woman might speak to a child or a pet.

By August there were travelers on the roads all through the Berkshires—honest men searching for work, thieves looking for a window that had been left open, mothers with children to feed—many of whom had already lost their faith. A group set up a camp in Band's Meadow. Shacks were thrown together with planks and old nails collected from the railroad tracks. Bonfires burned through the night. Mrs. Jacob at the church went around collecting what little food there was for the needy. When she called on the cabin by the river, the fisherman's wife contributed more than anyone else. Whole smoked fish. Shad that were filleted and ready to cook. The fisherman's wife didn't speak as she packed the fish into a basket. Instead, she held a finger to her lips to make her message clear: the fisherman was not to know there had been a donation.

Most people did what they could for the lost and forgotten. Women gathered in the evening to sew and knit clothes for the dozens of children who were suddenly members of the community. The church pews were full on Sundays, perhaps because the pastor gave out apples and bread at the end of every sermon. He vowed that faith in the future would see the town through, although some people wondered if the country could withstand such strife, let alone their little village. From a distance, Blackwell looked the same, but the closer a person came, the more changes he noticed. Fences were falling down. Men sat on chairs outside the meetinghouse, idle, with no ready work available. Collie dogs clustered in the shade. Before long the collies began to hunt rabbits in a pack, and on at least one occasion they were so hungry these gentle shepherds took down a small deer near the pond. They came home to their owners with blood on their muzzles and coats.

AT THE END of the summer another group of outsiders arrived in the Berkshires, sent by the WPA. They were five men in all—a children's book author, two professors, and two newspapermen. The men had been directed to collect folklore. It was part of the Federal Writers Project, and, frankly, it was sheer luck to have any work at all. They took the train to Albany en masse, sharing some whisky and a few laughs. All five were embarrassed by their current circumstances and by their foolish task. But they were broke, without serious employment, and so they decided to make the best of it. On their journey they poked fun at one another and one-upped each other. They told New York City big fish stories while the train rumbled upstate—where they'd been published, whom they had interviewed, who'd gone to Harvard or Yale, whose byline was bigger, stronger, better. They made a bet before they got to Albany, the end of the road, where they would split up to go in different directions to collect local legends. Whoever caught the best and biggest story and found the most extraordinary life would be bought drinks at the Oak Bar at the Plaza by the rest of the gang on New Year's Day of the following year. They shook hands on the platform, then went their separate ways.

Ben Levy, who had written for the *Herald Tribune* and had half a novel in his knapsack, headed out in the direction of Hightop Mountain and the towns east of Lenox. He had a map and the names of several contacts—mayors, pastors, schoolteachers. He was thirty, a city boy, but he found he enjoyed walking along the country roads. He liked the sensation of the sun beating down on him and the silence of the countryside. He had the urge to do a cartwheel, and he might have, if he'd known how. He'd spent the better part of his life in classrooms, newspaper offices, and libraries. He was smart and passionate, political by nature, but he didn't know the first thing about the natural world. He had no idea that the white things growing in the ditches were called Queen Anne's lace or that the berries on the bushes he passed by were gooseberries—which he actually found to be quite delicious—or that the spindly-legged dogs he spied as he was making camp were actually coyotes. He'd grown up in the Bronx, on Jerome Avenue, where there was only one kind of tree. He'd never thought to ask exactly what kind it was. Now he had a tent and a lantern and blisters on his feet. Once it rained while he was sleeping, and when he awoke in the morning, the whole world seemed blue and fresh. He felt weirdly hopeful out in the middle of nowhere, even though the whole country was crashing down around him.

As he approached Blackwell, Ben stopped at the Jack Straw Tavern. He took out his notebook so he could jot a few lines about it, then went inside. He had little enough money, but he ordered a whisky, which he savored. Some things were still the same, and just as good. Jack Straw's was dark and smoky. There were no other customers. The tavern had managed to get through Prohibition because the town council had graciously turned a blind eye to liquor sales after 10:00 p.m. But the current economic situation had made people stay home. Plus, there'd been the somewhat suspicious fire, which had left a mess. The beams in the ceilings were charred and pitted.

"Business bad?" Ben asked the bartender, who was Joshua Kelly, a nephew of Horace the fisherman's, and the son of Arnold, who had last owned the Jack Straw and had recently shot himself in Band's Meadow due to his financial woes. He'd been buried two days earlier. His brother hadn't bothered to attend. Joshua still wore a black armband on his sleeve.

"You might say so," he said to the newcomer.

"No interesting characters around?"

"Characters?" Joshua didn't like New Yorkers, and this fellow sounded like one. He looked like one, too. He wore glasses and a hat tipped back on his head. He had on fancy shoes even though he swore he had walked all the way from Albany and had been camping along the way. "Like Mickey Mouse? Is that what you mean?"

"Not at all." Ben decided to order a second whisky, which meant he would have very little spending money during his time in Blackwell. But buying another whisky might make for an easier time asking questions at the bar of the Jack Straw. "People with interesting stories. Oral history project."

"The government send you around?"

"Something like that."

"Nope. Can't help you out. Unless you count my uncle's wife. She swims with eels."

"Not exactly what I'm looking for." Ben thanked Joshua Kelly and put his money down, gazing at it tenderly, for it would be a long time before he saw any cash. Then he set out in the direction of town. He took notes as he went along. If he didn't find any worthwhile folklore, he'd have to invent some. He was a newspaperman, but he was a novelist as well, even though after writing half a novel he had pretty much hit a wall. It was a story about a student at Yale who felt alienated from everyone, then found his calling in political action but still couldn't get over the fact that his older brother, the smarter, more talented of the two, had died of typhus. Ben's own brother, Seth, had died at the age of fourteen, from an ear infection of all things. The infection had spread and in less than twenty-four hours Seth was dead. Ben couldn't write past that moment. He was glad to be in Blackwell. To be outside himself, looking for other people's personal histories.

He walked through an apple orchard where some local boys were climbing trees. He was told the local variety of apples was called Look-No-Furthers and that the trees had been planted by Johnny Appleseed himself. Whether or not it was true, Ben got to writing, pleased by the information. He wandered on, searching for what the boys had called the Tree of Life, the oldest apple tree in town. He found it at the edge of the meadow, standing alone. A small twisted black specimen laden with dusty leaves, drooping in the summer heat. An old woman passing by told him that one year the Tree of Life had bloomed when all other crops for miles around had failed. In this way the citizens of Blackwell had been saved from starvation. The old woman's grandmother had been there and seen the boughs bloom with her very own eyes as the snow was falling in heaps. Ben wrote that down, too. When he admitted he was starving, the old woman took him home and made him something she called red flannel hash, fixed from scraps of beef and potatoes and cabbage fried in oil. Considering Ben had had nothing but bread, hard cheese, and whisky since getting off the train in Albany, the food seemed especially delicious. The recipe merited an entry in his notebook.

The old woman, whose name was Ruth Starr Carson, lived in a cottage behind the Blackwell History Museum. For years she had been the curator, but now there were no funds for such cultural institutions, so she'd draped white muslin over the displays to keep them from fading and locked the doors. A few neighbors had helped to board up the windows, and still there'd been that awful robbery. She'd heard the thief rustling around—she continued to be blessed with good hearing and eyesight—and she'd gone out to her porch with what was said to be the founder's rifle. But the stranger had disappeared into the woods. Ruth was afraid she'd break her shoulder if she fired that old gun, if the thing even worked at all, so she let him run. Her family had lived in the grand house that was now the museum. They'd had so many children every room had been filled. But things had changed. Now she resided in the cottage that had once been a barn where sleighs and carriages and horses were kept. She had a son, but he'd gone off to California with some of the other young men in town, and although he kept promising to come back home, she had yet to see him.

Ben Levy kept writing as he ate his red flannel hash. He was starving, and his feet hurt from all the walking he'd been doing in his best shoes. His only shoes, really, since his boots had fallen apart right before he left New York. He thought about New Year's Day at the Oak Bar at the Plaza Hotel. He imagined walking in, tossing his files on the table, perhaps even reading his case studies aloud. Listen to this one, he'd call, recounting the story of the old woman who had lived in the museum, reciting the recipe for red flannel hash as if it were Hamlet's soliloquy, amusing the other men with his research and wit, winning the bet hands down.

In exchange for room and board, Ben worked on the cottage, which was in sad shape. He repaired the roof, cleared the wooden gutters, took down the dilapidated fence that was listing to one side, rebuilding it with the use of old slats and wire. In the evenings, Mrs. Carson let him wander through the museum, where he faithfully took notes. He described the wolf in a glass case, the ragged stitches crisscrossed through the threadbare pelt, the mouth pulled back in a snarl. He drew pictures illustrating the smooth, snail-like fossils that had been found in Band's Meadow, made sketches of the founding families' wagon wheels and pots and pans, and wrote descriptions of the bats that hung inside a glass case, yellow eyes forever open.

Ruth did him the favor of making introductions in town. When he said he wanted "characters," she did her best. She took him to the Jacobs, who lived behind the church. Ben took notes while speaking with Mrs. Jacob, who organized the food drives and the knitting and sewing circles, then he interviewed Mr. Jacob, who had fallen from his position of bank president to become church janitor and was now convinced the Lord had a lesson in mind: Money was the last thing he should think about. Redemption, he insisted, could be found in the churchyard, which he faithfully raked every morning.

Ben thanked them and set off to go. As he was leaving, one of the Jacob sons, Calen, the bookish one, heard that the stranger interviewing his parents had gone to Yale. The Jacob boy followed and asked if he could walk Ben back to Mrs. Carson's. On the way Calen told him there was a mermaid living in the Eel River and that for two dollars he could show Ben exactly where she could be found. Calen was an individual who knew what he wanted, and that included getting out of Blackwell and the church cottage. He disagreed with his father's philosophy concerning money and redemption. Perhaps Yale was in his future as well.

"Let me guess," Ben said, thinking back to his encounter with Joshua Kelly at the bar. "The fisherman's wife."

"Yes, sir," Calen said.

"Well, I don't believe in such things, and I don't have two dollars." Ben Levy clapped the boy on the back. "Nice try," he said, and kept walking.

Ben had a busy schedule with little time for nonsense. That afternoon, after lunch, Ruth was taking him to meet Lillian Gale, a distant cousin of the Partridges, direct descendants of the town founders. Miss Gale, the oldest woman in Blackwell, lived up the hill with an assortment of animals she'd rescued. She had a raccoon that sat on a chair and drank tea from a cup, along with two hound dogs that had come wandering out of the woods one day, a tame crow, and a lynx, which looked like nothing more than a huge gray-brown housecat until Ben bent to pet him and he bared his teeth.

Out in the barn Lillian Gale had chickens and two goats. The local children told her there was a stray donkey stranded in the woods. She planned to go out in search of it that very day, as soon as her company left. Miss Gale was starving herself in order to continue feeding her animals. On most days she had little more than two cups of oatmeal and a pot of tea. Ben was taking notes so fast his hand was cramping. Today their hostess was especially talkative and outraged because she'd taken the lynx, named Amos, down to the river on a long leather leash the evening before. In this way Amos could hunt for himself without running away. He was missing an eye, Ben noticed, and would probably not survive in the wild if set free. Miss Gale assured him that Amos was still hunter enough to take down rabbits, which he had for his dinner. When he was finished, she collected the bones and gristle to cook into a stew for the dogs.

"Do you have a recipe for that?" Ben interrupted. His own mother hadn't been much of a cook. Her specialties had been potato dumplings and potato bread, with a dried roast whenever she could get something on sale at the butcher's. He couldn't imagine her getting by on oatmeal, or being resourceful enough to fix a gristle stew.

"A recipe?" The two old women looked at each other and laughed. "You cook it, add water, then you serve it. I'm not talking about a custard pie here, mister. Let's just call it Whatever You Have Stew and leave it at that. The dogs like it, and so do I."

"I see." Ben was wondering what was in the tea he'd been drinking, which had a faint yellow hue. It had probably been made with *whatever,* and that was worrisome since he'd had allergies as a boy. Later, he would ask Ruth what they'd been drinking and she'd tell him it was chamomile, but for the time being he only took a polite sip, then pushed his cup away.

"Anyway, I decided to try Amos down at the river," Lillian Gale went on. "I figured he'd be a pretty good fisherman, and the shad were running. There are always eels, as well, if you know where to look. We went down to the bank, and I sat down and let him have a bit of freedom. Amos traipsed on and stood in the water, still as a statue, waiting. That's what fishermen do, I suppose, and it comes to him naturally. I guess I fell asleep because the next thing I know Amos is yowling and someone is shouting at him. He comes leaping back up the riverbank soaking wet with a gash in his head." Sure enough, there was a cut above the lynx's single good eye. "It was the woman who'd done it."

"The fisherman's wife," Ben Levy guessed.

Lillian Gale nodded. "Something's not right there. That's all I'll say."

"She always donates food for the poor," Ruth reminded her friend.

"She can donate till she turns blue, that won't change the facts. My Amos has a scar on his head and I know who did it. And I know the reason why." Miss Gale leaned forward. "She's more fish than wife."

When they left, Ben gave Lillian Gale the last of the cash he had left—ten dollars he'd been given for train fare back to the city. "For your menagerie," he said. "Wouldn't want them to starve."

Miss Gale took his hand in hers and kissed it. "I don't care if you don't believe in Jesus Christ," she announced. Of course the whole town knew Ben wasn't a Christian, with a name like Levy and a hometown like New York. "You're a fine man."

"That was a good deed you did," Ruth Carson said as they set off on the winding road back to town. There were blackcap raspberries growing, which Ruth pointed out. They stopped to pick some so she could make a pie.

"It's called a mitzvah," Ben explained. "It's a person's responsibility to help those around him." He had no idea how he would get back to New York City now, not that he was in any hurry. "Whatever good you do comes back to you in some way."

"For instance, a raspberry pie after supper," Ruth said.

Ben grinned. "Something like that."

"I suppose you'll want to talk to her as well." Ben gave the old woman a look, not quite following. "The fisherman's wife," Ruth Carson said.

"I don't know. I've still got quite a few on my list. There's the fellow who runs the apple orchard that you told me about. There are the Partridge sisters. Then I have to travel to three other towns, and make my way over to Hadley to interview the pastor there before I pick up the train in Amherst and head back to New York, if I can get the train fare together."

"You said you wanted a character," Ruth Carson said. "Well, this woman is a mystery. No one knows where she came from or why she's with that old man, Horace Kelly. If you find that out, maybe you'll win your bet."

Ben had told Ruth about the Plaza Hotel, and the other folklorists, and even about the half a novel in his knapsack. He talked more out here in Massachusetts than he ever had in New York. That evening he almost told her about his brother, but since he'd never been able to get past that particular story and didn't know what he'd find on the other side if he ever did tell it, he held his tongue and ate raspberry pie instead. Another recipe for him to write down, one he might actually try someday, if he ever found blackcap raspberries while walking in the woods.

HE WENT DOWN to the river early Sunday morning with a lunch Ruth packed him just in case his wanderings lasted till nightfall. It was the end of August and the river was low, the green water murky and slow. When Ben spied the shack on the riverbank, he stopped in order to describe it in his notebook. The ground was boggy, so he took off his shoes and socks, slipped them into his rucksack, then rolled up his pants legs. Ben had never walked barefoot through mud before and he thoroughly enjoyed it. His feet were black in no time. There was a gray cloud spiraling up from the smokehouse, but all was quiet. He peered in the window of the shack—there was a bed, a woodstove, a rough-hewn table and chairs, along with some clothes hung up on a hook, and a braided rug on the floor.

After jotting down these details, Ben walked along the river for a while. He noticed a trail, not footsteps exactly, but some broken brush, so he followed along. He came to a spot that looked much like the bend in the river Miss Gale had described, where her pet lynx had been attacked. He put down his rucksack. Because he was alone, he took off his shirt and pants and folded them. Then he made his way down the bank, which was thick with ferns. He'd never gone swimming, but now he stepped into the water, wanting to experience the river. The shock of how cold it was surprised him and made him shout. He was glad none of the fellows he knew in New York City could see him, startled by a little cold water, standing in his underwear, his skin pale, his bare legs muddy. He went in a little farther. There were birds singing, but of course Ben Levy had no idea that they were meadowlarks. He didn't know that the swirls of insects were blackflies or that the tiny mouselike creature running near the riverbank was a pygmy shrew, so light it could race across the water.

He heard a woman laugh, then turned to see the fisherman's wife crouched down in her black coat, wearing her heavy mud-caked boots, her long black hair wound up. He was already knee-deep in the river, just about naked, looking only the more foolish for what little clothing he wore.

"I must look like an idiot," he said, mortified.

She nodded, laughed again, said, "Yes." She rose and walked toward him. "Careful. The mud there is deep."

Ben Levy realized he was indeed stuck, as if he'd landed in quicksand. When he tried to move, he just sank in deeper. He let out a string of curses, and his pale skin turned red with embarrassment. The woman laughed again, then came to the edge of the water and reached out a hand. Ben gazed at her, puzzled. After all he'd heard, he had a moment of doubt.

"I won't bite," she said.

Ben Levy was surprised by how strong she was as she pulled him out, up toward the safety of the riverbank. He was slick with mud, a laughable fool, but she didn't laugh again. He saw then how beautiful she was and how Calen Jacob might have mistaken her for a mythological creature when he'd spied her swimming in the river. Then and there Ben found himself envying Calen for what he'd seen.

"I think I've been looking for you," he said.

"You shouldn't be. I'm a married woman." The fisherman's wife smiled, but only a little.

"I'm a writer," Ben told her. "I'm collecting folklore and oral histories."

"Is that what you were doing in the river?"

They both laughed then. She turned around while he took up his clothes and got dressed. When he asked her to join him for lunch, she sat down and accepted one of the sandwiches Ruth Carson had made him, but she ate only the bread. He asked her a list of questions, the sort he asked everyone he interviewed.

Where and when she was born, when had she come to Blackwell, when had she married, the simple facts of her life.

"I don't like to talk about myself," she told him.

She looked skittish and Ben didn't want her to leave, so they spoke of other things, mostly about Ben. He found himself telling her about his brother. At last, he got past the part of the story where his brother cried out in pain while Ben hid in a closet so he couldn't hear. He choked up afterward and had to turn away. That was at the other side of the telling, his great despair and loneliness. Perhaps it was because this woman had come upon him nearly naked that he felt as though she had seen through him already and was at last able to show the deepest part of himself. It was getting late, and the woman grew nervous as darkness began to fall. When he asked her to tell him one thing about herself, anything, she relented and told him her name. It was Susan. She laughed and said, "Don't tell anyone. It's a secret." He nodded, but she pressed him for a promise, so Ben crossed his heart.

THAT NIGHT HE couldn't sleep. He thought of his brother tossing and turning in his bed, fevered, losing consciousness. He thought about how beautiful the woman at the river had been and how he'd felt alive in her presence. The next morning he went looking for her again. When he found her, they sat together by the river. She was both intensely present and inaccessible. There, and yet removed. Once more Susan wouldn't answer any of his questions. The day was far too short, and before they knew it the afternoon was gone. All at once she told him he had to leave. It was evening; the lack of sunlight panicked her once more. Ben, too, should hurry, she told him. He should run back to Mrs. Carson's house before anyone else might appear. Indeed, Ben saw a boat coming down the river in the darkening light.

"Your husband?" he asked, for there was old man Kelly, a lantern on the bow of his boat, not three hundred yards away.

"You think he's my husband?" Susan laughed and sent him off.

That night Ben Levy went back to the Jack Straw Tavern. He needed some company.

"Find yourself a character?" Joshua Kelly asked.

"A few." Ben nodded.

"And did you meet her?" Joshua wanted to know. "My uncle's wife?"

"She says she's not his wife," Ben confided. He had been wondering if perhaps he should do something to save Susan. He couldn't stop thinking about her. Although he had never thought of himself as heroic, any man with half a soul would have begun to imagine he might rescue her and have her for his own.

"Is that what she says?" Joshua gave Ben a drink on the house, since he was going bankrupt anyway. "Well, that's what happens when you find your wife in the Brattleboro Asylum up in Vermont."

Ben Levy walked back to town in the dark, baffled by the way he felt. He had no idea why he couldn't stop thinking about a woman who was a stranger and nothing more. It would soon be September, and the air was cool after the sun went down. He reached Ruth Carson's house, but continued walking, through the woods and the low bogs, to the river. He felt confused, as if he had drifted inside a dream. Waking up was out of the question.

He now understood himself to have fallen in love, like a stone dropped into a river. He was a man quite out of his senses. He went to the place where he had found her, and soon enough she came to sit beside him in the dark. They held hands. She told him that she was married.

"You can come to New York with me," Ben said. "No one will know you're married."

"I'll know," Susan insisted.

She stood up and took off her clothes. Her black coat, her boots, her dark dress. He held her there right on the ground, not thinking about the mud or the cool air. He felt the way a drowning man might, gasping, barely surfacing until they were done. At last she pulled away. "If I was yours," she said, "I know you'd set me free."

She told him never to look for her again or to speak her name. Before he could argue with her, she went to the edge of the river and dove in, leaving her clothes behind. Ben ran after her, calling, but she was soon submerged under the water and quickly swam away. Ben ran through the woods, but when he reached the shack, he saw the fisherman at his door with his lantern. There was no choice but to make his way back to town.

In the morning, he couldn't eat the breakfast Ruth prepared for him. It was the date he was meant to leave and travel to the other Berkshire towns, but instead he sat on the porch steps thinking all day. He felt maddened by the crickets calling, by the faint watery air. He told himself he should go home where he belonged, get himself to Albany or Amherst and take the first train. At twilight he went back down to the river. There was the fisherman, Horace Kelly, filleting trout and tossing the fish into the smoker.

"Are you looking for something?" Horace said when he saw Ben Levy in his good shoes with his shirt buttoned to the collar and a set look on his face. "I think you made a wrong turn at Wall Street."

"I came to talk to you about Susan." Ben hadn't planned to talk about her at all, but there it was. He'd said her name.

"Susan?" Horace Kelly said. "So she told you her name. Well, she's right there."

Ben looked around. There was no one.

"Right over there." The fisherman pointed to a rope stretched from tree to tree. On it hung a burlap bag that twisted back and forth as if caught in the wind. But there was no wind. It was a still evening.

"Go on," the fisherman urged with a laugh. "Tell her you want her to run off with you. That's what you came here to say, right?"

"I don't think this is funny," Ben Levy stated.

"No," Horace said. "You wouldn't."

Ben noticed Susan's black coat and boots in a heap near the smoker. He looked at the fisherman, who'd gone back to filleting his catch. Ben went over to the burlap bag. He took it down and opened it. Inside was a black eel struggling to get out. Ben shut the bag.

"That's her," the fisherman said. "Still want her?"

Ben went to sit in a chair by the smoker.

"I caught her one night and I kept her," Horace said.

Ben understood that he was sitting with a lunatic. He wondered if it was the fisherman and not his wife who'd been incarcerated up in Brattleboro.

"She was so beautiful I couldn't throw her back," the fisherman went on. "Even though she's asked me to again and again.

She says she has a husband, and that he's waiting for her, and that she can only be true to him. I've caught thousands of eels, but I can't catch him. I try every night because I know he's right around here, trying to get her back. I've seen them talking. I've seen them do more than talk."

Ben Levy had a fleeting thought of Jerome Avenue, and the one kind of tree that grew there. He thought about his mother sleeping on the couch, and his brother's funeral, and the night he stopped writing his novel, and the drinks he'd had on the train up to Albany. He felt sick at heart.

"As for me, I've had enough of her," the fisherman said. "I was thinking of cooking her. Throwing her into the smoker. But now you've come along. What would you give me in exchange for Susan?"

Ben Levy laughed despite the madness of the evening. "I have nothing, sir."

"I doubt that," the fisherman said, looking him over. "I'll take your shoes."

"My shoes for Susan?"

The fisherman nodded. Ben Levy slipped off his shoes. The fisherman got up, retrieved the burlap bag, and tossed it at Ben's feet. Ben took it and made his way through the woods. He half imagined that the fisherman might shoot him in the back, or perhaps Susan had been hiding in the shack and would come running after him, but the woods were silent. He walked on, barefoot. The mud was cold, and the dark was sifting through the trees. When he got to the clearing where they'd met before, Ben went down to the water. New York City seemed like a dream, and this, the dark river and the burlap bag in his hands that he lifted into the water, was all so real. He opened the bag.

At first nothing happened, then the eel swam out in a dark flash. It was a large eel, much larger than most, and there was another like it waiting in the shallows. Ben Levy watched them and then he walked on, back to Ruth Carson's.

Ruth got him a pair of boots from the used clothing box at the church. Ben waited for seven days thinking Susan might return to him. He had Calen Jacob and the other boys in town search for her in all the secret hiding places they knew around the river, but they found nothing. He asked the pastor to send out a search party; he even had the sheriff called in from the next township, but in the end everyone agreed. The fisherman's wife must have left the old man, hardly a surprise to anyone in Blackwell. She'd been young and beautiful. A man like Horace Kelly would never have been able to hold on to her for long.

When Ben left Blackwell, he didn't bother to collect stories in any of the towns along the road to Amherst. He got on the train, buying his ticket with a donation Ruth Carson insisted he take. He was more than a week behind schedule, but no one at the WPA faulted him for that. People got lost out in the countryside. That's what maps were for. On New Year's Day Ben went to the Plaza. He told his colleagues about the banker's family who lived in the church, and the lynx with one eye, and the tavern where the owner had shot himself after a fire. He left out the story of the fisherman's wife, however. That one he kept for himself, and he wasn't surprised when he lost the bet, or when he proceeded to buy a round not just for the winner, whose story concerned a beekeeper who'd been stung a thousand times, but a drink for one and all.

KISS AND TELL

1945

Hᴀɴɴᴀʜ Pᴀʀᴛʀɪᴅɢᴇ ᴡᴀs ғᴀᴍᴏᴜs ғᴏʀ ʜᴇʀ garden. That year, she had planted more than eighty tomato seedlings. She'd worked all through June, crouched down on her hands and knees in the dirt. Her tawny blond hair had turned red from the gritty soil. In the evenings, when she showered, the tub needed to be scrubbed every time. Now it was August and the fruit was ripening. In all the belladonna family, only tomatoes weren't poisonous, though the leaves could be lethal if boiled into a tea. Tomatoes hadn't even been considered fit to eat in Massachusetts until the mid-1800s. Now there were hundreds of varieties for cultivation. On summer evenings when Hannah's neighbors walked by, they could smell the bitter green scent of the vines. They peered into the huge yard, where the twilight gleamed green and shadows stretched far into the woods. If they stood still enough in the first humid waves of nightfall, it was almost possible to hear the plants growing.

The large farms around town had closed down, the fields were bare, the barns empty. Food was at a premium when not homegrown, costly and hardly first-rate. Even in a small town such as Blackwell, beef and butter were rationed. There was a war to fight, and many of the young men who would have been working the local farms had been sent overseas. Thirty women in town had husbands in the armed services. Another twenty were the mothers of sons who had enlisted. Few people bothered to cook sit-down dinners these days, especially those who were missing a husband or son. The coffee shop had a new Victory menu, with simpler, more inexpensive fare. That was the extent of nightlife in town. People went to bed earlier than they used to, frightened by the darkness of the world beyond Blackwell.

Hannah was thirty-five that year. She was young and attractive, yet she felt her life had not yet begun. Why then did it seem as if it were already over? Hannah's sister Azurine, who had studied to be a nurse, had gone off to France to work in the ambulance corps. Azurine was in the battle zone, facing the terrors of the world, driving over muddy fields, performing surgery she hadn't been trained for should a doctor be unavailable, falling madly in love with one doomed man after another, spending torrid nights in their beds, and mourning each one before he had walked out the door. *There may not be another chance to live,* she wrote to her sister. *If not now, when?*

Hannah sat in the parlor in the evenings to read Azurine's letters. The windows of the house were open and a fan was set up, yet it was beastly hot. Hannah wore a slip and nothing else. She kept her long, graceful feet in a pan of water in an attempt to stay cool.

The only way to fight evil is with joy, Azurine had written. *Forget everything we've ever been taught.*

Hannah's skin was blotchy with heat, her pale hair was pinned up. Her knees were still dusted with red earth from her day's work in the garden. Hannah considered herself to be plain, especially when compared with her sister, but her face in repose was incandescent. Had any man in town seen her at that moment, had he walked past and happened to have spied her, he would have realized she was beautiful. But no one saw her, and she couldn't have cared less about the impression she made. The moths repeatedly hit against the windows, convinced they were headed in the right direction, heedless of the wire screens that stopped their flight. Hannah pitied them. Who but a fool would stay in one place and butt her head against the same window time and again? A fool who should have been in Paris, who never should have stayed home, but one who seemed tied to this garden and this house.

Hannah retained a stony aloofness. She had always been known as the serious sister, absorbed in her chores, tending to be somewhat standoffish. Still, people were drawn to her. She had an uncanny ability to gauge who was in need, often appearing at someone's back door with exactly what they yearned for most: a pot of split pea soup, a bottle of milk, a blanket for an ailing baby, a spray of red phlox from her garden. As the summer went on, she had less to give, with nothing more than tomatoes to offer her neighbors. There was a glut of them, so many they fell from the vines in the night. The patter of falling fruit sounded like hail, waking people who lived nearby from their sleep. A rumor began that if Hannah Partridge came to your door with her wicker basket, your wish would be granted. It started when ten-year-old Eric Hildegarde found a rabbit in the grass after Hannah stopped by. Eric had always wanted a pet rabbit and was overjoyed to find one beside the back door. His father built a hutch in the yard the next day, and maybe that was what Eric had wanted most of all but hadn't known it: to spend the day with his father learning how to use a hammer and saw.

Mae Jacob, whose husband, Steven, was serving in Belgium and had been out of contact for weeks, received a letter from him the afternoon Hannah delivered a bagful of crimson tomatoes that were perfect for sauce. The next day Mae told her neighbors she'd dreamed of her husband when she slipped his letter beneath her pillow. She didn't dare to share the details of the dream, which were far too personal, but she credited the tomatoes from Hannah's garden for her new hopeful outlook, as well as the letters that had begun to arrive on a regular basis.

Hannah was unaware of the rumors about her garden until the evening she decided to hike over to the Jack Straw Bar and Grill. She had walked to the edge of town in search of a place where she could escape the heat, but even the countryside was stifling. With its darkened windows and its long wooden bar, the Jack Straw seemed promising. Hannah wore a summer dress and sandals. As soon as she was inside she perched on a wooden stool directly under the ceiling fan. She whirled around once on pure whim, then ordered a cold beer.

"You didn't bring me any tomatoes?" the bartender, Bob Kelly, joked. They'd gone to high school together and were vaguely related through marriage. Hannah had been Bob's tutor for a season or two. He couldn't write an essay to save his life. He was deaf in one ear, so he hadn't been called up to service. "Now I won't get my wish," Bob said.

"Meaning?" Hannah had decided to order a meatloaf sandwich even though she usually only had a salad for dinner. She was suddenly hungry. She had been working hard, forgetting meals, existing on iced tea, tomatoes, and Popsicles. Canning and putting up chutney and tomato sauce had taken up every other evening this week. The rims beneath her nails were scarlet. Her fingertips were scorched.

"People get their heart's desire when they eat the tomatoes from your garden," Bob informed her. "Or so I've been told."

They both laughed. Hannah was a good egg when she let her hair down.

"People are pathetic." She shrugged. "They'll believe anything. If it's true, then where's my heart's desire? I've practically eaten a bushel of tomatoes just this week."

"Hard times make for simple minds," Bob suggested. "What do you hear from Azurine?"

Half the men in town had been in love with Azurine at one time or another, and Bob had been among them.

"Out saving the world," Hannah remarked. She missed her sister terribly.

"I'll bet she'll come back speaking French," Bob said wistfully.

Hannah laughed. "Are you expecting my sister to come back?" Hannah had finished her sandwich and beer, so she stood up to go. It would still be broiling in her parlor when she got home. "Would you leave Paris to come back here?"

❧

THE TOWN HAD decided to go forward with the yearly Founder's Festival, even though so many of Blackwell's sons were posted overseas and would be absent. A stage had been built in Band's Meadow. Every year the drama society mounted a play about the plight of a local ghost called the Apparition. This summer Jenny Linden, aged five, had been given the starring role. As Hannah walked home from the Jack Straw Bar she spied a crowd huddled around the child, who was sprawled out in the grass, crying. No one could get Jenny to stop wailing— not the drama teacher, Grace Campbell, nor the other children gathered in a circle. Even Jenny's own mother couldn't comfort the child. Hannah felt herself drawn across the lawn. She sat down beside poor Jenny and patted her hair. When she heard children cry, she was always undone. She had lost a sister when she was quite young, and in some ways she'd never gotten over her grief.

"I was the Apparition when I was your age," Hannah told the distraught little girl. Jenny looked at her, baleful, still tearing up. "I was nervous, too. But I remember how I felt when everyone applauded. I felt as though I was a star in the sky."

Jenny hiccoughed, but she'd become attentive. The Apparition only had two lines. *It's me, sister,* and *I'm leaving this earth, but I'll never leave you.* Under Hannah's tutelage Jenny practiced her part even though tears still shone on her face. She quickly improved with a little coaching. Hannah clapped her hands appreciatively.

"I can always tell who'll make a good Apparition. You'll be perfect," Hannah encouraged Jenny, who had forgotten all about crying and had instead begun to think of stars up above and how brightly one might burn on the wooden stage if it should ever fall from the sky.

By the time the adults thought to thank Hannah Partridge, she was gone, walking through the meadow, burning not with light but with despair. She would never get her heart's desire. More than anything, she wanted a child. Find a husband, someone might have told her, get married, have a baby or two—all easily accomplished even in a small town such as Blackwell. But Hannah was not interested in men. She never had been. She refused to speculate on what this might mean, or admit to the crushes she'd been aware of. She only knew that if she didn't wish to be someone's wife, she couldn't have what she yearned for most in this world.

THE FOUNDER'S DAY celebration was not as elaborate as it had been in past years. In order to conserve electricity, the fairy lights weren't strung through the trees. No new costumes were sewn, and instead, the old ones were patched and seamed. The wooden bleachers were hammered into place even though they were rickety and should have been replaced. Still, there would be great fun at last. Carnival rides were set up on the green, and food stands sold homemade cookies and cakes. Ice cream could be had in paper cups or piled into cones made of waffle batter. Although there was no circus this year, no musicians, not even the chorus from Lenox, a troupe of actors had been hired to come from New York and present a series of skits.

The actors were staying at the Lamplighter Motel. Within two hours of their arrival, they had grown bored with Blackwell. The town council was paying a small fee and expenses. When split among four people, it was barely worth the effort, but the two couples had decided to think of the job as a vacation.

They would do their best to take advantage of what little Blackwell had to offer. They swam in the Eel River, which they found shockingly muddy and cold. They hiked up Hightop Mountain, where the women, Charlotte and Abbey, panicked when surveying the wilderness, vowing they'd spied a bear. They ate peach pie at the coffee shop and peered through the dusty windows of the history museum, which had been closed since the war had begun. The foursome wound up at the Jack Straw, where the men played darts with the locals and the women asked for whisky sours, not that there were any maraschino cherries to be had in all of Blackwell. Hannah was at the bar when the request came in. She grinned at Bob Kelly, then took two cherry tomatoes from the basket she'd brought him, placing one in each glass.

"They're city people," she said, looking over her shoulder at the two actresses. "They'll never know the difference."

After the drinks were delivered, one of the actresses came up to the bar. Her name was Charlotte Scott and she was tall and elegant, with long dark hair. She wore a black dress and high heels. She didn't look like anyone in Blackwell.

"Was that supposed to be a joke?" she said.

Hannah turned, ready with a smart remark—something about it being a cherry tomato, and wasn't that what she'd wanted? But when she faced Charlotte she said nothing at all. Her face flushed and she felt a fool.

"Cat got your tongue?" Charlotte had her hands on her hips. Her eyes were piercing.

"I have no idea what you mean," Hannah said.

"I mean come sit with us, we're bored to death."

Hannah might have stayed at the bar, finished her beer, and

left, but Charlotte took her by the hand. "Someone has to entertain the entertainers."

The actresses had a second round of whisky sours, and Hannah ordered another beer. She was talked into recounting the history of Blackwell, since the museum had been closed to visitors. She told all of the stories she could remember. How the founders had been stopped by a snowstorm on their journey west, how Johnny Appleseed himself had planted the oldest tree in town, how Emily Dickinson had visited before shutting herself away from the world. Hannah was more entertaining than she'd ever imagined she might be, perhaps because of the beers. She ended the history lesson by enacting the meeting between the Apparition and her older sister on the banks of the Eel River from the second act of the Founder's Day play.

"'I'm leaving this earth, but I'll never leave you,'" Hannah quoted and was met by applause. She felt somewhat flushed by the turn her solitary evening had taken and the praise for her sudden starring role. The men came over and introduced themselves, James Scott and Stanley Franklin. James was Charlotte's husband and Stanley and Abbey were engaged.

"Real name, Fishman," Charlotte whispered gleefully about her spouse. "Men." She sighed. "All is vanity."

At the end of the evening, Charlotte decided they should trek over to see Hannah's house, since it had been the founder's home, and they had come all this way for Founder's Day. It made sense for them to steep themselves in local lore, adding bits and pieces of Blackwell's history to their skits. The group walked along in the green-tinged summer dark, drunk and cheerful, out for a lark. It was good to forget the war and all the losses in life for a little while and just let loose. In the space of an evening, Hannah and Charlotte and Abbey had become great friends.

"I'll bet you're dying to get out of this town," Charlotte said. She lowered her voice conspiratorially. "Considering."

"Not at all," Hannah answered, confused. "I can't imagine living anywhere else."

"Oh, come on." Charlotte gave her a look. "This isn't for you."

They'd reached the front door, which Hannah proudly informed them was the original, the first door on the first house in Blackwell. When she led them on a tour, they were particularly impressed with the rifle over the mantel that had belonged to the founder.

"You know what they say," James Scott announced regally. He was handsome and lanky with a wonderful, deep voice that sounded vaguely British. "If you see a gun in act one, it had better go off in act two."

The gun hadn't worked for years, Hannah informed him. Someone had broken the triggering mechanism ages ago. "Act two had better be something completely different," she said, and again everyone laughed, charmed by her matter-of-fact humor.

They went out the back door, up to the gardens, past the gate into what had always been called the red garden, now planted with more tomatoes than the four New Yorkers would ever have imagined could be found in one town, let alone on a single plot of land. The scent of the vines was overwhelming, a mixture of sugar and sulfur.

"Hence the tomatoes in our drinks." Charlotte laughed. "Now I get it."

She and Abbey danced through the rows of tomatoes, their arms linked around each other's waists, as the men applauded.

Then Charlotte grabbed Hannah and they danced as well. When they came to the end of the row, where the vines were overgrown and met to form a bower, Charlotte leaned forward to kiss Hannah. The kiss was so hot and fast Hannah thought she had imagined it. But when the actors left, waving from the street, she was still burning.

IN THE MORNING, Hannah stood at her window and drank iced tea. She gazed at her garden, but she didn't bother to water or weed. At last she left home and walked to the Lamplighter Motel. At the desk she asked Betty Harkness where the actors were staying, fumbling over her explanation, finally saying she was their official guide. It was even hotter than the day before. There were hawks circling in the blue sky, and the asphalt in the parking lot felt as though it was melting as Hannah walked across to the Scotts' room. It was number seven and she wondered if that meant good luck. She stood and tried to peer through the curtained window, agitated, there to accuse Charlotte of misunderstanding. She knocked at the door. Her head was spinning. When at last Charlotte appeared, she grinned, then grabbed Hannah's hand to lead her inside, saying, "What took you? I could only get rid of them for so long. Now we only have an hour at best."

There were two double beds. They went to the one that was unmade and fell into it, already kissing. In moments they were naked and entwined. Hannah felt the way she had when she'd been cast to play the Apparition, her body in one place, her mind racing. She'd been terrified then. She remembered what her sister had told her on that long-ago evening, to let go and not think about anything else. She did that now, even though she could hear a car in the parking lot, though she knew that outside the sky was bright and the hawks were still above them.

They were dressed and sitting on the bed when the others returned from their outing. Charlotte's hand was inching up the back of Hannah's blouse and her touch was burning. Hannah wished she wasn't so fair; surely her blushing would give her away. The actors filed into the room groaning, exhausted from their hike, kicking off their shoes. Their second foray up Hightop Mountain had been just as much a failure as the first. This time Stan had been stung by a wasp, and they'd stopped to get ice at the coffee shop on their way back.

"God, I hate the mountains," Abbey exclaimed. She rubbed her feet and poured herself a drink from a bottle of vodka. "What I wouldn't give for a bucket of ice."

"Take this," Stan said, offering the small wedge of ice that had helped bring down the swelling on his arm. "It'll put a sting in your drink."

James threw himself onto the bed and grabbed Charlotte around the waist, pulling her back with him.

" 'O, that this too too solid flesh would melt,' " he intoned regally as he sank into the mattress. "If I ever mention hiking again, slap me," he told his wife. "Hello, local girl," he murmured to Hannah, pulling her down on the bed as well. "I'll bet you don't mind wasps and mountain trails and bears."

Hannah laughed and pulled away, quickly rising to her feet.

"I only stopped by to wish you luck," she remarked.

"Never do that!" Abbey cried. "You'll put a curse on us. Luck has nothing to do with good fortune."

"You look like the heat is getting to you," Stan noted as

Hannah edged away from the bed. "Maybe we all need a dip in the Eel River," he suggested.

"Tonight," Charlotte agreed. "When the sun goes down. After the festival."

"Brilliant," James said to her. "Eels and mud and cold water and starlight."

"Go with us," Charlotte urged Hannah. "Meet us after the performance."

Hannah looked at the clock. She had no place to go, but the sudden desire to leave was overwhelming. "Good Lord, I'm late," she said. "See you!" she called as she went out the door. She was reeling, walking as fast as she could. She thought of how irresponsible she'd been today. She hadn't even bothered to water the garden despite the heat wave.

Behind her, a door opened, then slammed shut.

"Hey," Charlotte called. "Hannah. Wait."

Charlotte came running across the parking lot, barefoot, her feet burning. "You forgot this." Charlotte had Hannah's hair clips in her hand. She stood in the one pocket of shadow cast by a tall sycamore tree, wearing only her slip with James's shirt thrown over it. "Are you angry?" she wanted to know. "He's my husband, after all."

"I'm not angry," Hannah insisted.

Charlotte walked up to her, over the melting tar. "It doesn't mean I'm not crazy about you."

"I doubt that." Hannah sounded hurt, even to herself. It was ridiculous. Charlotte was a married woman. They'd only just met.

Charlotte gazed at her, amused. "A girl's got to do what a girl's got to do." She looped her arms around Hannah and drew her close. "James has no idea what a good actress I am. You know the real me."

HANNAH HURRIED HOME. She decided to run. When she ran, she didn't think; and when she didn't think, she was better off. She didn't go inside when she reached her house. Instead, she went directly to the garden and watered, then set to pulling weeds from the damp, ruddy ground. It was so hot she couldn't breathe. She hosed off the dirt when she was done, then went inside to look at herself in the mirror. She looked exactly the same. No one could see that her world had been turned upside down.

When it was time to get ready, Hannah chose one of her sister's dresses. She pinned up her hair with the tortoiseshell combs. Everyone in town was out for the evening. The paling sky was clear, but no cooler. Hannah splurged on some ice cream from the food stand. She realized she hadn't had lunch or dinner. Instead, she ate vanilla and chocolate swirl from a paper cup while standing beneath one of the old apple trees. The light had begun to fade by the time the Founder's Day play began. Everyone had seen it before, yet the audience was riveted. Jenny Linden's little ghost drew the largest applause, especially when she cried *I'm leaving this earth, but I'll never leave you.* Hannah felt oddly proud and moved.

After the curtain call, the children in the drama society trotted out to take a bow and their teacher, Grace Campbell, thanked the town for their continuing support even in these dark days of war. Then it was time for the players from New York. They were nearly unrecognizable in their costumes. James was a swashbuckler who recited bits of Shakespeare. Abbey was dressed in swirling, filmy white. She'd taken on the persona of Emily Dickinson, thanks to the information Hannah had provided. Stan and James presented a comic skit about Johnny Appleseed. People roared when Johnny didn't know the difference between a seed and a stone. Then Charlotte came onstage. She played the part of the town founder with a Spanish accent, clearly undertaken so that the skit could end with a tango danced by Charlotte and James. The acting had been mediocre, but the dance was something much more. Slinky and erotic and wholly absorbing. Music from a record player drifted over the meadow, and as the couple danced, the darkness became blue and deep. It was easy to forget there was a stage, or that this was still Blackwell. People left their lives at that moment, imagining they were in Spain, under a starry sky. Beneath the tree, in the gathering dark, Hannah felt entranced.

When the performance was over, she waited for the crowd to clear, then found her way to the back of the stage. The only one there was Grace Campbell, packing up costumes and props. Hannah's disappointment must have shown in her face when she realized Charlotte and the others were gone.

"If you're looking for the actors, they've just left," Grace told her. "I warned them the Eel River wasn't a place for night swimming, but they wouldn't listen. That's where they've gone."

Hannah made her way toward the river. She'd been invited, after all. She slipped off her sandals and carried them in her hand. It was easier to make her way barefoot. After a while she heard them on the riverbank. She peered through the dark and saw them as they began to strip off their clothes. They were still wearing their costumes, and they looked like strangers, clothed and then unclothed.

"Thank God that's over," she heard James say.

"Small towns and small people," Charlotte crooned, slipping off her black lace dress.

The men leapt into a deep pool, shouting at the cold.

"Holy mother of God," James Scott cried. "It's pure ice."

"Will you miss your little friend?" Hannah heard Abbey ask Charlotte.

"I have no idea what you mean," Charlotte said.

Charlotte waded into the water now, up to her knees. Abbey followed suit.

"Don't give me that," Abbey protested. "You think I don't know you by now?"

"She wasn't so little," Charlotte remarked. "She was taller than I."

The women laughed and waded farther. There were mosquitoes and gnats, which they slapped away, hitting their own naked bodies. Together they dove right in.

In the dark, standing in the tall weeds, Hannah felt her heart bumping against her chest. What would happen if she ran to the river? What if she threw her arms around Charlotte, packed up all her worldly belongings? Before she could think any further, she spied a spot of blue moving along the riverbank. It was a little girl, heading toward the water. She was there, and then she disappeared, as if swallowed by the dark river.

Hannah ran toward the far bank. People had faltered here, carried away by the currents, but thankfully Hannah was a strong swimmer. She went right in, chasing after the child, but no one was there. The blue dress Hannah wore spread out in a circle as she paddled to stay afloat, shivering. All at once she knew what had happened. She felt she had witnessed a miracle, a moment so private it could never be shared. Hannah could hear the actors joking with each other, but she didn't listen to what they were saying. She was convinced she had seen the Apparition, the child who'd drowned so long ago.

WHEN AZURINE CAME home that autumn, Hannah went to the train station in Albany to pick up her sister. Azurine had been gone a long time, and she hadn't come back alone. Hannah was so overjoyed, she nearly sank to her knees when she saw the little girl. Azurine admitted that she planned to tell everyone that she'd been married in France, and that the father of her child had died in battle. In truth she didn't know who he was. She'd been in love a dozen times or more, but she was giving all that up now. Hannah laughed and said she was doing the same. Love was for fools and dreamers. On this they agreed.

The sisters were glad to be together. They had the easy sort of relationship where they didn't have to speak to be understood. For as long as the weather held they took their meals on the porch, looking out toward Hightop Mountain. They moved the kitchen table and chairs outside. Lunches often lasted an hour or more as the weather continued to be fine even after the maple trees were already turning. Little Kate was already a charmer. Her red hair was tufted and shimmery in the daylight.

"What do we want for her?" Azurine wondered as they watched her, both sisters ready to dart over should she begin to fall.

Hannah was about to answer true love, but love alone was never enough.

"She'll have us," she told her sister. "That should do."

They were finishing the last of the summer's tomatoes. They'd picked them that morning, just after breakfast, scrambling into the garden barefoot, racing to see which sister could collect the most. Now, when Kate came skittering back to the table, they let her take a bite, even though some people might say it was best for children to eat only simple things. In their experience, nothing was simple.

THE MONSTER OF BLACKWELL

1956

Hᴇ ᴡᴀs ɴᴏᴛ ꜰʀᴏᴍ Bᴇʀᴋsʜɪʀᴇ Cᴏᴜɴᴛʏ or from anywhere in Massachusetts. He didn't know where he'd been born or who his parents were. He lived with an aunt in Albany, near the railroad tracks, but he didn't expect to be there for the rest of his life. He was convinced that something else was out there for him. He'd decided he would be ready, whatever his future might bring, whenever it might appear before him. He was prepared to vanish, take chances, disappear if need be. He thought perhaps he was enchanted. He was exceedingly ugly, so ugly he couldn't look at himself. He'd always known this. People had told him so often enough, and, although he avoided mirrors, he'd glimpsed himself and had come to the conclusion they were correct.

He expected the reaction he caused. People ran from him, and he didn't blame them. If he could, he would have gotten as far away from himself as possible. His features didn't go together; they were misshapen, large and broad, pushed in as if the doctor had made a mistake during his birth and tried to throw him back into the place where he'd originated, pushing in on his nose, and ears, and mouth. His shoulders were broad and his arms muscular, but he seemed twisted and tended to be hunched. His eyes, however, were dark and beautiful. People didn't notice. They didn't look him in the eye. They were gone before that.

He'd always kept himself hidden. In school he hadn't let on that he was smart. He'd made sure to sit in the back of the room, face averted. He'd been too big for his age, those big hands, big feet, big arms. He was as tall as a man by the time he was ten. His back was misshapen, pushed up onto his shoulders. That was why he hunched, in the hope of disappearing. When he was younger, the boys at school had him lie on the floor so they could climb over him. They said he was a mountain. They beat him. He stayed still and let them. He could have easily crushed his attackers, but it wasn't in his nature to do so. He felt like a mountain, alone, far away.

Perhaps there was a spell to undo what he was, one that would lead him to become something better. He prepared himself with a feverish attempt at self-improvement. He read voraciously at night while his aunt was sleeping, not just novels and poetry, but how-to books. He studied the skills he might someday need in another time and place: how to make a fire, how to gauge which plants were poisonous and which were edible, how to build a house out of sticks and stones. All the while he was getting ready for the life he yearned for, though it was so distant.

❧

HE LEFT THE year he was seventeen. To earn money he had worked summers in a foundry where he could wear a mask when he welded, an old iron thing that made him look as if he had crawled up from the Black Lagoon. It was time to leave Albany and he knew it. His aunt didn't want him. He shouldn't have ever been her responsibility or her shame. He had gotten a wreck of a car and rebuilt it. He was a fast learner, and hard work didn't bother him, not if it meant getting away. Maybe his aunt knew what he was planning as he worked on the motor all that year. Maybe she heard him leave. He drove for hours. He was looking for a place where his aloneness would feel right. He found exactly that when he happened onto a road that curved upward, in a county he'd never been to before. He was headed toward Hightop Mountain. He felt something inside him shift as he drove. It was the first time he'd felt hopeful or alive. He was struck by the beauty of the countryside—the hay fields, the orchards, the delicate leaves on the birch trees. As he drove through small towns, children who spied him ran after his car pretending to shoot at him with their toy guns. He understood why they would chase him and shout out names.

The more he drove, the better he felt. At last he was free. He stopped for gas on Route 17 at twilight, hat pulled down so no one would see him. He didn't want to scare anyone. That had never been his intention. He gassed up his car, mumbled to the mechanic, handed over some cash. He wasn't used to country roads, and it was growing dark the way it does in the mountains, suddenly, as though a curtain has been drawn. He kept on even though he was tired. Maybe he was light-headed or falling asleep.

All at once something was in the road right in front of him. When he swerved too quickly, he lost control. The car flew into a ditch nose first, wheels spinning. It rolled over, and he rolled over inside of it. There was the sound of the axle cracking, the windshield breaking. He could hear his own hoarse breathing.

In a rage for all he'd just lost, he quickly climbed out of the car and started up to the road, indignant, ready for a fight with whatever creature had done this to him, ruined his car and his getaway plans. There it was. A six-hundred-pound male black bear. The bear didn't scare him—he was used to being the one who frightened people. They faced each other and neither one backed down. The air was hot between them and then it wasn't. Each took a step away into the dark, endless night. It wasn't worth fighting over a mistake. Plus the bear was so beautiful the boy was glad not to have run him over. A car was just a car.

HE LIVED IN the old wreck for a while, down in the ditch. He had a sack of groceries in the backseat, a pile of books. After a while he began to explore, tramping up the cliffs, growing stronger every day. He found a meadow at the top of the mountain and a series of caves, some of which had recently been inhabited by bears. He discovered freshwater and streams running with fish. He'd brought along a saw and a toolbox and his how-to carpentry books. While he was still living in the car, he began to build the frame of the shed that would eventually be his shelter. He collected rocks ribbed with mica for the foundation and the fireplace. He liked working outside in the sun. He took off his hat, his shirt. He stopped thinking. He got away from himself at last.

By midsummer, branches were growing up through the rotting undercarriage of the wrecked car; vines twisted around the rusting axles. The woods were full of miraculous things—fossils, bats, grass so tall a man could stand in it and disappear. The boy was glad to be hidden, away from people. He'd gone to the nearest town only once, late, when everyone else was in bed. He felt as if he had wandered into a dream. All those houses with their dark windows. The bark of dogs tied up in the yards. The shuttered library, the town meeting hall. It was a world to which he didn't belong. He jimmied open the back door of the AtoZ Market and hurriedly collected some items into a paper sack—a small bag of concrete mix, rice, matches, tinfoil, a frying pan—then left twenty dollars beside the cash register.

Occasionally he and the bear saw each other, but they had a truce and ignored each other. The bear was old, and although this was his territory, he didn't seem to mind the company. Perhaps the boy was himself a bear, a foundling left on a step in Albany, raised among humans but reviled for his innermost traits. In the woods, he did feel himself becoming more of whatever he was. He ate blueberries and looked at leaves. He didn't think about winter, but he was well aware of its approach. He worked more quickly on his shelter. He knew everything ended.

ONE AFTERNOON HE heard voices ringing. A group of children were climbing down from a hike in the woods. It was a field trip from the local summer camp, fifteen or so boys and girls from the Blackwell Community Center along with a counselor, a teenaged girl named Kate Partridge. Kate had long hair that was so red it didn't even look real. She had a take-charge manner and a luminous complexion, even though her face was now smudged from hiking with a bunch of eight- and nine-year-olds. Her job earned her extra credit at school and twenty-five dollars a week. She had her charges paired up and holding hands. The children were kept busy by singing "A Hundred Bottles of Beer on the Wall." Kate knew the camp director probably wouldn't approve of the song selection but she didn't care. Kate was fifteen and felt the world belonged to her, or at the very least, this section of Berkshire County did. She lived with her mother and her aunt Hannah in the oldest house in town. The women doted on her. When they told her she was a brilliant, beautiful, one-of-a kind girl, she had no reason to doubt them.

Kate could be selfish or selfless depending on her mood. She had definite ideas about everything, including politics (she was a Democrat) and education (she intended to go to Wellesley).

People said she'd be a heartbreaker soon, if that wasn't already the case. Neighborhood boys already had begun to follow her home, and although they tried their best to get her attention, she had no interest in them. She wanted to study art history and live in Paris, as her mother had. That was where her parents had met, but her father had been killed during the war and her mother came home to Blackwell to live with her unmarried sister. Kate had grown up knowing that she wanted to travel the world. She wanted to get as far away from Blackwell as possible, to fall in love fifty times over, to swim in the Nile, walk along the Seine, see war and life and death.

Kate was one of those girls who thought she knew exactly what fate would bring her, but that was all about to change. Halfway down the road, as they were heading down Hightop Mountain, Cal Jacob disappeared. Cal was nine years old and trouble.

One minute he was holding his partner's hand and the next he was gone. Another boy said he thought Cal had gone looking for fish. Kate didn't like the sound of that. Fish meant water and water meant drowning and drowning meant Cal would ruin both their lives. There had been a well-known drowning in their town over a hundred years earlier, in the Eel River, and it was said that the little girl's ghost could be seen on certain nights. They called her the Apparition and there was a play about her that was always staged by schoolchildren during the summer festival that celebrated the town founder's birthday. Kate had played the part of the Apparition when she was six years old. She'd been such a good actress that when she'd looked into the audience, she saw that both her mother and aunt were crying, as if she were indeed that little girl lost in the Eel River rather than their own darling, confident, one-of-a-kind Kate.

She went to the edge of the road and called Cal's name, but there was no answer. Kate went into panic mode. She had the other children hold hands and stay put, leaving Cal's sister, Lucy, in charge before dashing into the woods. Her heart was pounding; it was all she could hear, the thud of her own blood in her ears. She was the girl who won every contest, who always came out on top, the most beautiful girl in her class, the one who would travel the world and succeed at everything she tried, not the girl in whose care a local boy had gotten lost and drowned, the one gazing mournfully out her window while the entire town held candlelight vigils and blamed her for the tragedy.

THE WOODS WERE cool and deep and green. Kate called for Cal over and over. Her voice sounded thin and helpless even to her. The forest smelled of moss and earth. Bands of light streamed through the trees and left a delicate lattice of brightness. Kate could hear the children up on the road singing in their sweet high voices about bottles of beer. She reproached herself for losing Cal, for that was the unalterable truth. She had been in charge, and whatever happened next could mark the rest of her life. Maybe she wasn't who she thought she was. Maybe she wouldn't win everything.

It was then that she saw something in the underbrush. "Cal?" she said. She took a few steps forward. Something suddenly stopped her. It grabbed hold of her. Kate felt herself grow cold inside. She thought it was a bear that was upon her, and that her life was over even though she was only fifteen and hadn't even begun to live. He had his arm around her waist. She turned. Even when she looked at him, she still thought he was a bear until he spoke in a voice that surprised her by how human it was. "Stay back," he told her.

Cal was below them in a clearing. There was a stream filtering down from the mountain, and Cal had found little fish floating in it. He was crouched there, trying to stab at them with a stick. But he wasn't the only one in the clearing. There was a huge black bear beside some low-growing blueberry bushes. The bear was very still, and Kate remembered her mother once telling her that just because something was quiet didn't mean it wasn't dangerous. A wasp, a snake, a deep pool in the Eel River, a bear.

The creature Kate had at first thought to be a bear left her to creep down the hillock. He was quiet and quick. He grabbed Cal before the boy knew what had hit him and carried him toward the steep embankment, his hand placed firmly over Cal's mouth. Kate blinked back tears. She thought Cal might be torn apart, fought over by animals, but when the bear eating blueberries stood up and made a sound deep in his throat, the one carrying Cal leapt onto a log and made himself taller. The big black bear backed away, and the one with Cal came up the hill. When he handed the boy over to Kate, she understood he wasn't a bear at all. Just a young man. Kate stared at him, rudely, mouth open.

"Run," she thought he said, and so she did, dragging Cal with her, ripping her clothes on stickers and briars, breathing so hard her chest was nearly bursting. She gathered the children together and got them running, then flagged down a passing truck. She safely deposited all of her charges into the flatbed. She quieted the crying ones and told the rowdy, overexcited ones to sit still. The truck was from the local orchard and it smelled like apples. Kate's heart was racing. She thought about his hand on her waist, the look in his eyes. She wondered if it had all been a dream, a vision brought on by the strange circumstances of the day. She gazed back into the woods and thought about bears and men and how life was already not what she had thought it would be.

SHE NEVER TOLD anyone about what had happened. She wasn't sure they would believe her, but there was something more. She was flooded with shame, but the truth was she didn't want to share that boy in the woods. All the same, rumors began. The gardener at the church said he'd spied someone rummaging through the old clothes bin. The stranger proceeded to run away when the outside light was flicked on, but his shadow was seven feet tall. Several boys in town said they'd seen a creature at the Eel River that looked like a cross between a bear and an ape. It had slunk off when they threw rocks at it, tail between its legs.

Doug Winn, who owned the AtoZ Market, began to notice that on days when items were mysteriously missing from the shelves, there was cash left on the countertop. He rigged a Polaroid camera with a string and left it by the register, set to flash if anyone broke in after closing. When it happened, he showed the photo to nearly everyone in town, insisting the image he'd caught was that of a monster. People laughed and said Doug had merely recorded the presence of an individual who'd thrown his hand in front of his face, startled when the camera's flash went off. After a while things quieted down. The rumors faded and people got more interested in starting a petition requesting that a stoplight be put in at the corner of Highland and Main, where there had been three accidents in a single year. Folks stopped talking nonsense about monsters. Still, they locked their doors at night.

KATE WENT INTO the garden in the evenings in order to be alone. She wasn't the same since the incident on the mountain. She had a secret, one she could hardly admit to herself. She had the urge to be away from other people, to banish herself from the future she'd always planned. The garden was old, and Kate's aunt Hannah grew tomatoes and red peppers and watermelon and radishes. One day Kate filled a basket and told her mother she was taking it to the town hall as a donation to the food pantry. But when she got to the town hall, she kept on. She carried the basket along Route 17 and set it on the side of the road in the spot where Cal Jacob had disappeared. She waited there for quite some time. When the stranger didn't appear, she walked home, disappointed.

Kate grew even more moody and dissatisfied. People in town seemed provincial and small-minded. Her third cousin, Henry Partridge, came from California to stay before he went on to Harvard. He was predictable and safe. He asked her to the movies, but even though he was a distant cousin, once removed, Kate wasn't interested. At the end of August there was the Founder's Day celebration. This year Lucy Jacob was playing the part of the Apparition. She forgot her lines and had to be coached from the wings by her mother and wound up in tears.

"You did fine," Kate reassured Lucy when she went backstage after the play. "You were a better Apparition than I ever was."

The stage was part of an open-air theater that was set up on the town green once a year. Cal Jacob was there, standing in the grass. He'd grown quieter since his runaway episode in the woods. When anyone addressed him, he shifted in his shoes and looked the other way. Now he waited to speak to Kate until the other children went off for cookies and punch. "There really is a monster," he said quietly. He'd been wanting to talk to Kate for some time. He knew no one else would believe him.

There were rides set up beyond the green—a little Ferris wheel and a Whip and bumper cars. White fairy lights had been strung through the branches of the trees.

"There's no such thing as a monster," Kate told him.

Cal shook his head, stubborn. "He was."

"No. That's not what he was."

"Okay," Cal said. He had the jitters and was tapping his foot. Anyone could tell he wasn't convinced. Kate put her hands on his shoulders.

"Listen to me," she said. "He was just a man."

THE NEXT TIME she brought a basket of food she also left a note. She ran home afterward, embarrassed, her face flushed with heat. She wasn't herself anymore. She didn't know what she was thinking or why she'd become so absorbed in searching out a stranger. Summer was fading and the dark came earlier now. Kate felt as though her fate had split in two on the day Cal ran into the woods. She could have gone in one direction, a life in which she might have been home reading, or at a sleepover with the other girls in town, or visiting her cousin in Cambridge. Instead, she came back to Route 17 again and again.

High school would soon be in session, and Kate had begun to feel an odd sort of desperation. The note she'd left had exact instructions. On the appointed date and time she went to Band's Meadow. The meeting place was on the far side of the orchards. It was off-season so there was no one around. Kate walked through the tall grass. He was waiting there for her, hidden. He watched her as though she were another dream, like the town at night when everyone was asleep in their beds, a dream so distant all he could do was watch in the dark. As she drew near he called for her to stop and she did. She sat down in the tall grass, legs crossed.

"Now what?" she called.

"Close your eyes," he told her.

When she did, he came to sit across from her.

Kate lifted her face and squinted, but all she could see was a shadow. "Can I open my eyes?"

"No." He laughed.

"This is silly," Kate complained, grumpy. Then she added, "All right. Fine. I won't look." But only to ensure that he wouldn't run away. She introduced herself, her eyes shut tight, then asked for his name in return.

He studied her beautiful face. He hesitated. He had never thought of himself by name. He was simply himself.

"Matthew James," he said. Matthew was the name his aunt called him. James he plucked out of the air. He had passed a town called Jamestown; maybe that's why it came to mind. He'd never known his surname. He'd never even wondered until now.

"Matthew James," Kate said approvingly.

He told her about the house he was building, and the collection of books he had. He had run out of novels and was now reading science fiction magazines he had picked up from the AtoZ Market. She promised to bring books from the library, along with pens and paper, and anything else he needed. She didn't have to be told why he wasn't living in a city or a town. He didn't belong there. She felt older when they said good-bye, as if time had shifted while they sat in the meadow and knowing him for this one evening had made her grow up fast. She opened her eyes and watched him walk away. From this distance, he looked like a tall young man. He turned to wave when he thought he was far enough away so that she couldn't see him. But she could.

THE FIRST WINTER was the hardest. Some days he didn't leave his house. The snow fell and kept falling, and he stayed in and read the library books she'd brought him. He liked rebels. Lawrence, Dostoyevsky, Miller, Kafka. He had a rain barrel of melted snow, and he boiled the water for coffee and tea. After a while he began to feel deeply at home on those winter evenings. He made a set of weights out of a tree limb and rocks to keep himself fit. On days when it was clear enough he went out to trap game. He broke through the ice of a nearby stream to fish. He didn't mind crouching down in the snow, waiting to see a flash of silver in the water.

He waited for her visits, fewer in the winter, more frequent the following spring. In time he forgot to tell her to close her eyes, or she forgot to listen to him. Once, when they were together in the woods, she took his hand. He burned and had to look away. He warned her not to do that again. How could her hair be so red? She'd unplaited it while they were in the woods, and he'd been made mute with desire. How was it possible for her to be there with him? Why would she search him out? He thought perhaps he had invented her the way some cruel soul must have surely dreamed him up. She was quiet when he told her not to touch him, her mouth set. She became upset when he then suggested that perhaps she should go home. She walked through the orchard on her way back to town, confused because he'd told her to go. She broke off budding branches and set them in her bedroom in vases. She told herself she was done. Nothing would come of tramping through the woods, playing at love. She told herself she needed to get back on course. It was her senior year of high school and her future was at stake. She dreamed of apples all night. When she opened her eyes the next day, she was still thinking of him.

❦

SHE APPLIED TO Wellesley but didn't want to go. Her mother and aunt sat her down and convinced her it was best. They knew something was wrong with Kate. Her moodiness, her solitary ways, her refusal to see friends. She got a summer job at the library and she took home armfuls of books and locked herself in her room at night. Once their cousin Henry came all the way from Cambridge to take her out to the movies in Lenox, but when he brought her home he confided to her mother and aunt that Kate didn't seem to be there with him.

When Hannah found a bone in the garden that same summer, she thought perhaps their food had been contaminated. She had worked in that same garden all her life and had never found anything odd before. She wasn't the sort to believe in curses, but there it was, a smooth, white bone. Kate's aunt and mother dug up an entire section of the garden and found more bones. There were rumors that this area had once been a burying ground. Perhaps it was bad luck. They reburied the bones they'd found, filled in the holes, then tore out the seedlings and the old vines. They locked the gate and decided to forsake their garden that year. Kate no longer had homegrown vegetables to take to the woods. Instead, she saved the money she earned from her job at the library and bought food at the AtoZ Market to carry up to the mountain. Once she made a cake. Her mother spied her walking down the road with the cake tin. Then she knew there was a man.

When Kate told Matthew she was going to Wellesley, he said he understood, and he did. He took her to his house soon

after. She'd always asked to see it, and he'd always been standoffish, but now he changed his mind. He took her there when it
was dark. He hoped she couldn't see him when they went inside
the one room where he lived. She kissed him first, and all the
rest followed. He led her back to the road in the dark so that she
would be home before morning. It was not only to keep her
mother and aunt from knowing she had vanished. He was afraid
that the things they did and said would melt in the light.

They were together from midsummer on, and then there
were no more nights and the summer was through. He'd known
it was a stolen time, but he felt crushed when it was over. Before
Kate left for college, he gave her a poem. He told her not to read
it until she had gone to Wellesley, but she read it in her room
that night.

> You told me to wait in a field.
> It was dusk and I could smell summer. The world was green.
> I had been a bear for so long I couldn't imagine anything human.
> There was nothing I missed living in another world
> Except this:
> A woman cutting through the field to meet you
> Grass in her hair, pollen on her fingers, your name in her mouth.

She folded the poem into a box, which she then stored on
the top shelf of her closet. If she had chosen to read it again, she
might not have left.

SHE DIDN'T SEE him all year after she went off to college. When
she came home at term break, there was a snowstorm and the

mountain roads were impassable. She sat in her room and looked into the garden they didn't use anymore. She kept her hair pulled back. She wore glasses now. She felt desperate for him, and then just desperate, and then she felt nothing at all. Her mother and aunt still worried over her. Kate assured them she was fine. Her life was back on course. She decided not to see him. What good would it do? He belonged in one world, she in another.

He came one night before she went back to school, even though the snow was deep. He stood outside and watched her through the window as she read a novel. She was beautiful and far away even though he was standing in her yard. He knew that coming into town was a mistake. That next spring he found the old bear, dead, in one of the caves. He slept beside the body. He dreamed the bear was his father. That was when he gave up being human. He gave her up as well.

IN THE SUMMERS Kate went to Paris, where she studied at the Sorbonne and took a position as a counselor at an American camp for girls. In her senior year at Wellesley she became engaged to Henry Partridge, the young man she'd once ignored who was the cousin of a cousin once removed, hardly a cousin at all. After graduation Kate came home, to plan her wedding and to care for her mother, who was ill with cancer, bedridden, with only a little time left. Kate sat by her mother's bedside and read to her in French. She gazed out the window. After that first year they spent apart, on the day before she went back to school, she'd seen the trail his boots had left in the snow. She'd known he'd come, then turned away.

"We found bones in there," her mother told her one night. She was delirious sometimes and Kate had to lean in close to hear. She was talking about the garden and about that time when Kate seemed so distant. "We thought that was why you were acting so peculiarly that summer when you were fifteen. We thought you were under a spell. Then I realized it was a man."

"There was no man," Kate said.

Later when she went out to sit on the porch with her aunt, she asked Hannah about the bones.

"We stopped using the back garden after that." It was true; the lower, newer garden where the soil wasn't as rich or as red was now the plot of land they cultivated. Tomato plants had been set in a row, but after Kate's mother fell ill, no one had bothered to weed and there were brambles everywhere.

The wedding date was pushed up, to ensure that Kate's mother would be able to attend. Kate had already bought her dress in Boston. It was June, but overcast. Kate had an argument with the pastor, who would not shorten the service to accommodate Kate's ailing mother, who often needed to lie down. Kate was defiant and wouldn't back down, and in the end the pastor agreed to a truncated ceremony.

"If you're getting married on your mother's account, don't," Hannah said to her the week before the wedding. "All she wants is your happiness. She's convinced there's another man."

KATE WANTED TO see him before she was married. She found the place easily enough, as if she'd been there only the day before, even though it had been years. When she reached the clearing, she stopped and gazed at the house. She thought about the first time she'd gone inside. There were still stories about him in town. Every new group of elementary school children started the rumors up all over again. There was a monster in the woods they said, he'd eat you up, leaving only the bones. He was half ape, half bear, but he knew how to speak. And he knew tricks as well. He could call to you as if he was injured, then leap upon you. Mothers and fathers in Blackwell told their children that if they didn't finish their dinners, the monster wouldn't be very happy. They used him as a cautionary tale: That was what happened to bad boys and girls, they were banished to the woods.

There was a flurry of panic when Lucy Jacob was murdered on Route 17. Kate had been away in France that semester and hadn't heard the sad news until after she came home. Lucy had been riding her bike and someone had abducted her. She was missing all winter long until the snow melted. At last they found her with her neck broken out in the woods. She'd only been fourteen. People went out in search parties, but they found no evidence of the monster or of anything else. Things quieted down after the pastor gave a sermon in which he stated that monsters were men's imaginings and that men had to take responsibility for the horror in the world. Be sure of one thing, he had told them. It was a man, not an imaginary being, who had taken Lucy from them.

When she was almost at his door, Kate couldn't bring herself to go farther. She didn't know how to explain her long absence to Matthew, she didn't understand it herself. She clearly didn't understand anything, so she went away. It was not until she was home that night that she dared to speculate that perhaps if she had actually seen him, she would not have gone back to town. She might have been ready to give up the world that she knew. But even if she'd gone forward that afternoon, he hadn't been there. He'd been at a lake miles away, up in the mountains. He'd caught several fish and spied some herons. When he returned, he found a long, red hair in the grass outside his door. He wrote a poem that night and went into town. He crept into the yard and left it inside the old garden. Kate found it there the next morning.

If I met you now, I would tell you to
beware of men who think they're bears and bears who think
    they're men.
Here's my advice:
Run over the mountain.
Run as far as you can.

Your mistake was walking down the road where I was.
My mistake was everything else.

I want the words you hold in your hand, lamplight in a jar.

We met here.
But it could have been anywhere
the next road on the map
the one that curled around the mountain like smoke and
    disappeared.

I walked you home and didn't say much.
You were the one who kissed me.
Remember that, but remember I was the one who wanted it.
Sometimes I think I forced you to kiss me with my wanting.

I was no one. Nothing. A handyman, a jack of all trades
Winner at none. But I was the one who fell in love with you.

I never told you why I was there.
My car had broken down.
I left it in a ditch.
The sunlight was blinding. I couldn't even see you at first, only
your outline against the trees.

But it was enough.

These are the things I would have said to you as I held you closer,
As I told you to run,
Making certain to speak in a language
You didn't understand.

She went inside and folded the second poem into the box with the first. She moved a stack of sweaters in front of it, but it didn't matter. She knew it was there.

THE WEDDING WAS on a Sunday, at the Hightop Inn. The next week Kate's mother died. Kate and Henry decided to stay on. They moved in with Aunt Hannah, who was undone by the loss of her beloved sister. Kate took a job at the high school, teaching French, and Henry joined a law firm in Lenox. Sometimes Kate felt that they rattled around the old house. Everything seemed empty. But she got used to it. People welcomed them to town and were glad to have Kate back among them. One night Kate and Henry met a group of their friends at the Jack Straw Bar and Grill. They were nearly through with their meal when Kate spied Cal Jacob at the bar. He was a grown man now, one with a drinking problem. Although she hadn't seen him for years, Kate went to say hello. She still thought of him as nine years old.

"I'm so sorry about Lucy," she said.

There weren't many murders in the county, certainly not in their town. For everyone who'd known Lucy Jacob, the loss still stung, but Cal was nonchalant.

"Yeah. Thanks." Cal made it clear she should drop the topic. He didn't talk about his sister. He was a man with a swagger, one who indulged in petty crime and thought the world owed him something. "Let me buy you a drink. Come on, sit down with us."

Cal was accompanied by some of his no-good friends from Albany, one of whom, a thin dark man with hooded eyes, looked Kate up and down.

"Do you mind?" Kate said, offended by his indecent gaze. She felt undressed in some way.

"I wouldn't mind at all." Cal's friend snickered and all the men laughed. He grabbed her arm, which would later leave a mark on her creamy skin. "Let's go out to the parking lot and do it right now."

Kate pulled away. "I just wanted to say hello," she said. "Clearly a mistake." She went back to her table, rattled. "What's happened to Cal?" she asked.

One of their friends, Leo Mott, was on the Blackwell police force. "He's a bad apple," Leo said. "His buddies are worse."

"I think it's my fault," Kate said to her husband as they walked home that night.

"Your fault?" Henry laughed.

"I was his camp counselor and he disappeared into the woods on my watch. I should have kept a closer eye on him."

"But he didn't disappear. You found him," Henry reminded her. He'd heard the story before, or at least that part of it.

Kate and Henry held hands, but as they walked through town everything looked odd to Kate, the way things do in a dream, or in any place where you know you don't belong.

YEAR IN AND year out, Kate left baskets on Route 17. She went at least once a month. She packed warm sweaters, novels, notebooks, coffee, chocolates, packets of nails, wire. Items she thought he might need or desire. Her aunt Hannah went with her sometimes, for the exercise. She never questioned why they were taking a basket into the forest. Once Kate had said, "It's for lost travelers." Hannah didn't ask for any further explanation. She was fairly certain it was for that man her sister had believed existed the summer when Kate seemed so changed.

IT WAS AUGUST when it happened, the month when she'd first met him. She packed up tomatoes, lettuce, a copy of *Great Expectations,* a few issues of *Life* magazine. The air was amber, the way it was in late August. Kate and her aunt took their time. Hannah had changed since Kate's mother had died; she didn't often go out socially, and her one enjoyment was her walks with her niece. It was a perfect day. Cars passed by occasionally, but Kate and her aunt paid them no mind. One car pulled off to the side of the road into a scenic overlook. From there you could see all of the valley below. The town of Blackwell looked like a child's toy.

Kate and her aunt had gone past the overlook on the side of the road when a man came up behind them. He was running, slinking through the trees. He had the speed of a whirlwind. He hit Hannah so hard that she sank down immediately and rolled into the weeds. It happened so fast Kate didn't understand. She hadn't seen him yet. She wondered if there had been an earthquake or if her aunt had had a sudden heart attack. She dropped down to her knees to try to stop her aunt from drifting any farther downhill, and that was when he hit her, too. Once she was down, the stranger grabbed Kate by her hair and dragged her farther into the woods. She was on her stomach, trying to get away, clawing at the ground. There was blood running from her scalp, and she could feel its heat. He got on top of her, pushing her face into the dirt so she couldn't move while he fucked her. He tore at her clothes so they were half off. He was strong and maddened. He told her he would kill her if she made a sound, so she did what he said, thinking he would let them live. She caught a glimpse of him. He seemed familiar but no one she knew. He was rough with her even when she promised she wouldn't fight him. He wanted to hurt her. Then she remembered. Cal's friend at the bar.

She let her mind leave her body. She imagined she was walking through the woods. She was far away and soon it would be over. When he was done, he didn't keep his word. She should have expected as much. He told her she was a whore who deserved to die. He hit her again with a rock, harder. She felt a flash of white-hot pain. She went under, then came back. She decided to pretend she was gone so he would think she was dead and leave them be.

She thought he would go back to his car, make his getaway,

but that was not his intention. He scrambled up to the ditch where Hannah was unconscious, limp and forsaken in the dirt. That was when Kate knew she couldn't pretend to be dead. She pulled her clothes on and took up the bloody rock. She pounced on him while he was leaning over her aunt, talking to her even though she couldn't hear, telling Hannah he was going to do to her what he'd done to Lucy and to Kate, but he would break her neck first so she'd continue to be quiet. Kate hit him hard. She could feel the strike through the bones of her arm. He jerked forward as if he was going to turn to her, so she hit him again. She kept hitting him. By the time she was finished he wasn't moving anymore.

Kate sat back on her heels and tried to catch her breath. Blood flecked the ground. It pooled beneath the leaves. She pulled herself together and scurried over to her aunt. She put her ear to Hannah's back. She thought she could hear her aunt breathing, but she wasn't sure. She took off. Inside something cut through her like glass. Kate ran across the road and up the hill. She felt as if she was broken and if she stopped for an instant she would fall into pieces.

Matthew was there when she got to his house, stunned by her appearance. She didn't have to say much for him to understand. He went with her back down the mountain, across the road. He knelt beside Hannah and took her pulse. He had a medical book and knew what he was supposed to do. He breathed into Hannah's mouth and pushed on her chest. At last she took a gasping breath. He said he thought she had a concussion and maybe some broken bones. He lifted her in his arms and stood there on the side of the road.

"What are you doing?" Kate asked.

"I'll carry her home. Then you'll call the hospital. You'll say someone broke in to your house and hurt you both. Then he ran away."

"I killed him," Kate said, astonished by her own actions.

"No," Matthew told her. "He disappeared. He came into your house and you don't know what happened to him. I'll come back and get rid of him later."

The light was fading when they reached Blackwell. They went the back way, through the orchard. No one saw them. Kate had imagined being with Matthew in town a thousand times, bringing him home, but not like this. They hurried through the yard, up the porch, into the house. Kate was sobbing, but she didn't know it. Matthew took Hannah into her bedroom. When he came back into the parlor, Kate told him he had to leave. People would think the wrong thing if they saw him. He said he would, but he didn't make a move to go.

Kate realized then that she felt so filthy she had to take a shower and change her clothes. She knew she wasn't supposed to clean up before she called the police, but she couldn't stand the stranger's touch on her. She undressed in the kitchen, crying, and Matthew folded her ruined clothes into a paper bag. She stood in the shower and wept, her forehead against the tiles, hot water falling over her shoulders and her head.

Matthew was sitting in a chair in the parlor when she came out wearing a blue dress, her long red hair wet. He knew he had to go, yet hadn't.

"I just wanted to know what it was like to sit here and wait for you," he said.

She sat in his lap and kissed him. She felt undone and crazy. The world was nothing like she'd imagined it would be. She would have left her life right then, traded it in completely, if he had asked her to. Instead, he went out the back door. He left town the way he'd come, through the orchard. There was barely any light by then, but some boys out playing baseball thought they spied a monster and they all took off, running for home.

When he returned to the woods, he dragged the man's body into the forest with him. He covered his tracks. He took the body to the bear's cave and hid it beneath a heap of branches. The old bear's skeleton was in there and Matthew kept one of the bear's teeth for luck. He could guess what people in town would think. He set fire to his shed that night. He packed up only the belongings he would need and watched the rest of it burn.

He took the car that had been parked in the scenic overlook. It was a better specimen than the one he'd arrived in, with four new tires. Cal's friend had left the keys in the ignition for a quick getaway. When Matthew opened the glove compartment, he found Lucy Jacob's hair ribbon, a token her killer had kept. Before he left, he buried the ribbon in the woods. He didn't drive through town on his way out of Blackwell. That would have been too much for him. Instead, he went north, toward New York State, where he supposed he'd come from. He avoided Albany, which meant nothing to him and had never been home, but some months later he did venture into a small town near Saratoga, where he went into the post office, ignoring the stares of the clerks behind the counter, and bought stamps for an envelope addressed to Blackwell.

When the letter arrived, Kate didn't open it until she was in the woods. She went off alone, as solitary as she had been ever since she'd met him. It was bear season, November, when the bears were most active, preparing for winter. After the incident on the road, a band of Blackwell teenagers found the charred remains of Matthew's shed. They carted their findings down to the police station. There were some books, along with pots and pans, the remnants of clothes, pieces of what looked like a handcrafted table and chairs. People were stunned. There had indeed been a monster up on Hightop, although now he was clearly gone. Everyone assumed he was responsible for the attacks in the woods. Lucy Jacob's parents were relieved they could have some sort of closure in the matter of their daughter's death. Cal even accepted some cash from a journalist in exchange for telling his sister's story. Kate ran into him once, in the AtoZ Market.

"I guess you were right," she said to Cal. "There are monsters."

He'd been so intent on looking for them, he'd brought one to town in the form of his so-called friend, a man who had disappeared, whose car Matthew abandoned when he reached Saranac Lake, from where he made the rest of his way on foot.

Kate sat in a clearing. She was certain they would be growing worried at home. They would be standing at the door wondering why she went off walking when the woods were clearly dangerous. She opened the letter only to find it wasn't a letter at all. It was the first poem her beloved had written, on the evening after Cal Jacob wandered off the road into bear territory, when he first knew what they were to each other and she didn't want to know.

It was a decision before it was a question.
That was the way things happened in the human world.

In our world, a leaf falls one day and we know it's time.
We feel our hearts slowing down.
We try to fight it with cold water, bee stings, fresh kills.
But the leaf has fallen, the water doesn't rouse us.

When we sleep we dream more than any other creatures.
We dream of entirely different lives.
We are men and women.
We walk and talk in houses, and fields, and farmyards.
Leaves mean nothing to us. Thousands can fall and we look
    the other way.

A beautiful woman walks toward us and we fall in love.
We feel it happening, but can't stop it.

In your world, love pins you to the ground.
You take it to bed and wake up with it.
You dream it and it becomes your life.
I knew I'd never sleep through a winter again.
I took a knife and cut myself to see how fast I would bleed.

Slow, and I would be a bear forever.
Fast, and I was yours.
I nearly died from a single wound.
That was what it meant to be human.

SIN

1961

IT WAS EARLY SUMMER WHEN THE NEW people moved into the cottage behind the Blackwell History Museum. The museum had once been the grandest house in town, a gabled three-story building with arched windows, but for many years those elegant rooms had held displays of dinosaur bones, cases of beetles and butterflies, and shelves of unusual rocks. There was a collection of tools the first settlers of Blackwell had used—wagon wheels, axes, a black frying pan—as well as an exhibit of local mammals, which included a wolf that was coming apart at the seams, two moth-eaten foxes, and several large desiccated brown bats that frightened visitors from the elementary school. Local children swore the museum was haunted. They whispered that the bats came to life at night. If you stayed past closing, they would tangle into your hair, biting your neck deeply enough to draw blood.

The cottage had been occupied by the groundskeeper until the museum's funding dried up. Now it was rented out, and the new people were set to arrive. The cottage was small with a wraparound porch and a tilted chimney. There was a twisted wisteria vine all along the porch railing and red roses growing up a trellis that reached to the roof. Carla Kelly watched for the moving van, but there was only a station wagon with New York plates, packed to the gills. There was no man around, no father or husband, only Ava Cooper, a woman in her thirties dressed in blue jeans and a white shirt. She was surprisingly young and beautiful, almost as if she were a movie star, with her honey-colored hair pulled back into a tortoiseshell clip and her mouth streaked with scarlet lipstick. She didn't look like someone's mother, except that her daughter, Tessa, was equally beautiful, resembling her mother, only her long hair was a shade paler, an ashy blond. The daughter was also wearing blue jeans. She had on a red shirt that flared out behind her as she carried bundles back and forth from the station wagon to the cottage. The radio was still turned on, as if mother and daughter had no idea that a car battery could quickly go dead, which Carla knew only too well since she worked weekends in her father's gas station, a job she despised. The car radio was playing "Will You Love Me To-morrow?" It was Carla's favorite song. The Kelly property met up with the museum acreage in the back, so Carla had slipped through the woods into the yard to spy on her new neighbors.

Blackwell was an isolated town in the Berkshires. The closest movie theater was forty miles away. People went to bed early and worked hard. Carla was bored out of her mind. Moving in from a hidden spot behind some pine trees, standing in a cool green pool of shadow, she surveyed the cottagers. The air was fragrant with honeysuckle and the bitter sulfur-tinged scent of bridal wreath that grew along the lanes in Blackwell. Carla imagined that she'd known the new people forever, that the new girl was her best friend. When they walked through the high school corridors the following autumn, everyone would call out hello, but they'd be far too busy with their plans to bother answering.

Ava Cooper tossed down a bundle of blankets and pillows. Fed up with work on such a gorgeous summer day, she began to dance to "Will You Love Me Tomorrow?" She threw her arms into the air as though it was the most natural thing in the world to be dancing in the driveway. Her daughter applauded, and the clapping startled the birds in the woods. All at once some crows flew up from the trees. When the Coopers turned to watch the birds, there was Carla watching them in return.

"Hey there," Ava called, gesturing for their new neighbor to come over.

Carla walked out of the woods slowly, ashamed to have been caught spying. She was wearing pedal pushers and an old blouse that looked dingy compared with Ava's. Her black hair was pulled back in a ponytail. Some of the girls at school whispered that she smelled like gasoline.

"Thank goodness," Ava said as Carla approached. "You're just what we needed." The sunlight fell over mother and daughter as they stood there grinning, hands on hips. "A friend for Tessa."

✺

AFTER THAT CARLA was at the Coopers' every day. She could hardly imagine what life had been like without them. All that first week she came over early while Tessa was still in bed. She'd sit with Ava in the kitchen, drinking coffee—something her own mother would have never allowed. Ava was divorced and her ex, Tessa's dad, was an actor. "I should have been smarter," Ava confided to the teenager, as if Carla was her girlfriend, too. Both Ava and Tessa called her Carly, which made her sound exotic, even to herself. "Anyone who falls in love with an actor should have her head examined," Ava joked.

When Tessa would finally wake to join them at the table, she'd be wearing a white silk slip instead of pajamas. The fabric had a blue ribbon stitched prettily through the hem. It took Tessa an hour to wake up and at least three cups of black coffee. It wasn't that she was lazy, it was simply that she was out of sync with the pedestrian everyday world. She was a night owl, often reading until dawn. She was madly in love with Jack Kerouac and before long lent Carla her dog-eared copy of On the Road. As far as Carla could tell the author was a drunken lunatic who rambled on about nothing in ridiculously long paragraphs. She told Tessa she thought the book was fascinating, but really she'd stopped reading halfway through.

"The only woman stupider than one who marries an actor is one who marries a writer," Ava told them both at breakfast. Ava was an amazing baker. They were having honey buns along with their cups of black coffee. The combination of caffeine and sugar woke a person up, pronto, even dreamy Tessa.

"I don't care. I'm in love," Tessa remarked stubbornly. "Someday I'm going to get in a car and drive across the country to California and find him."

"That's far, honey," Ava said wistfully. "By that time Jack Kerouac will be dead if he keeps living the way he does."

"'Tiger, tiger burning bright.'" Whenever Tessa wasn't quoting Kerouac she was quoting Blake. *Songs of Innocence and Experience* was the next thing she tried to unload on Carla, also gone unread, although Carla had skimmed a few pages for appropriate quotes. Tessa told Carla that when she and Jack Kerouac had a child together, they would name it Blake, whether it was a boy or a girl. "It's better to burn out beautifully when you're young."

Ava got a funny look on her face when she heard her daughter say that, as if she'd thought similarly once, and had lived that way, and was only now realizing the flaws in such a philosophy.

WHEN THE GIRLS went down to the Eel River, Tessa confided that even though her mother joked around, she'd been terribly wounded in love. They'd come to Blackwell to start a new life after the mess of the divorce. Frankly, there had been a few men since then, but it never worked out. Her mother always chose the wrong ones. Tessa hadn't bothered to change out of her slip to go to the river. She'd merely added plastic flip-flops and a brimmed straw hat, and she looked like a fashion plate.

Tessa and Carla spent most of their days lying on beach towels, using baby oil to improve their tans, although Carla had fair and irritable skin that burned to a crisp. Carla would reveal juicy bits of gossip about everyone in town as they baked in the sun, adding a few invented details to make life in Blackwell more interesting. The girls who never included Carla were turned into sluts, kleptomaniacs, and runaways. It wasn't payback, not really. They were more interesting that way. Carla's brother, Johnny, who worked at the gas station and was known for speeding around town like a demon on his motorcycle and getting into fights at the Jack Straw Bar and Grill for no particular reason, became a haunted loner in the telling of his story. Carla presented him as a deep, moody young man à la Jack Kerouac, rather than a self-centered lout who insisted that Carla not speak to him when she ran into him because he didn't want to be seen with her. At least when Carla spiced up the truth, she had something to say that held Tessa in thrall, even if it was a lie.

The homespun village lore about Blackwell was probably lies as well, invented by the town's forefathers, but the stories seemed interesting to an out of towner. Carla told all the old tales she'd heard since she was a child. There were the museum bats coming to life, and the rumor that Johnny Appleseed had passed through town, and, perhaps most interesting, the little ghost girl who wandered along the banks of the Eel River. They called her the Apparition and said she was searching for her sister. Whoever spied her on a summer's evening would be lucky in love. Tessa adored Blackwell and all its stories. She loved the countryside and declared the Eel River to be a state treasure, one of the wonders of Massachusetts. She wished Jack Kerouac could see it, how the sunlight glinted over the green water, how the cattails grew so tall. She said that when the weather got hotter in late summer they would swim the length of the river. Carla agreed even though after a lifetime in Blackwell she had never done more than wade in the shallows. She had a wicked fear of eels.

❧

AFTER THE COOPERS had been in town for a while, rituals were slowly established for the girls: breakfast, then suntanning at the river, then back to the cottage for supper. Usually they had macaroni or hamburgers, comfort food, all delicious, but it was Ava's desserts that were truly amazing. That first week she made one of her Seven Deadly Sins cakes—devil's food for greed. Each night thereafter there was a large gooey piece for dessert. It was the kind of cake that could make you want things you hadn't even known existed. It made you yearn for more, especially when the last piece of cake was shared and devoured. Too soon the twilight would begin to turn into darkness and it would be time for Carla to go. Tessa always walked her halfway home through the woods. There were fireflies glinting in the underbrush, and branches broke beneath their feet. The girls usually took to whispering. They made up stories about what had happened in these same woods in days gone by. They imagined the pioneer women who had traipsed through the snow, and the strong men who had planted all the apple trees in town. There was also a ghost said to haunt these woods as well, the sister of the river ghost. People said she'd left town in the middle of the night with her beloved, but had always yearned to come home for she knew that her little sister searched for her from beyond the grave. Locals swore that if you saw her, there'd be a journey in your future.

The girls ambled along, telling stories, but as soon as they reached the huge old oak that signified the borderline of the Kellys' property, Carla would shout "See you!" and take off like a shot. Sometimes she'd glance over her shoulder and Tessa would still be watching her, her pale hair framing her beautiful face. Even when Tessa called out, "Wait! Carly! I'll walk you all the way home!" Carla kept running. Where she came from was so plain, so ordinary, she didn't want Tessa to see it and think less of her. Carla's mother was upset with her because she was never home anymore, but who could blame her for choosing the Coopers' cottage over her own house? As for Marian Kelly, she didn't like what she was hearing about Ava Cooper, who was going around town looking for work, chatting people up, offering free cakes to the folks at Hightop Inn and the coffee shop and even at the Jack Straw Bar and Grill as she looked for a position that would pay the bills.

"What's she like?" Marian asked Carla.

"She's an amazing baker." Carla knew enough to keep her descriptions brief. No stories of Seven Deadly Sins cakes, particularly Lust Cake, a lemon poppy seed triple layer with sugary frosting that was impossible to resist. She wisely failed to mention that Tessa carelessly walked around town wearing little more than her underwear, unaware that this might be considered unusual. She certainly didn't tell her mother that Ava served them coffee at breakfast or that on that very first night, when the Coopers had moved into the cottage and there were still unpacked boxes stacked everywhere, Ava had allowed the girls small glasses of champagne and they'd all made a giddy toast. Once Carla let slip that Tessa's father was an actor, but she quickly fell quiet when she saw the look on her mother's face.

ON SATURDAYS CARLA never went to the Coopers. "I'll meet you at the river before supper," she told Tessa. When asked why she was never around on Saturdays, she said only that she had family obligations, or errands to run. The truth was she had to report to the gas station. She prayed Ava Cooper's station wagon didn't need gas while she was at work. Carla counted the minutes while she sat behind the cash register or helped her father bleed the brakes on Leo Mott's Chrysler. Her brother, Johnny, often had a hangover, and when he was in a bad mood, Carla stayed away from him. He was the sort of young man who could charm someone one minute and have a fistfight with him the next. He had the up-and-down personality many of the Kellys were said to have. Women couldn't stay away from him.

Carla bolted her lunch while working the cash register and ducked her head when a group of girls she knew from the high school walked by. One of the girls, Madeline Hall, was sent in by the others to ask if Johnny was around. They were all much too young for him, yet they yearned for him, or who they thought he was. They'd become something of a fan club.

"He's in the back working," Carla said.

"Well, we're all going to the movies in Lenox next weekend," Madeline told her. "You could come, too, and bring Johnny."

"Thanks, but no thanks," Carla replied.

Before, she would have died for an invitation. Now she had plans with Tessa. Carla sat there the rest of the day dreamily biding her time. She had her bathing suit on under her clothes. As soon as the clock hit five, she headed out.

The high school girls were gathered on the steps of the library when she passed by. "Hey, Carla," one of them called. It was Jennifer Starr. "Don't forget the movies next Saturday."

Carla wished those girls would disappear into thin air. They were so small-town in their shorts and T-shirts, their hair braided or pushed back with headbands. They'd never been anywhere at all, let alone seen Manhattan. They probably didn't even know who Jack Kerouac was. And they certainly didn't have Tessa Cooper as their best friend.

As it turned out, Tessa seemed to need Carla just as much as Carla needed her. She had confided that she was frightened of crowds. She grew uneasy on buses and in theaters. Sometimes she couldn't speak in class. She became totally tongue-tied. She was smart and beautiful and there was no reason for her to be shy, but she was.

"Don't worry," Carla had assured her. "We'll be in all the same classes. If you can't speak, I'll just say you have laryngitis."

Tessa had thrown her new friend a grateful look.

CARLA CUT THROUGH the woods after work. She followed along the marsh where there were cattails and the ground turned spongy. There were little frogs in the puddles and white butterflies with green specks on paper-thin wings circling the purple thistle. The sun was like honey, falling in splashes. It was a relief not to be on Main Street, in her father's gas station, where everyone knew her and everything about her. Carla hadn't imagined the ways in which her life might follow a different path until the Coopers moved into the museum cottage. Since then she'd been seized with the impulse to create a more intriguing persona for herself. Lately, everything seemed brand-new, including Blackwell, even though Carla knew every street and lane.

She heard the murmur of voices as she approached the river. There was Tessa sitting on her beach towel, laughing in the dappled sunlight, wearing her white slip with the red blouse thrown over it like a jacket. Next to her in the grass were Frank and Jesse Mott, both sixteen. They'd seen Tessa and Carla walking through the woods day after day, arms thrown around each other, beach towels over their shoulders. It was Tessa they were interested in. Once she was alone, without the pesky Kelly girl hovering, they'd been bold enough to introduce themselves. As Carla drew near, the Mott brothers stopped talking.

"Hey!" Tessa signaled her over. "Where've you been? Come on," she called to Carla. She patted the picnic basket beside her. "My mother sent a treat." Tessa turned to the boys. "We'll share if you're good."

"I will be," Frank offered. The boys were twins, but Frank was the tenderhearted one who played by the rules. "I can't speak for my brother."

Jesse was already opening the basket. He had his eyes on Tessa's tanned legs.

"Quit it," she said, pushing him aside. They looked at each other after they'd touched. Then, as quickly, they looked away. Carla had a strange feeling in the pit of her stomach. Jesse was the boy everyone in town was in love with. "Oh," Tessa said, bringing forth a half of a cake. "It's Gluttony Cake! Devil's food with chocolate pudding and chocolate chips inside."

They cut the cake into pieces and wolfed it down—at least the Mott brothers and Tessa did. Carla took a neat bite, then tossed her portion into the woods when no one was looking. She felt sick. She was quiet that afternoon, more audience than participant, and she was glad when the day was over. When the girls left, the boys followed until they had to split up at the road and go their separate ways.

"See you tomorrow," the Mott brothers called.

"Maybe," Tessa called back. "Maybe not."

For a shy girl she seemed entirely comfortable with the boys' attentions.

"Are you madly in love with Jesse?" Carla asked once they were alone. "Be honest."

"Of course not!" Tessa laughed.

"That's good," Carla lowered her voice. "He's ruined a lot of girls' reputations."

Tessa glanced over at her friend. "Reputations don't mean a thing," she said. "Jack Kerouac couldn't care less about a person's reputation."

"Well, he didn't live in Blackwell," Carla said emphatically. "That Jesse is bad news." It wasn't completely true, but it was true enough, and Carla felt satisfied that she'd warned her best friend against him.

THE NEXT DAY was Sunday and Carla had to go visit her grandparents for lunch. On the way home, she was in the car with her parents and Johnny when they saw a station wagon pulled up at the gas pumps.

"Someone broke down," Carla's dad, Bill, said.

They were closed on Sundays, but steam was rising from beneath the station wagon's hood. All at once Carla realized it was the Coopers' car. Ava was standing there smoking a cigarette, a worried expression on her face. Carla slunk down in the backseat. Her face flushed, and she could feel her heart hitting against her chest.

"I'll take care of it," Johnny said. He got out and went over to Ava. She laughed and curtsied as though he was a knight who had come to her rescue. Carla looked through the rear window of the car as her father drove away. She watched until they turned the corner and couldn't see anymore.

The next day when Carla went to the cottage, the Coopers' car wasn't in the driveway.

"My mother broke down. She got a ride back here on the back of a motorcycle. The guy driving it looked so much like Jack Kerouac I couldn't believe it."

Carla worried all that week that she would be found out. She was nothing in this town, just a gas station girl. As soon as Tessa knew who she was, she wouldn't want her as a best friend anymore. Carla carried her dread around with her, knowing her happiness at being someone brand-new would soon be over. Sure enough, on Saturday Ava Cooper showed up to collect her car. "Carla," she said, delighted when she came upon her daughter's friend in the office. "I didn't know you had a job!" Ava had a cake tin with her. "The gentleman who worked here was so helpful I brought a Gratitude Cake." It was angel food with vanilla icing. "It's even better than Gluttony Cake, although nothing is as good as an Apology Cake. That is by far my best recipe."

Johnny waved from the garage. "Car's all ready," he called to Ava.

"Great," Ava called back.

"Don't tell Tessa," Carla said.

"What?" Ava was distracted. She grabbed the cake tin to take out to the garage.

"Don't tell her I work in a gas station."

"There's nothing wrong with working. You should be proud of it."

"Please don't tell her," Carla begged.

Ava looked at Carla, her brow furrowed. "Okay. Fine. You tell her."

AT THE END of the day Carla ran all the way to the river. She and Tessa always wore their bathing suits, but they never went swimming. There were the eels in the water, and if that wasn't enough to keep a person out of the river, there were fast eddies and little whirlpools even in the summertime. Carla had warned Tessa that the Eel River was dangerous. But on that Saturday, Tessa and Jesse Mott were in the water. Carla could hear them whooping as they encountered the shock of the cold currents. She stopped at the edge of the pine forest. The sunlight was blinding. There they were, swimming around, laughing. Then Jesse moved in close, as if he was going to tell Tessa a secret. Tessa laughed and swam away to the bank. She pulled herself out. She stood there in her slip, now see-through in the sunlight, water dripping from her arms and from her long pale hair. She looked like a nymph. She had an unreadable expression, but she broke into a grin when she spied Carla standing in the woods.

"Hey, you!" Tessa waved. She looked like herself again.

Carla could hear Jesse mutter "Shit" under his breath as he dragged himself onto the riverbank. He certainly wasn't pleased to see her. Carla walked toward them with a sour look.

"There are eels in there," she said of the water. "Where's Frank?" she asked Jesse. Just the two of them meant something. She felt as if she had stepped into a pool of treachery even though Tessa seemed glad to see her.

"He's going to meet us tonight," Tessa said.

"Tonight?" Carla said.

"We're going to have a party," Jesse remarked. "Unless you can't come," he said pointedly to Carla.

They were to meet at midnight on the steps of the museum. Carla and Tessa walked home together, slowly, for the day was still brutally hot. "What if it's haunted like people say?" Carla wanted to know of their planned nighttime foray. "What if we see the sister who ran away?"

"Then we'll prove there are ghosts, and I can write to Jack Kerouac and he can come here and rescue me."

Carla was surprised to hear that Tessa of all people thought she needed rescuing.

"I thought you liked Blackwell," she said reproachfully.

"Not from Blackwell." Tessa made a face. "From myself."

When she stopped, Carla did, too.

"You promise you won't tell?" Tessa said.

Carla crossed her heart, which was pounding against her chest. Tessa lifted up the sleeves of her red shirt. There were marks on both wrists.

"Is that from the eels in the river?" Carla said, confused. "Were you bitten? That stupid Jesse, he should have never taken you swimming."

Tessa smiled, then shook her head sadly. "It's from before we moved here."

Suddenly Carla realized these were the marks of a razor blade.

"Why would you cut yourself?" she asked.

Tessa shrugged. "After my father left, I didn't see the point of things. I wanted to burn bright. To feel something deeply."

"Tiger, tiger," Carla murmured softly.

"Exactly." Tessa glowed. "You understand me, Carly. But it was a mistake. My father never even showed up at the hospital. And they made me leave school. That's the real reason we moved here."

"Sometimes I feel like leaving school," Carla admitted. "People make fun of me because I work in my father's gas station."

There. It was out in the open. Carla looked sideways at her friend.

"They're probably just jealous because you have a job," Tessa said. "You're more mature and responsible."

Carla didn't think that was the reason, but she was pleased to hear that Tessa did.

"Hey, you two," Ava said when they approached the cottage. She signaled them into the kitchen, where she'd been baking all day. The owner of the Hightop Inn had been interested when Ava went up there with a sampling of cakes. He said he might be willing to take six cakes per week. "Try this," Ava said, cutting them slices of yellow coconut cake. "Envy Cake. Everyone wants the recipe."

"It's unbelievable," Tessa said. "I'm going to send one of these to Jack Kerouac."

"You don't know where he lives," Carla reminded her.

"I'll send it via his publisher. I'll write a note that will make him burn with desire. *I envy your life on the road. Take me with you!*"

THEY SNEAKED OUT at the midnight hour. It was the Fourth of July, so no one would notice. Everyone would be out in Band's Meadow watching the fireworks or they'd be at the annual Independence Day party at the Jack Straw Bar and Grill. Carla had come through the woods alone. She was nervous in the dark. She was nervous about meeting the Motts. She wondered what it felt like to cut yourself, to be so daring, to be asked to leave school, to not care about your reputation.

Tessa climbed out her window while Carla waited in the yard. She shinnied down the drainpipe, then jumped down from the porch roof. There were red roses growing there and the thorns had torn into Tessa's skin, but she didn't seem to mind. She and Carla looped their arms around each other and went toward the museum.

"Who do you like better? Frank or Jesse?" Carla asked.

"They're just boys," Tessa said dismissively. "I need a man like Mr. Jack K. Someone with experience. Frank and Jesse have probably never been outside of Blackwell."

That was true of Carla as well, but she agreed with Tessa. "They're mere babies," she remarked, even though she herself would have run off with Jesse in the blink of an eye.

The Mott brothers were waiting behind the museum. Their mother volunteered in the gift shop, and Jesse had swiped the key to the back door. They stumbled inside, laughing, giddy, then stopped so their eyes could adjust to the dark. There was the wagon wheel that had been on the first settlers' carriage. There was the wolf someone had shot up in the mountains when there were still wolves slinking through the woods in Massachusetts. They stood in front of the bats in the big glass case. When Jesse made a *whoo whoo* noise, the others all jumped in a fit of fear, then exploded into laughter.

"Come over here," Jesse said, grabbing Tessa by the arm. "I want to show you something."

When he led her into the rocks and minerals exhibit, Frank

and Carla stood there uncomfortably. They knew what Jesse was initiating—a kiss, maybe more. Still, they had nothing to say to each other and were somewhat grateful when Tessa shrieked. They both ran into the room where there were fossils and samples of the local mica.

"I saw the ghost," Tessa cried. "The runaway sister. She was right outside the window, with her horse."

Jesse rolled his eyes; he had one thing on his mind, but Frank said they should go out to investigate. Carla and Tessa held hands. "What did she look like?" Carla asked.

"She was about our age. Long hair. She looked sad."

"There's nothing here," Jesse said, disgusted.

Frank was kneeling on the ground. "Look," he said.

They all crouched down. There were the marks of something that might have been a horse's hooves. Tessa sat down in the ivy. She declared that she thought she might faint, and in fact her creamy skin had paled dramatically.

"Come on, Tessa," Jesse urged. "It was probably some kind of joke."

But Tessa was so upset it was decided she would go home with Carla since Ava was out at the Independence Day party. The boys walked them through the woods, then regretfully said good-bye. Although Carla was pleased to have Tessa to herself, she worried about having her worlds collide. When she took Tessa in to meet her parents, the Kellys were wary but polite. The girls went into the living room and looked through a copy of *The History of Blackwell.* They found a reference to the two sisters who were said to be ghosts, both from the Starr family. They had lived in the museum when it was still a house. One was a little girl who had drowned, the other was her older sister who had run off with a horse trader. There was a hazy photograph of the elder one, whose name was Mary.

"That's her!" Tessa said. "I'm not kidding. She's the one I saw tonight." She took Carla's hand and whispered. "It means someone will be leaving Blackwell to go on a journey. Probably me."

"Don't say that!" Carla cried.

Because it was so late Mrs. Kelly asked Johnny to drop Tessa at home on his way out to the Jack Straw Bar and Grill. She didn't want her daughter's friend to be wandering through the woods all alone.

Tessa was absolutely thrilled when she saw Johnny's motorcycle. He was in the driveway wearing boots, torn jeans, a white T-shirt. She remembered him from the time the car broke down. "Let's go to California!" she said. "We won't stop till we get to City Lights bookstore."

The idea of Johnny in a bookstore made Carla laugh out loud.

"Who's paying for the gas?" Johnny said in a jokey way. He was especially nice to Tessa, flattered by how thrilled she was over the prospect of getting on his motorcycle. He had never once taken Carla for a ride. "Hop on," he said grandly.

Tessa hugged her friend good-bye, then got on. She put her arms around Johnny when he told her to, to make sure she wouldn't fall off once they began to soar down the bumpy road. Carla stood watching them. When her brother gunned the engine, dust rose up. Carla had grit in her eyes. He came so close when he took off he almost hit her and she'd had to jump back, heart pounding.

Carla's mother stepped onto the porch. There were still fireworks going off and sprays of red, white, and blue filled up the sky. Carla thought about the disappearing sisters who had once lived in the history museum. The motorcycle tore off down the street.

"Pretty girl," Mrs. Kelly said.

Carla looked over at her mother, who was gazing at the fireworks display.

"She's the kind who will always go far."

CARLA WOKE UP in the middle of the night. At first she thought she heard thunder, then she realized there were still fireworks being set off, homegrown ones, cherry bombs and sparklers, the kind that always sent someone racing to the emergency room of the Blackwell Community Hospital. Carla got out of bed and got dressed. She felt restless and spooked, trapped in her little bedroom. She climbed out her window and went through the woods. Because the moon had risen, the path wasn't as scary as usual. When she reached the edge of the woods, however, she stopped. She thought she saw the ghost weaving past the museum. She went forward, straining to see. A girl with blond hair was in the yard. Johnny's motorcycle was up against an old oak tree.

Carla could feel her pulse pounding. The girl disappeared into the woods, so Carla went on, following, toward the river. She felt reckless, the new her, a girl who refused to be frightened by imaginary creatures. There were still splashes of fireworks up above, and the sky was ashy and bright at the same time. She heard voices, so she slowed down a bit. When she looked over at the river, she felt her heart jolt. There was something blue on the riverbank. She thought it was the Apparition, the ghostly little sister in the blue dress, perhaps going to meet her older sister Mary. But when Carla crept closer, she saw it was only a pair of jeans. They'd been tossed onto a tangled pile of clothing. White T-shirt, boots, a black belt, a red shirt.

Carla leaned against a tree and listened to them as they dove into the water. There was the rise and fall of their muffled, watery voices. She heard their laughter and their desire. She felt dizzy in the dark, consumed with hatred. She saw them in a still deep pool, arms around each other, kissing. The girl's cascade of blond hair looked green in the dark. Carla's brother looked like a stranger. They were naked in the water, wrapped around each other. He was running his hands over her breasts and she was letting him. Carla crouched down and watched the stranger who was her brother. She realized that he was fucking the blond girl. The girl arched her back, her neck. He put one hand on her throat and brought her close to him. He kissed her until it seemed they might drown. And she kissed him back. She kissed him like crazy.

Carla turned and ran back through the woods. It was a long way, and she was out of breath when she got home. She was shivering even though the night was hot. In the morning, she reported the incident to the other girls in town, Jennifer Starr and Madeline Hall and all the rest. She told the Mott brothers, who looked dumbfounded. Jesse said, "She wouldn't even let me kiss her." Once she started telling she couldn't stop. Right before supper she told her mother, who slapped her face, then called her father home from work.

From her bedroom Carla could hear her parents arguing with Johnny when he came home, and Johnny shouting back, then her father's angry voice telling him to get the hell out.

Johnny slammed the door and left, and they could hear his motorcycle roar away. Carla stayed in her room all the next day. That week she didn't go to the Coopers'. She didn't go the whole rest of the summer. She started to spend afternoons with Madeline Hall when Jennifer went to Maine with her family. Her brother gave her murderous looks, and once he said, "How does it feel to be such a bitch?" but after that he stayed clear of her, which frankly was a relief. He drank too much, and at the end of the summer he moved into a room in a house full of college students from the community college even though he didn't know a single one. He continued to show up for work. Carla, on the other hand, had been allowed to give up her job. It would have been too uncomfortable for her to be there, considering the animosity between brother and sister.

Once, Ava Cooper came to the Kellys' house, carrying a cake tin. She was wearing the red blouse Tessa had been wearing on the day they moved in, the one Carla had spied on the riverbank the night she'd stumbled upon the lovers. Mrs. Kelly went out to meet Mrs. Cooper in the driveway. Carla watched through the window for a while, then she got into bed. She had a sinking, sick feeling. It was the red blouse. She hadn't known they shared clothes. She started to feel confused about what she had seen that night. Her mother knocked on her door, then opened it.

"Your friends sent you something."

Carla sat up. Her mother was holding a red velvet cake.

"She said it was an Apology Cake."

"I don't want it," Carla said.

When school started, Carla felt anxious. She started biting

her nails. She didn't know what she would say if Tessa tried to sit with her and Madeline and Jennifer at lunch. Maybe Tessa would accuse her of being a liar. Well, then, she'd just say Tessa was a slut, even though she now knew it wasn't true. But Tessa didn't show up on the first day of school. Later that week, Carla went past their house. The station wagon wasn't there. The shades were drawn.

"They've moved," her father told her when she asked if he knew what had happened to the Coopers. "The mother came and got the car serviced before they left. They went to California."

Carla thought about them often, how the ride to California must have taken days, through wheat fields, across the desert. Once she got a cookbook and tried to make a red velvet cake, but it was a disaster, all tilted and mushy, and a single bite turned her mouth red. She worried that she was cursed, that her mouth would stay red forever. But it was just the red dye in the recipe. It washed away after she drank some cold water. When the following summer Johnny was killed in a motorcycle crash, Carla was the one who had to clean out his room. Her mother was too distraught. Her father couldn't bring himself to go over to the house where Johnny had lived since the falling-out in their family. A young man let Carla into the house. She was surprised to see how small her brother's room was and how neatly he'd kept it. Searching through his bureau she found a packet of letters addressed to Ava Cooper that had been returned to him. ADDRESSEE UNKNOWN had been stamped on the envelopes. She'd heard that Ava had opened a restaurant in San Francisco, that people stood on line on Saturday nights, hoping to get in. She thought her brother had the address right, on Montgomery

Street, but that the Coopers most likely didn't want anything that had been mailed from Blackwell and made sure it was sent right back. They probably never even thought about the Eel River anymore, the way the sunlight fell across the water, the fact that it was one of the wonders of Massachusetts.

BLACK RABBIT

1966

THE MOTT BROTHERS WERE IN TROUBLE from the time they could crawl. Their mother, Helen, had grown up in Hartford, Connecticut. She was a sheltered woman, educated at private schools, known for her sweet temper and lovely singing voice. She'd been engaged to a medical student, but when Leo Mott came tearing through Hartford on a lark with some of his buddies one summer night, Helen fell for him on the spot and moved to Blackwell. She appeared to settle easily into small-town life. But something happened to her during her pregnancy. She seemed unsettled. She kept to herself and didn't return phone calls. People saw her wandering through town, as if she were lost. One day she started off at a brisk pace as if she could walk her way out of Blackwell and a pregnancy that had caused her to become enormous, a stranger to herself. She might have made it all the way back to Hartford if she hadn't come face-to-face with a bear on Route 17.

Helen closed her eyes and waited to die. She said a silent farewell to her children-to-be who might never be born and to her husband and to everyone else on earth. She made a vow that if she did happen to survive, if some miracle occurred even though she hardly deserved such good fortune, she would never again complain about Blackwell. When she opened her eyes, the bear was gone, but there was his footprint, huge as could be. Helen ran home, then drove back to the site, having stopped at the hardware store for a sack of plaster of paris and a thermos she hurriedly filled with water so she could set the footprint and bring it home. That way people would believe her.

Every time the Mott boys got into trouble, people said the twins' fearless nature had been formed during that ill-fated meeting. The boys were named Jesse and Frank before their mother understood that these had also been the names of the notorious James brothers. Frank was dark and intense. Jesse was blond, always the favorite in town. His appearance was so angelic that his antics were usually overlooked. He stole his father's car at the age of thirteen and drove it into Dead Man's Pond, but no charges were brought. He burned down the bookstore, but it was declared to be an accident; he was merely setting off a cherry bomb on the Fourth of July, and insurance paid for the rebuilding. Jesse usually got off scot-free, leaving his brother behind to clean up the mess, which Frank did willingly because of his bond with his twin. He insisted that he was the one who'd forgotten to test the brakes of his dad's Chevy and swore he'd bought the cherry bomb. For as long as they'd lived, the brothers had never spent a day apart.

But in 1966, the year Frank was drafted to go to Vietnam, Jesse Mott ran off to California. He did everything he could to convince Frank to go with him. They would slip out of town in the middle of the snowy midnight, escape from the backwater where they'd never belonged in the first place; even their mother had known that in the months before their birth when she tried to return to Hartford. To Jesse's surprise, Frank wouldn't go. He was more stubborn than people might guess. He wasn't the sort to run away from his responsibilities, even if that meant fighting a war he didn't believe in or even understand. There was a big blowup between the two brothers at the Jack Straw Bar and Grill. Both men were hammered; they swung wildly and slugged each other. They called each other names, then wound up crying together in the parking lot in the snow.

It took a lot to get Frank Mott to cry, but if anyone could manage to bring him to tears, it was his brother. Some people joked that they were two halves of the same person: the quiet, dependable one, and the one who was willing to do just about anything on a dare. On the night of their fight, Frank held his head in his hands as he sat between two parked pickup trucks. His jaw was throbbing from a good left hook, but that was the least of his problems. His whole world was coming apart. His parents planned to drive him down to New Jersey the next day for his induction. He wished someone would run him over in the parking lot, just mow him down and be done with it.

"We'll just get out of this fucking town," Jesse kept saying. He had a bruise rising around one eye and his knuckles were raw, but he sat down beside Frank and threw an arm around his shoulders. "It will be you and me against the world. Come on, brother. Don't you get it? I'm doing this for you. You're the one who's being drafted."

As for Jesse, he was the one with all the luck. He was a wild man, well known throughout the Berkshires because of the time he'd jumped off a cliff on Hightop Mountain. His friends had turned away after he leapt, too frightened to watch as he careened to earth with no safety net other than his leather jacket, which he held over his head like a parachute. Anyone else would have surely broken his neck in such a fall. Jessie had let out a joyous shout and wound up with a shattered leg.

"Just give me drink," he'd said when his friends raced to find him in a heap. They took him to the hospital with Frank driving, muttering curses as he broke the speed limit. The girls had gone even more crazy for Jesse after that; his limp added to his mystique. He had half the girls in town in bed before Frank had his first sexual encounter with René Jacob. Frank had felt trapped into remaining in a tortured relationship with René for the rest of high school while Jesse did as he pleased, getting stoned every day, screwing every girl who came his way, making the varsity basketball team despite his limp, even though Frank was the one who had coached him and taught him his jump shot.

On the night when Jesse took off, both brothers were too drunk to drive. Not that that had stopped Jesse before—but this time they actually couldn't remember where they'd parked their car. Jesse rose from the snowy curb, then reached out and pulled Frank to his feet.

"Last chance. I'm leaving right now. I'm not waiting to be inducted into their war. Come with me."

Frank shook his head. He was dizzy as hell. He was going to fight in a war that had nothing to do with him; but he knew how his parents would feel if they woke up in the morning to discover both their sons gone.

Jesse walked off into the snow. One minute he was there, railing at Frank, telling him he was an idiot who would miss out on all those beautiful California girls, and the next he had disappeared into the swirl of snowflakes. Frank sat there for a while, in the quiet of the falling snow. He was the one who'd been drafted, but Jesse was taking the opportunity to go AWOL. Frank's blood was pounding. He could feel his aloneness deep inside. All at once he realized his mistake. He had to get out of Blackwell and out of the army and out of his life. He took off after his brother down Route 17, but Jesse was nowhere to be seen. Frank shouted out Jesse's name as he loped along, then blinked in the lights of an oncoming car. A drunk driver headed to the Mass Pike skidded out and knocked Frank Mott for a loop. When he woke up in the Blackwell Hospital two weeks later, his memory was gone.

FRANK'S PARENTS SAT by his bedside each day. The nurses spent hours reminding him what year it was and who was president. It was all a blur to him. Friends patiently listed the names of their teachers back in high school, trying to conjure his previous life outside the hospital. René Jacob, now René Link, having married Brian Link, one of their classmates who had been sent to serve in Vietnam, visited the very first week even though they hadn't spoken in ages. She had a baby girl she'd named Allegra. She pulled up a chair next to Frank's hospital bed and took his hand in hers as her baby slept in a stroller. In the hopes of jogging his memory, René told him everything about the first time they'd had sex in the back of his father's car. She described it in such detail, Frank felt himself wanting her. His sudden desire shocked him. Then René bitterly reminded him that he'd broken up with her in their senior year.

"I'm sorry," Frank said.

"You weren't then," René informed him.

Even though she'd known he hadn't loved her, she'd been crushed. "Remember when I told you I wished you would die?" René said in her soft, pretty voice. Frank thought that he might. Either way he got a chill. "I didn't really mean it," René admitted. "I meant I still loved you."

Little flickers of memory came back slowly. Frank recalled the dog he'd had as a boy, a collie named Cody. He remembered his father teaching him to ski. He had flashes of the past while he was undergoing physical therapy for his shattered leg. Two months after the accident he was transferred to a rehab center. When he swam in the pool there, he'd often get an image in mind—a face, a tree, a cloud, a moment in time. All the same he felt lost, a man without a past, turned out into the world all alone.

THEY LET HIM go home in March when the weather was windy and the sky was overcast with clouds thickening over Hightop Mountain. There was a surprise party for him at the Jack Straw Bar and Grill and everyone in town showed up. Aside from a slight limp, Frank appeared to be perfectly fine. He had a scar under his eye, but that seemed to add something to his appearance, a scrim of daring. Frank thanked his parents for their forbearance and his neighbors and friends for their kindness. The one person he didn't thank was his brother, Jesse. He didn't remember him at all.

They showed him photos and told stories of the twins' exploits, with Jesse always taking the starring role, but nothing came back to him. They said he had shattered the same leg that Jesse had, and wasn't that a strange coincidence, but Frank merely shrugged off the alleged similarity of their injuries. By now he could remember his math class with Mr. Shannon in high school, but he still couldn't remember his own brother. He could remember kissing René and wishing she was someone else, just as she'd said. He remembered his neighbors and the names of their pets, the many holidays spent at his grandparents' house, but his brother and best friend, the person who loomed largest in his life, was gone. When Frank sat in his parents' darkened living room and watched home movies, he didn't recognize the boy he had always trailed after and made excuses for. People continued to swear that he and his brother now had matching limps, and that they used to joke about them being two halves of a whole, but he didn't remember the day he'd rushed Jesse to the hospital or how worried he'd been.

The Mott family's physician wrote a letter and Frank was excused from active duty due to his brain injury. "It's nothing to get upset about," the doctor explained to Frank. "Just some aftereffects of the coma. It doesn't mean your brain isn't perfectly good for most things."

Still, he felt damaged. That spring he let his hair grow long. He spent hours gazing at the trees in his parents' front yard. He was looking for answers in the way the light filtered through the leaves. He had to have several drinks before he could manage to get even a few restless hours of sleep. He usually had two or three more beers when he woke up as well. One day he drove past an abandoned farm near the Eel River and saw two women with long skirts walking barefoot down the road. They were young, and their hair was long and shiny. The clouds were billowy and the wind was blowing and all of a sudden the rain began to come down hard. Frank pulled over and offered the girls a lift. He had that scar now and his long black hair, and the girls laughed and shouted "Hey, gorgeous!" and got in. They gave him his first taste of marijuana in exchange for the ride. At the end of the road they told him to stop. They were home, they said, even though there was nothing much around but Band's Meadow, a desolate stretch of scrub grass and brambles under the slate-gray sky. The girls got out, but Frank stayed in his parked car thinking about things he'd never thought of before he smoked the joint. He wondered if it was possible for a person to leave his body, if that's what he'd done when he was in the coma. When the car was still there after an hour, one of the girls came back to check on him. She laughed when he kissed her, which he did because the dim afternoon was suddenly beautiful and hopeful now that this lovely creature in the car with him raised her warm, moist mouth to his. The girl said, "Go ahead. What are you waiting for?" Since he had no idea what he was waiting for, he had her there in his car, but it was utterly different from those furtive fucks with René Jacob. It was a like a dream, no strings attached, something loose and easy.

The girls were part of a group of young people who'd set up camp in the meadow. They had recently arrived from New York.

They'd come to Blackwell to live on this soggy, river-drenched stretch of land, intent on creating a communal farm with one of their members' inheritance money, not that they knew anything about farming. The men were Pete and Rattler; the young women were Jenna and Simone and Rose. Rose was the one Frank had been with in the car. She was gorgeous, with dark auburn hair and breasts that swayed under the thin fabric of her blouse. The group slept in tents and were trying their best to put up a house, so far without much luck. Pete had nearly cut off most of his thumb with a saw. Since Frank knew how to build things and had nothing better to do, he offered to help them. He drove out every day. When his mother asked where he was going, he said, "Just driving." Because of his accident she was afraid to pressure him, but Helen knew where he was going. The whole town did.

He wound up moving out there with them, getting stoned every night, sampling mushrooms, peyote, hashish. He took to drugs like an eel to water, but he also took to physical labor. He worked like a madman on building the house, splitting logs in the sunlight with his shirt off, aching from the hard work. He was glad to be doing something—anything—that let him stop wondering about what he had forgotten. He went swimming with his new friends in the Eel River late at night, sinking into the mud and cold water, floating and looking at stars. He took them climbing on Hightop Mountain and showed off the deep, blue view. All three women fell in love with him. He had become that kind of man—edgy, a loner, the sort of mystery man women thought they could save. As it turned out, Rose and Pete were a couple, as were Rattler and Jenna, so it was only natural for Frank to be with Simone. Simone had curly dark hair and a beautiful smile. She had been at NYU before coming to Black-well and was the one with the inherited money, the main reason she'd been invited along. She didn't seem to know the others that well. Technically she owned the Farm, not that she believed in ownership. Simone didn't talk much, and that was fine with Frank. He didn't want to talk. He just wanted to be. There was something wrong with him, some kind of emptiness, as if he had been turned into a shadow on the night of his accident, as if he had snow in his veins rather than blood. He remembered who he was, all right. He just didn't feel a thing.

People in town wondered if it had been wild Jesse who had kept Frank steady and if in losing the memory of his brother, he had somehow lost himself. When Frank drove into the village for supplies, they could hardly believe he was the same Frank Mott. His hair was down past his shoulders, he was deeply tanned, and his arms were huge and muscular from all that work he was doing out on the Farm. He could lift a two-hundred-pound bag of cement despite his bad leg. He always wore the same jeans and a T-shirt, along with a pair of cowboy boots he'd inherited from Rattler.

"What the hell do you think you're doing out there?" his father said to him when they met up in the parking lot of the hardware store. Bob Starr, who owned the place, had phoned Leo to give him the heads-up that his son was in town. The loss of both his boys had worn Leo down and confused him.

In response, Frank shocked his father by embracing him. He remembered his father teaching him to ride a bike; he remembered how they would fish along the banks of the Eel River on summer afternoons. He knew that Leo Mott was a good man who deserved a better son.

"Don't worry, Dad," he said. "I'm fine."

It was generally agreed that he wasn't. He seemed so obviously different it was entirely possible that he'd fallen under a spell. Girls he'd grown up with wondered why they'd never noticed him before. Guys he'd hung out with his whole life passed him on the street without recognizing him. When he brought his new friends to the Jack Straw, nobody talked to them, and a few people grumpily whispered that New Yorkers would be better off in New York. There were little digs about the Yankees, and what a crappy team they were, as if anyone from the Farm cared about baseball or recognized that what was said was meant to be insulting. That's what they called their commune, the Farm, not that they'd managed to grow a thing out there in that swampy acreage. Rattler got pretty smashed at the bar that night and quickly turned obnoxious, talking loudly about the little people in the world, which he meant to be a compliment to the workingmen of Blackwell, but which really got some folks' dander up. If Frank hadn't been a local boy, there probably would have been a fight out in the parking lot.

"Hey, Frank. What are you thinking?" the bartender muttered as they were leaving. He was Jimmy, one of the Kelly cousins who'd known Frank forever. "Go home. At least you have the option." Jimmy handed over *The Blackwell Herald*. Brian Link, René's husband, had been killed in Vietnam, buried on the previous Monday.

A few days later Frank went to pay his respects to René. She was living with her mother and her little girl in the house where she'd grown up. When Frank knocked at the back door, René looked over her shoulder and stopped what she was doing in the kitchen to slip outside. They stood in the shade of an oak tree. Frank thought he remembered coming here to pick her up when they were young. He'd sit in the car and honk rather than come up to the door.

"I just wanted to say how sorry I was," he told René.

"For what? Breaking up with me?" René had a catch in her throat.

"For Brian."

"I killed him," René announced.

"No," Frank said. It was so preposterous he nearly laughed.

"Do you think it's funny to destroy someone?" René asked.

"No. I don't."

René was wringing her hands. She hadn't slept in a week. "Before he left I gave him a rabbit's foot for luck. It's what killed him."

"Rabbits don't kill people, René. War does."

"I gave him a black rabbit's foot. I think it brought him bad luck."

"It didn't," Frank said evenly. "I don't know much, but I know that for certain."

René's mother was at the screen door, watching. For a while they just stood there, until René's mother went back to the stove.

"I hear you're not the same man anymore," René said then.

"That's what they say," Frank replied.

"Well, that's too bad," René remarked before she went back into the house.

THE FARM FELL into disarray that summer. It came apart just as quickly as it had begun one stoned night in a bar near Penn Station when Simone mentioned she'd come into some money due to the death of her grandfather. The first sign of bad luck was when Pete stumbled into a thicket of poison ivy and had to be admitted to the Blackwell Hospital. It was such a bad case, the doctors thought he might go blind. After Pete's parents drove from Manhattan to claim him, the Farm began to falter. Romance was the cause, or maybe it was only thoughtless desire. Rattler started sleeping with Rose as well as with Jenna and all hell broke lose. People stopped talking to each other, and then there was a week of rain, which put everyone on edge. They sloshed around in the mud, grumbling, the sexual tension turning to despair. One night there was screaming and fighting, all of which Frank ignored as he cooked lentil stew over the fire. He hated scenes and shows of emotion. He heard car doors slamming and wheels spinning in the dirt. When he went to investigate, the only person left behind was Simone, who was sitting cross-legged on a blanket, crying. He drove her to the bus stop in Blackwell the next morning and waited with her on the bench until the bus pulled in. They held hands because they'd been through something together, not that either one imagined they'd ever see each other again. When Simone got on the bus, Frank realized that he didn't know her last name. He'd never bothered to ask.

PEOPLE THOUGHT HE would move back into his parents' house then, or rent a place for himself. He'd get a job, be the person he'd once been. But he continued to stay away. A couple of his old friends drove up to the Farm late in July. They figured they'd ambush Frank and give him a good talking-to; they'd set him straight. There were coyote pups yelping somewhere close by, and the sky was bright with the last of the day's light. The guys from town found a lot of trash strewn around, and the half-built log house, abandoned now, but no sign of Frank. His friends shouted his name, but nothing came back. Just an echo and the lulling sound of the Eel River, slower now that it was midsummer.

It was said Frank was sleeping in the caves, where there were known to be bears. Some kids in a Scout troop camping up there had seen him. They thought they spied a ghost, or maybe a bear, but it was only Frank, wearing jeans and an old leather jacket and the cowboy boots, cutting down firewood. Leo Mott went out searching for his son soon after. He didn't find him, but when he came back to his parked truck, there was a note stuck on the windshield, the message scrawled on a brown paper bag.

I'm fine, Dad, Frank had written. *Don't worry about me.*

FRANK TOOK EVERYTHING worthwhile that had been left behind at the Farm. A tent, some pots and pans, blankets, matches. He had a rifle that Rattler had bought, but he had no idea how to use it. He was sleeping in the tent, spending his days converting one of the smaller caves into a house for the coming winter. He insulated the walls with ferns and grass, then covered the insulation with planks of wood. He had the saw and toolbox from the Farm and was fashioning a hole in the top of the cave. He planned to rig up an exhaust system for smoke to escape, which would allow him to keep a fire going all winter. He'd build a door, a bed, a table, some chairs. He was growing marijuana in a pasture between the highest cliffs, a place of great beauty where he spent his afternoons. He thought he lived the way most people dreamed. In slow motion, in the dark, alone.

One day he heard a truck straining to get up an old logging road that cut through the mountain. The road was nearly impassable and not many people knew about it. Frank was in a section of the woods where there was a litter of fox pups he liked to watch. The foxes had gotten used to him and mostly ignored him, but they too heard the truck and they scampered away. Frank climbed down to an overlook, rifle over his shoulder, careful to ensure that no rocks would roll down into the road. If you could even call it a road. It was more of a trail, seeded with ferns, and moss, and young birch. Down below there was a Jeep, stuck in the mud.

The driver got out, pissed. He was a tall, handsome blond man, wearing jeans and a suede jacket. He had on expensive cowboy boots, handmade. He had a noticeable limp.

"Fuck this Jeep," he said. "I thought it could go over anything. What a rip-off."

A woman with long pale hair stepped out on the passenger side. She was the most beautiful woman ever seen on Hightop Mountain, the kind who could make men stupid with longing.

"I told you not to drive up here," she said. She wrapped her arms around herself and looked warily at the shadows cast by the trees. "We'll probably be eaten alive."

The man went over and linked his arms around her. After a while, the beautiful woman backed away.

"Did your mother know she was naming you after outlaws?"

"I'm not such an outlaw," the man said, sheepish.

"Not you." The woman laughed. "Your brother."

That night Frank thought about the man who was clearly his brother and who hadn't seemed familiar in the least. Frank had been doing his best to try to learn the constellations and he lay outside in the tall grass staring up. There was an awful lot they didn't teach you in school, important things like how to survive. He thought he'd be ready to be sent overseas if he was drafted now, not that the army would ever have him at this point, not that he wanted to go. All the talk that people at the Farm had tossed around about getting back to the land was actually true for him. He felt wrapped up in Hightop Mountain, a part of it, as if the cells of his body had expanded to include fir trees, foxes, streams of green water. He had no plans to go anywhere.

He heard the Jeep again a few days later, honking its horn, driving up another logging road that wound even higher into the mountain. It was startling to hear so much noise in the deep quiet of the forest. The Jeep stopped and the driver got out. Frank could see his brother clamber on top of the roof. He started shouting Frank's name like a madman.

"I know you're out there," Jesse called.

Frank said nothing. He knew how to wait. After a while, Jesse went away. Then it was quiet again.

The third time Jesse came searching for Frank, the beautiful woman was with him again. She was wearing shorts and hiking boots and a white shirt. They got out of the Jeep, slamming their doors. Birds took flight. The sky was filled with sparrows.

"You know where you're going, right?" she said.

"I grew up here," Jesse told her dismissively. "Of course I do."

Frank followed them at a distance. They were making a loopy circle through the thick part of the woods.

"Did you ever think he might not want to be found?" the woman said.

The couple kept walking, annoyed with each other, getting scratched by brambles and bitten by flies. Before long even they could tell they were getting nowhere. They were utterly lost. There'd been a murder up here once, but Jesse didn't mention it. They sat on a log, backs to each other.

"Fuck," Jesse said. He looked over his shoulder. "There are bears up here."

"Well, great, Jesse," the woman said. "Perfect."

It was late in the day. The sky was ashy. The woman was so beautiful she was like a magnet. Frank stepped out of the woods. He seemed like a shadow and then like a man. His own brother didn't recognize him, so on that point they were even.

"What do you know!" Jesse crowed when he realized it was Frank who'd found them. "It's you." He leapt to embrace Frank, and Frank allowed himself to be hugged. Jesse took a step back, grinning. "You're a fucking mountain man."

The woman came over and stuck out her hand for Frank to shake. "Tia McCorry," she introduced herself. "Thank goodness we found you. We are so lost."

Jesse grabbed Frank by the arm. "They're telling me you don't remember me. That's total bullshit, right?"

The blond man had green eyes. He was smiling at Frank, but he had a puzzled look under his smile.

"Total bullshit," Frank said.

Jesse let out a whoop. "I knew you were shining them on. You weren't going to forget me."

As Frank led them back to their Jeep, Jesse told of his exploits in California. He'd hitchhiked out and that had been a blast.

"Making sure to fuck every woman he met," added Tia. "You know your brother. Ultimate ladies' man."

"Yep," Frank said.

Jesse had hung out in San Francisco for a while, then decided to hitch down the coast for a weekend. When he wound up in L.A., he was broke. He'd been there ever since, working at a nightclub, managing a few bands. That's how he'd met Tia, who was a singer—or at least she planned to be. Several of his bands had broken through. He was making a ridiculous amount of money at this point.

"You've got to come with us," he said to Frank. "I told you this town is nowhere."

It was growing dark. Frank had good night vision, but it was difficult going for the other two. They stumbled over rocks and their clothing snagged on thornbushes. When they reached the car, the sky was inky. Jesse reached for his keys, but dropped them in the underbrush. "Fuck," he said.

"Your brother's a city boy," Tia murmured to Frank. He noticed she smelled like vanilla. Perfume drew mosquitoes to you. It was hot and buggy, and Tia raised up her length of blond-white hair in one hand and fanned her neck. Frank felt dizzy looking at her.

Jesse was still rooting around in the tall grass for the car keys when Frank heard the bear. He was used to quiet, so he took notice of the sound of the bushes being flattened as the bear headed their way.

"Get on top of the car," he told Jesse and Tia.

"If I had a lighter, I could see," Jesse complained.

Tia was looking at Frank.

"Do it now," he said. "Be quiet."

Tia scrambled up.

"I think they're over by the tire," Jesse said, still searching through the brush.

Frank leaned close to his brother. "Shut up and get on top of the car."

The intensity of his tone made Jesse get on top of the Jeep, fast.

Frank had his gun, but he didn't want to use it. He'd shot at squirrels and practiced with targets. In the winter he'd have no choice but to go after rabbit and deer, but he'd never entertained the notion of shooting a bear. There was something wrong about that. Something unmanly. He stood with his back against the Jeep and watched the bear amble along the logging road. There were overripe blueberries and wild raspberries. The bear was an old male, big. He was so close they could hear him grumbling to himself, the way some folks hum when they're going about their business.

It was true twilight now, darker by the instant. The mosquitoes and midges were something you had to get used to on the mountain or you could easily be driven mad. The bear looked at Frank standing there. He made a deeper growling noise and stopped. He moved his head back and forth the way bears sometimes did before they charged. Frank could hear Tia making little sobbing sounds even though she was covering her mouth with her hands.

"Shoot it," Jesse urged in a whisper. "Go ahead, brother."

The bear smelled like leaves and mud. He was so close that his musky scent was already clinging to Frank's clothes. The bear hadn't seen the other two, flattened against the Jeep's roof. He was just looking at Frank.

Frank thought of the way the snow had been falling when he was walking down the road before the car spun out and hit him. He thought of how the cold water in the Eel River had been such a shock to him when he dove in with Simone and Rose, floating in dreamtime. He felt ready to be over with something, although he wasn't sure what that something was. All at once, there in the buggy twilight, he felt intensely awake.

"I know this place is yours," he said to the bear. "I'm just passing through."

The bear stayed on for a moment, then went in the other direction, rambling up toward the meadow, where there were dozens of honeybee hives in the fallen oak trees. Frank waited in silence for several minutes, then he climbed onto the roof of the Jeep. The three of them looked up at the sky.

"Los Angeles, here I come," Jesse said.

Tia and Frank didn't say anything. They watched the stars appear. Frank took out a joint, which they shared, and afterward Jesse fell sound asleep.

"He talks about you a lot," Tia said. She was lying between them, her arms crossed behind her neck, cushioning her head. "He says you're the good one."

"He's wrong," Frank said.

Tia raised herself on one elbow and kissed him. It was the most delicious, hot, crazy kiss Frank had ever experienced. He felt as if he could fuck her right there on top of the car. He wanted her so much he felt certain he'd become the victim of temporary insanity.

Soon, though, he pulled away.

"He's right about you," Tia said. She kissed him again, but it wasn't as good the second time because they both felt guilty.

They slept on the roof with Tia sandwiched between the brothers. In the morning, Frank found the keys in the grass. Tia and Jesse were covered with bug bites. They couldn't get out of the woods fast enough. Frank drove into town with them. When they got to the house, his mother cried and hugged him and his father took him aside and told him he was glad Frank had gotten it all out of his system and had snapped out of it at last. Frank took a shower and let his mother wash his clothes. He was sitting at the desk where he used to do his homework, staring out the window, when Tia slipped into his room. She came to sit on his lap even though he was naked and the whole family was downstairs. They kissed for a while. They did things they shouldn't have done. It seemed like a dream and then it didn't.

Frank told her to wait, he'd be right back. He went downstairs and got his clothes from the dryer. He dressed right there in the laundry room, then went out the back door. He remembered that his brother always stole his best clothes. It was easy enough; they'd been the same size. Frank had never cared; he'd felt honored that Jesse wanted something he had. That was back when they were brothers. Now he walked three blocks and made a left on Main Street. He kept going until he got to the house where René had grown up, and as fate would have it, she was waiting at the door.

THE RED GARDEN

1986

Blackwell had always had a problem with flies. They appeared every spring, swarms rising up from the cold water of the Eel River and the rushing eddies of Hubbard Creek in such great numbers that some of the women in town covered their windows and doors with garden netting during the first two weeks of April, the kind you throw over blueberry bushes to protect the fruit from bears.

Louise Partridge didn't remember that there'd been so many while she was growing up. Living away from home for a few years had changed her perception of just about everything—animal, vegetable, and mineral alike. Louise had come home from Radcliffe in her junior year to nurse her ailing mother until Mrs. Partridge's death that past winter. Louise hadn't really liked Cambridge, all those know-it-all girls, the smart-aleck pot-smoking boys who thought no one had ever had an original idea before they came along. But she missed the libraries, and the classes, and the bookstores. She missed Cambridge, as a matter of fact.

Louise was a fixer; she didn't throw up her hands when confronted with a problem, she took charge. She got to work on her grandmother's ancient sewing machine and made a hooded cloak out of mosquito netting. She had decided to replant the back garden, the half acre of land her mother and great-aunt Hannah had always told her was of no use. They'd always insisted that whatever was planted there would grow into the opposite of what anyone expected, almost as if the earth had a mind of its own. But the old garden was on higher ground, and the blackflies weren't as plentiful there, so Louise decided she would find out for herself.

She was the closest blood relative to the town's founding families, related on her mother's side to Hallie Brady, as well as to the Partridges, who had also been among the first settlers. There were still plenty of Partridges around. Louise's own father had been a long-lost Partridge cousin, one of the ones who'd gone off to California, probably driven off in the first weeks of spring, unable to think straight because of all those flies buzzing around. Louise's father had come back east to go to Harvard and had fallen in love with her mother. He'd died when Louise was ten, and not long after, her beloved aunt Hannah passed on. Their Thanksgiving dinners, at which the traditional Brady Indian pudding was always served, had shrunk from four to three, and then there was only Louise and her mother, Kate. Now, when next November rolled around, Louise would be eating Indian pudding alone. She'd been practicing the recipe—cornmeal, milk, molasses—and had scalded it every time. Fixing the pudding made her miss her mother, who had died far too young, and she wished she had paid more attention to details. While she was growing up there were times when she would glance out her window at night to spy her mother out in the garden amid the green shadows. Louise had never even asked her why she was out there at such a late hour.

Louise had inherited the Brady house, the oldest in town. If she hadn't been her mother's sole beneficiary, she might have gone back to Cambridge and finished her classes. She'd been studying biology and had even considered med school, but after her mother's long illness, a ferocious battle with bone cancer, she never wanted to enter a hospital again. Her mother had been delusional at the end. She insisted she was in the wrong life, that someone from her other, truer life came to sit beside her late at night when the hospital corridors were empty and yellow light spilled across the parking lot.

"I'm the one who's here for you," Louise would say then, taking her mother's frail hand. "It's just me."

"Oh, I know," her mother would murmur. "That's why I love you so."

Love had never been discussed before. Louise's mother had tended to be undemonstrative, and hearing her speak so tenderly of love made tears well up in Louise's eyes. Now that her mother was gone, Louise always stepped down hard on the gas when she passed the Blackwell Community Hospital. She had the feeling that if she didn't, she'd be trapped. She'd never get away.

Louise planned to leave town as soon as she came up with a plan. Until then, she had nothing but time on her hands. The house was far too big for one person. The original structure had been added on to in a crazy quilt of rooms over the years. There were rooms where you least expected them—under the staircase, off the breezeway, through a crawl space into the eaves of the roof. There was a shed out back that had been a house at one time, rented out to schoolteachers, and was now home to shovels and peat moss. People in town said the big house had a buried history, just as they swore that Johnny Appleseed himself had planted the twisted old tree out in Band's Meadow—a local variety known as the Blackwell Look-No-Further, perfect for cider and pies. In the old days people had called this apple tree the Tree of Life and had insisted that the town of Blackwell would last as long as the tree did. There were still several cuttings, now grown into tall trees, all over town. They were extras, just in case the original should suffer from blight or be struck by lightning. No one in Blackwell was taking any chances.

THAT SPRING LOUISE took her mother's old Jeep down to Harvest Hill, a huge nursery off the Mass Pike. She came back with fertilizer and seedlings and flowers of every variety. After all those months in the hospital watching her mother die, Louise had a strong desire to witness something grow. She donned the mosquito net cloak, affixed it with one of her father's old eelskin belts, then got to work, pulling out brambles and weeds in the abandoned garden. Louise had no friends in town and only a few acquaintances, card-playing pals of her parents. But even the old guard had mostly retired to Florida or moved to the village of Lenox, where the long, snowy winters were better spent and there were card games galore in the summertime.

Although she'd grown up in Blackwell, Louise had always been an outsider. She was shy, red-haired and freckled, and that alone would have set her apart. Then her parents plucked her out of the local kindergarten and sent her to the Mill School in Lenox, where they felt she would get a better education. She'd never really made connections in town. Although she knew Latin and Greek and had the honor of dropping out of Radcliffe, she had never been in the Jack Straw Bar and Grill or had anything more than a hurried cup of tea and a slice of Look-No-Further Pie at the coffee shop or a wedge of their famous Apology Cake, made from a secret recipe a summer resident had once given the owner's grandmother. Louise had never been to a high school football game, even though the Blackwell Bears were ranked among the Commonwealth's top ten teams, nor had she attended one of the ballet recitals held at the town hall that attracted people from as far away as Connecticut and New York. She talked to people as if they were strangers, even though some were her very own cousins. She had attended several of the Hallie Brady festivals, held each August to commemorate the birth of Louise's ancestor who had founded the town, without whom the original settlers wouldn't have lasted past their first winter. But mostly she'd been gone in the summer, off to camp in Maine, or on trips to France to study the language or renting a cottage in Provincetown, where she worked as a waitress, rooming with a gang of college friends whom she imagined she liked until she got to know them, and vice versa if truth be told.

Living in the old Brady house, Louise simultaneously had the feeling of being at home and also being in a foreign land. She hadn't been up to the attic since she was a little girl playing dress up. She couldn't abide the sadness of entering the bedrooms where her aunt and her mother had slept. Sometimes she dreamed of burning the house down. Then she'd finally skip town. She'd have the freedom to head off to Vienna, where she'd buy a season ticket for the opera, or better still, she'd hightail it to Oregon, where it was leafy and green and there was rarely snow. Instead, she stayed on, making plans for the old garden. She was a big planner. She always looked before she leapt, so Oregon and Vienna were probably out of the question at the moment. It would take her months just to get through the guidebooks and come up with an acceptable plan of action so that she could finally fashion a life of her own.

AFTER HER FIRST week of work, the brambles in the garden were torn out and fertilizer was spread around. One night Louise had a bonfire and watched the weeds burn in a metal trash can, sending sparks blazing into the sky. After that, she started collecting the rocks that littered the ground, shards of mica-filled granite. She made a pile she intended to use for a rock garden, unless she wound up in Portland. She worked tirelessly. She had discovered that gardening made her stop thinking, and she was pleased by the effect of hard labor. When she realized her hands had become ragged from her digging, she found an old pair of her mother's leather gloves. Even they didn't do the trick; when she took the gloves off at night, her fingers were bleeding. She soaked them in a bowl of warm water and olive oil, then rubbed in some of her mother's lemon-scented hand cream.

One day Louise went to the hardware store to buy white paint. She planned to freshen the shabby picket fence that surrounded the garden. She hadn't even known it was there till she'd cut down the last of the brambles. The fence was falling apart, and she hoped a coat of paint might spruce it up enough to make it last a while longer. People thought anyone related to the Bradys was surely rich, but they just looked that way. After her mother's illness, the accounts had dwindled to almost nothing. Louise didn't mind being thrifty. She'd never had an extravagant personality.

The checkout girl at the hardware store was about her age, pretty, and extremely competent. "Hey," the girl said to her, tentative. "Don't I know you?"

"Nice to meet you," Louise said, not really listening in the way that people who live alone often ignore others, their heads filled with silent, argumentative dialogue. Right then Louise was busy thinking about paint, debating between Sherwin-Williams and Benjamin Moore. She made her decision and pointed to the shelf of Benjamin Moore. "I'll take two gallons of the white."

"No. I mean we've already met."

The clerk was Allegra Mott, a local girl. Her brother Johnny had gone to kindergarten with Louise and had hit her on the head one bright afternoon and made her cry, which was the reason Louise's parents decided to send her off to private school in Lenox. She'd had a bump on her forehead for weeks.

"Did you know you were wearing a mosquito net?" Allegra asked gently. She had heard rumors about the Brady genes. Everyone had. Some of the Bradys were said to be completely mad. In the old days, one of them ran around town swearing she'd slept with Johnny Appleseed of all things, as if he were Mick Jagger. Others had disappeared, drowned, married the wrong men, generally scandalized the town.

Allegra gave a little smile and touched her head, signifying that Louise had forgotten to remove the mosquito netting cape she'd fashioned to fend off the flies.

"Oh, crap." Louise quickly grabbed off the netting and scrunched it into a ball. "I haven't experienced blackfly season in some time. It's a killer. I'm trying to undermine the flies without losing my marbles in the process."

"Right-o," Allegra said, ringing up the paint.

She couldn't wait to tell her brother that the love of his life was back.

LOUISE FOUND THERE were fewer flies in the mornings, so she went out to work while the sky was still dark. Blackwell was known for its songbirds, and this was the hour when they were waking in the trees. Sparrow, mockingbird, lark. All of them sounded glad to be alive. Because the garden was elevated, Louise could see the crest of Hightop Mountain as she toiled away. For some reason the view caused her to experience a catch in her throat. She hadn't thought she cared much about her hometown; she wasn't a rah-rah sort of girl. Yet when she saw the mountain, she felt moved in some deep way, the way she had when her mother had squeezed her hand in her last moments. Louise had known it was her mother's way of thanking her for all the time she'd spent with her in the hospital, for coming home from school and insisting everything would turn out fine when clearly it wouldn't.

Once the garden was ready, the red soil turned, Louise planted a grapevine, cucumbers, green Zebra tomatoes. She added a yellow rosebush. She put in some bleeding hearts, irises, and several rows of lettuce; and she set up a trellis that would support peppers and runner beans. It was more work than she would ever have imagined. In the evenings she was so tired she didn't bother to fix herself dinner. She ate cold baked beans from the can spread onto toast or threw together one-step macaroni from one of the scores of boxes she found in the pantry, prepackaged stuff that her mother, who had always been so intent on proper meals while Louise was growing up, must have been living on once Louise was away at school.

By then rumors about Louise Partridge returning home and running around town dressed in mosquito netting had swept through the village. Some people were waiting for her to have a full-fledged crack-up, or maybe drugs were at the root of her odd behavior, or an addiction to alcohol—she had gone off and lived in Cambridge after all. There were bets not about whether she'd wind up at Austin Riggs for rehab, but when.

But if Louise had a drink, it was only a glass of white wine, one that she sipped in the bathtub while soaking off the garden's grime. The only drug she allowed herself was a mild sedative to help her sleep. She'd found Valium in her mother's medicine cabinet. Dozens of vials were stacked on the shelves. Evidently, her mother had been living on nothing but sedatives and instant macaroni and cheese during the entire time Louise had been away at Radcliffe. This sad realization made Louise even more convinced she shouldn't have gone to Provincetown to spend summers with people she didn't even like and instead she should have stayed home to work in the garden with her mother. Maybe she would have known her then.

THERE WAS A week of driving rain. Spring rain, spitting against the windows, flooding the lanes. During that time the blackflies, which anyone might have imagined would have been washed away by the deluge, multiplied. Louise was irritated beyond measure. She went back to the hardware store and found a sort of zapping machine that was said to make an area undesirable to insects. The zapper cost almost two hundred dollars, but she didn't care. Despite her mosquito netting outfit, there were dozens of raised red bites on her skin.

"My brother said he never was in love with you," Allegra, who'd recently been promoted to store manager, revealed to Louise as she deposited the zapper in a shopping bag. "He said I was very much mistaken."

"That's good, since I have no idea who he is." Whenever Louise got flustered or felt insecure, her demeanor became haughty. Anyone might suppose she thought she was better than they were just because she lived in that big, falling-down house. But her redhead's complexion gave her away. She was blotchy with anxiety. All of a sudden she recalled that sunny afternoon when she was still in the Blackwell Elementary School. She remembered someone hitting her on the head. Johnny Mott. "Tell him to drop dead," she said tightly, gathering up the bug zapper.

"Will do," Allegra said. "Gladly."

The next week a few of the new plantings died, withering, it seemed, overnight. That seemed like a rip-off. It didn't seem fair that after all those hours of hard labor she'd wind up with nothing. Louise drove back down the Mass Pike to Harvest Hill to complain. They said anything could have ruined the plants—not enough fertilizer, too much rain, shade, aphids. This made gardening seem like a much more precarious endeavor than Louise had imagined. She didn't have her receipts, so they wouldn't return her money. They suggested she buy more. Something heat tolerant, bug tolerant, water tolerant, she assumed. She chose lilacs, a hardy variety, and a few small azaleas, along with some beans and tomatoes. She kept the receipts this time.

She put in all of the new plants in a single day, wrenching her back in the process. When she was done, she was not only filthy, but famished as well. She really could have used a drink. She realized she had no food in the house, no wine. Nothing but macaroni and cheese and sedatives. She had the sense that she was becoming her mother in her saddest period, and she was only twenty-two, not sixty. Louise braved the town and went out, driving her mother's Jeep, which was nearly rusted out through the floor. There was the pizza kitchen, the coffee shop, and the Hightop Inn—the nicest place in Blackwell, mostly filled with tourists who couldn't find suitable accommodations in Lenox or Williamstown. Louise switched the radio on. Prince's "When Doves Cry" was playing. She felt old and out of it, no longer a college student and nothing else instead. She hastened over to the Jack Straw Bar and Grill. It would be her first time inside.

The Jack Straw was a casual, wood-paneled place, busier in the summertime and on weekends. On Friday nights there were dart games that had once or twice ended in tragedy when fights flowed out into the parking lot. Louise realized that she was both under- and overdressed. She had grabbed a light Chanel jacket from her mother's closet, but was wearing it over a white undershirt, along with denim shorts she'd had since high school and a pair of knee-high rubber gardening boots. She didn't have on a lick of makeup. Her red hair was hooked up with a thick rubber band, whirled into a crazy-looking ponytail with bits of grass threaded through the strands.

"Hey," she said to the bartender when she sat down. She

figured it was better to be alone at the bar than at a table meant for two.

"Hey," the bartender said back, not bothering to look away from the Red Sox game on the tube.

"I'll have a glass of sauvignon blanc," Louise told him.

"Chardonnay," the bartender offered. He turned and saw it was that girl everyone expected to go crazy. He quickly backtracked. "I could look for sauvignon blanc in the storeroom if that's what you really want. Like if you had to have it or something."

"Chardonnay," Louise said agreeably. She ruefully noticed mud streaking her arms. "And a grilled cheese sandwich with fries."

That had been her favorite meal when she was a little girl, only her drink of choice had been chocolate milk instead of white wine. She went to the toilet to wash up. There she learned that people in Blackwell seemed to fall in and out of love fairly often, and they could be vengeful when their romances didn't work out. Names and phone numbers were written all over the wall, along with several nasty remarks about the length, or lack thereof, of one gentleman's private parts. On this several women seemed to agree.

When Louise got back to the bar, her dinner was waiting for her. The place had begun to fill up. The Eel River Kayak Company had just let out and several of the boatmen were there. The hospital was changing shifts, and Kelly's repair shop had just shut down for the day. Someone had fed the jukebox. "When Doves Cry" yet again. Several men stood in a group at the end of the bar. One of them gazed at Louise, then whispered to his buddy, and they both laughed.

Louise hated being a redhead. She blushed to the roots of her hair. She signaled the bartender over. "Why don't you tell that guy to go to hell for me," she said.

"Tell him yourself," the bartender suggested, clearly not a believer in chivalry. "He's a cop."

Louise paid and stood to leave. She'd only eaten half her grilled cheese sandwich. She knew she looked ridiculous. Maybe that was why she felt so reckless.

"Go to hell," she called to the last man at the bar.

He turned to her, stunned. All conversation at that end of the bar stopped. There was a play being called on TV. The Red Sox were down one.

Louise suddenly thought that the man at the bar was too handsome to have ever bothered making a lewd remark about her. He was tall and lanky with dark hair, just gorgeous. Even a shy person like Louise could feel the heat he cast. She must have misunderstood. Who did she think she was anyway? She felt transparent and foolish. She turned and rushed out of there. No wonder she'd never come to the Jack Straw before. It was a dump. She was breathing hard when she got behind the wheel of her mother's old Jeep. There were thousands of blackflies in the air, so many that you'd probably choke if you tried jogging out there. Dusk was the hour they loved best of all. Louise's heart was pounding stupidly. That handsome man was staring out the window, watching her, but she sped away. If he wanted to give her a ticket, he'd have to find her first.

IT TOOK QUITE a while before Louise realized what was happening in the garden. Whatever she planted was turning red.

When she phoned about the lilacs, which she knew were supposed to be a pale purple—she still had the receipts and they were called Twilight Mist—the fellow at Harvest Hill said some of the new pink varieties glazed reddish in the sun. It was getting to the point that she couldn't believe a word anyone at Harvest Hill said.

By then the roses had opened to reveal crimson-colored flowers. Louise knew for a fact that the tag had said Sunburst, which were meant to have yellow blooms with deep coppery centers. She'd asked for butter lettuce, but it looked to be coming in ruby tinged. And then early one evening, when she was harvesting the first of the reddish string beans, something odd happened. It was a pretty summer evening, very quiet and blue. Louise looked more carefully at the garden, the one her mother and aunt always said to avoid. The vegetables had grown fast. The garden was doing quite well considering she was a novice. The peepers over at the creek had begun their mournful calling at night and the mosquitoes were out in full force. But now Louise noticed there was some other natural force to be worried about: the soil itself looked crimson. She reached for a handful and rubbed it between her fingers. When she let the soil fall, her hands were stained bloodred. There was a small bone sitting in her palm.

Louise left the garden and closed the gate. She went inside her house and phoned the police station.

"There's blood in my yard," she said to the operator who answered. After that got around, people in town thought she was pretty close to losing it and that anyone who had put his money down on a full-fledged crack-up by August would win the betting pool.

Frank Mott, who was the chief of police, sent his son Johnny to take a look.

"Remember," he said. "She's related to Hallie Brady. Be nice."

Johnny grinned and drove over to the Brady house. He knocked on the door, but no one answered. He ambled around toward the yard. He was going over all of the things he might say, stupid lines like *Funny meeting you here* or *Where have you been all my life?* as he came upon her in the yard. When he did, he stared and didn't say a thing.

"Are you kidding me?" Louise said when she saw him. The handsome man from the bar she'd told to go to hell. "Is this a joke?"

"Are you going to hold my hitting you on the head in kindergarten against me forever?" Johnny asked.

"I think you said 'knock-knock' when you did it," Louise said.

"I was just trying to get your attention."

Louise had been pacing off the garden when Johnny stumbled upon her. It was a surprisingly large space. She now stood by the fence she had recently painted white. It looked iridescent in the fading light. "Have there been any murders in town?" she asked.

Johnny came to stand next to her. The garden, he noticed, was quite beautiful. He'd never seen anything like it.

"You're a gardener?" he asked.

"Anyone missing, kidnapped, decapitated?" Louise wanted to know. "This could be a mass grave, a killer's depository."

"You're very single-minded," Johnny Mott said. When Louise turned to him, she had a hurt look in her eyes. "Not that there's anything wrong with that," he was quick to amend. "Believe me—I'm single-minded, too."

"Then check all the records and get back to me. Check Lenox, too. There might have been someone killed there, with the body later brought out to Blackwell."

"There've been no murders, kidnappings, or decapitations. Trust me on this one."

"Then why did I find this?" Louise held up the tiny bit of bone.

"A dog came through?" Johnny guessed. "Tim Kelly's basset hound killed a rabbit? I could have him arrested. The basset hound, I mean. Not Tim."

Louise backed away, shamed. She started at him. "You're making fun of me."

"I'm not."

Johnny noticed she was wearing some sort of mosquito netting tossed over her and a big pair of boots, the kind people used to go eeling in the river.

"Well, maybe a little," he said.

"You think I don't know there's some kind of betting pool about whether or not I'll go crazy? I heard people talking at the gas station. And your friends were saying something about me at the bar."

Louise's face was getting pink. In no time it would be red. That had happened in kindergarten after Johnny had hit her. He'd felt especially bad when he saw how blotchy she was. Afterward he used to watch her take the bus to the Mills School. She got picked up right outside her house.

"Actually, the pool isn't whether you will. It's when."

"What's your bet?"

They had come round to the front door. It was the original one, the very first door in town. In the winter, snow came through the cracks. In summer, hornets nested in the wood.

"I don't make bets," Johnny Mott said.

"Go to hell," Louise said to him again, and again he was stunned. Louise couldn't care less. She felt insulted and something more. She hurried inside and locked the door, not once but twice, even though everyone in town knew that the door to the Brady house was so unstable every time there was a storm it got knocked down.

SOON AFTER, LOUISE went to the Blackwell Museum, which was right across the street from the bookstore. The museum was in an old house, and one energetic elderly woman sold tickets, ran the gift shop, and gave guided tours twice a day. Louise remembered going there as a child, examining the few items still left from the Brady expedition, their spoons and forks, some pots and pans, a tilted wooden wagon wheel. There was also an exhibit of taxidermy, a glass case of local wildlife trapped a hundred years earlier: beavers, red squirrels, foxes, a wolf that was so poorly sewn together you could see the black crisscross of thread down his back, some old moth-eaten bats.

In a corner there was a case of fossils. One of the bits of bone looked very much like the one Louise had found.

"Were there dinosaurs around Blackwell?" Louise asked the ticket taker, who was having a tuna salad sandwich at her desk. She had the same thing for lunch at 10:30 a.m. each day.

"You bet," the old woman said. She was Arlene Kelly, whose son, Tim, and three grandsons ran the Kelly Gas Station. Someone from the Kelly family had always owned the station, and Arlene had bought it from her cousin Carla when Carla retired early on disability to Delray Beach. "Louise Partridge, right?

How're you feeling, hon?" Arlene had put her money on September 7, which happened to be her birthday. She herself always went a little crazy right around then, and she figured Louise might flip out on that day.

"I'm fine. Thank you. What kind of dinosaurs?"

"Eubrontes. They were carnivores. We've found tracks. It's all over there in the prehistory case."

After she took a look, Louise got back in her mother's Jeep and drove home. Lately she had been getting the kind of phone calls where someone hung up as soon as you answered. At first she thought it was someone calling from *The Blackwell Herald,* trying to sell her a subscription. But more recently she had come to believe it was Johnny Mott. Why a good-looking man who thought she was about to go crazy would be calling and hanging up, and acting crazy himself, she had no idea. But she could feel something through the phone, a kind of yearning. When she realized she was the one doing the yearning, she stopped answering and let it go on ringing.

Louise sent a formal letter to the dean's office at Harvard. She wrote that she was an alumna, more or less. She didn't mention dropping out or being so miserable in Cambridge. Before long she was connected to the paleontology experts at the Peabody Museum to whom she explained her situation. Three days later a graduate student named Brian Alter arrived in a Volvo station wagon filled with equipment. There were just a few stray flies around then and the days were getting hot.

"Beautiful area," Brian said, after shaking Louise's hand when she came out to the driveway to meet him. "Great house," he enthused.

"Yes, except for the bones in my garden." Louise led him around to the back.

"In my line of work, that's great, too."

They went up the stone steps, past the gardens Louise's mother and aunt had planted in summers gone by, predictable plots of land where nothing unusual ever happened. The old garden, however, was a riot of red. Everything was blooming so fast and so hard that the white picket fence had nearly disappeared into a tangle of bean runners.

"Wow," Brian asked. "What kind of vegetables are those?" He pointed to the blood-colored runners.

"Green beans," Louise said.

When she showed him the soil and the piece of bone, Brian pursed his lips. He did not make jokes about basset hounds. *See!* Louise wanted to shout, had Johnny Mott been anywhere near. *He doesn't think it's ridiculous.* She wondered if perhaps her garden had become red for a reason, the way maps turn up in your glove compartment right before you get lost. She wondered if the reason was Brian, and if the garden had brought him to her, magicking him along the Mass Pike right up to her door. In many ways he was a perfect fit: nice looking, Harvard educated, a scientist, clearly a gentleman. Maybe fate had sent her one true love.

"Unfortunately this means we're going to have to dig up the garden," Brian said.

Louise felt like crying at the idea of the garden being deconstructed, but she had no other choice if she wanted to get to the bottom of things. She fixed a bedroom for Brian, put fresh linens on the bed, stored away her father's collection of eelskin memorabilia, went to pick up some groceries at the AtoZ

Market, English muffins and coffee beans, since Brian would probably expect breakfast.

Although he was only a first-year graduate student, Brian was exceedingly professional. Soon enough the rear garden looked like a proper archaeological dig. It was roped off and divided into sections. The little white fence Louise had painted so carefully had been pulled down. She looked out her window and saw the roses and runner beans flipped over into a pile. Louise thought of all the money she'd spent on fertilizer as the mounds of dug earth began to collect. She counted all the hours she'd put in.

"Louise!" she heard Brian shout one day when she was sitting in the kitchen, drinking tea and reading a guidebook about Vancouver. In her plans to leave town she had begun to think the colder, the better. She had become interested in Canada and Scandinavia.

She ran outside in her pajamas and fishing boots when she heard Brian. He was covered with dirt, having been digging since 5:00 a.m. Actually, people in the neighborhood were beginning to be annoyed at the *chink clink* of his shovel so early in the day. He was standing in a hole six feet deep. Louise stepped over the dead roses and pepper plants and peered down. At the very bottom of the hole was a pile of bones, including several huge ribs.

"Hallelujah," Brian said.

THEY WENT OUT to celebrate at the Jack Straw Bar and Grill. This time, Louise had on a sundress and flip-flops and had run a brush through her hair.

"What an authentic place," Brian said, glancing around at the knotty pine, the fireplace that was always roaring in winter, the dartboard, which could look picturesque if you didn't know Tim Kelly was blind in one eye because of a fight with his brother Simon over whose dart had come closer to the bull's-eye.

Brian went to the bar and pounded his fist joyfully. "Jack Daniel's!"

"ID," the bartender demanded. Brian looked like a punk to him and was definitely an out of towner. "Hey." He nodded to Louise while Brian was thumbing through his wallet for his driver's license.

"Hey," she said back. "I'll have the chardonnay."

Louise gazed around. There were a few locals at the far end of the bar. Somebody was fooling around with the jukebox. If they punched in "When Doves Cry," she'd take it as a sign that she should never come back.

"He's not here," the bartender said when he noticed her looking.

"Who?" Louise gulped some chardonnay. Lately she hadn't been getting those hang-up phone calls.

Brian presented his ID and turned to Louise. "At this point, whatever's in your garden could be just about anything," he said, interrupting. He gulped down the first shot of whisky as soon as he was served. "We'll have to collect the bones, clean them, then send them to Cambridge and have them carbon dated. I'll have to call Professor Seymour in on this." He laughed, delighted. "I'm in way over my head."

When Brian turned away for a moment, the bartender leaned in. "He's in the hospital," he told Louise. "His appendix burst."

"People don't even need their appendixes," Brian assured

Louise when he noticed she looked stricken. He was already pouring another shot. He planned on getting drunk. "I'm going to be famous. Your house is going to be famous."

"It already is," Louise said.

THERE WAS NO chinking of the shovel the next day at 5:00 a.m. While Brian was sleeping off his hangover, Louise went out to the garden. She peered down at the pile of bones. She had a shivery feeling, as if they'd perhaps discovered something that was meant to be left alone. She gathered an armful of flowers from the piles that had been torn out, then set off in her mother's Jeep. It wasn't yet visiting hour at the hospital, but the floor nurse recognized her from all those weeks she'd spent at her mother's bedside and let her in.

Louise had told herself she'd never walk into another hospital, but here she was. Johnny Mott was sharing a room with Mr. Hirsch, who was the principal of the high school. Mr. Hirsch had had a seizure the doctors thought might have been a stroke and was there for observation. Johnny looked aggravated over being trapped in a hospital bed, especially in a room with Mr. Hirsch, who had suspended him from high school three times for ridiculous infractions. Johnny had had his share of trouble as a kid and was headed in the wrong direction, then had straightened himself out. He still had scars and tattoos that seemed to belong to somebody else.

When he saw Louise Partridge with her half-dead flowers, he thought he was hallucinating. They'd been giving him Percocet for the pain.

"I hate hospitals," she said.

"Agreed." Johnny sat up in bed. He assumed he looked like an idiot—he was wearing a hospital gown—but actually Louise felt mutely and stupidly drawn to him. He was half naked and staring at her. She sat down on the edge of Mr. Hirsch's bed. She thought she might have a hangover herself.

"Go ahead," Mr. Hirsch said bitterly. "Don't mind me. Make yourself comfortable."

He'd spent forty years being sarcastic, but as Louise had gone to private school she took him at his word and said, "Thanks."

"Allegra told me you're living with someone. She said he drives a Volvo." Johnny sneered. "Those cars are so overrated."

"Your sister isn't as observant as she thinks she is. Is that why you stopped calling and hanging up, because of the Volvo?"

"Calling?" Johnny said, feeling shifty, even if he was a police officer.

Louise rose off Mr. Hirsch's bed and came to stand beside Johnny. She had something in her hand. A smooth white arc. She couldn't help but notice that they kept the temperature much too hot in hospitals. They thought only of the dying, never of the living. But wasn't that always the way?

Louise thought she might burn alive standing there.

"I don't think a basset hound's behind this," she said, showing Johnny the bone she carried with her.

"You never know," Johnny Mott said. People who knew him would have been shocked to hear just how thoughtful he sounded.

"Really?" Louise said. "Maybe that's true for you, but I always do. I don't have to think twice about things."

❧

AFTER A TIME, Brian had collected all of the bones and washed them in a bucket. They were then spread out on Louise's porch, to dry in the sun. A spine, ribs, long femurs, knobby things that Louise assumed were some kind of elbows or knees. Everyone in town was talking about the dig. Brian had to chase groups of interested ten-year-old boys off the property. Skittish teenagers came creeping around at night, daring each other to walk past the bone house.

Then one Saturday morning the board of trustees from the museum unexpectedly came to call. The board consisted of Mrs. Gerri Partridge, who was a cousin of Louise's, once removed; Hillary Jacob, who ran the faltering bookstore; and Allegra Mott, who seemed too young and snippy to be on the board of anything.

"Hello," Louise said when she opened the door.

Thankfully she was dressed in an A-line skirt and a blouse, both found in her mother's closet. The outfit looked half decent if you didn't notice the fraying seams. The women from the board had already turned their attention to the pile of bones. Brian was up in bed, sleeping it off. He had taken to visiting the Jack Straw Bar and Grill every night, not coming home till the wee hours.

"So you told your brother about the Volvo," Louise remarked to Allegra.

"Sure," Allegra said mildly. "Why not?"

"No reason," Louise said. "None at all."

The museum ladies informed Louise that due to the potential historical nature of the finding on her property, they would like to have the skeleton on permanent display in the Blackwell Museum.

"I don't know about that," Louise hedged. "The expedition's being funded by Harvard."

"What gets found in Blackwell stays in Blackwell," Allegra Mott said. "You of all people should understand that."

It sounded like some sort of veiled threat. But as a matter of fact, Louise had been experiencing a sinking feeling every time she saw the bones on the porch or heard the *click clack* of Brian Alter's shovel. She was actually pleased the skull hadn't yet been found.

"I'll keep your request in mind," she said.

Soon after, a professor from Harvard phoned looking for Brian. Dr. Seymour, the professor in charge of Brian's research. Brian hadn't checked in or sent a report in some time.

"I'm certain he'll be in touch soon," Louise assured the professor.

In fact, Brian had taken to sleeping all day, then getting up and going directly to the Jack Straw. Louise thought she had a budding alcoholic on her hands, maybe even a full-fledged drunk. One night she heard a ruckus on her porch. She ran downstairs in her nightgown and was met by the Motts, Johnny and his father, Frank, there on police business. They had brought home a sloshed, argumentative Brian, who tripped over his own feet as he attempted to take off and go back to the tavern for last call.

"Sorry to disturb you," Frank Mott said to Louise. "This gentleman said he was staying with you. We'll haul him up to bed if you like."

"Your bedroom or his?" Johnny Mott asked.

"John," his father warned.

"When you see the mess, you'll know you've found the right

room," Louise told Frank Mott. "Just throw him on top of the mattress."

Louise went out on the porch. It was already the end of July. There were cicadas calling. In the Blackwell Museum there was a display of a dusty pile of cicada casings, including what was said to be the largest one ever found in the eastern United States.

"What does your expert say this thing is?"

Johnny had come outside while Frank went on to have a fatherly discussion with Brian upstairs, informing him that he was no longer welcome at the Jack Straw and that if he got caught drinking and driving in town, it would be good-bye to his license.

"Let me guess," Johnny went on. "He doesn't have a clue."

"Why don't you figure it out?" Louise said hotly.

She was furious. She'd been the one to write to Harvard, and now she resented the fact that her garden was a wreck. All the plants were dying. Even the poor lilacs, uprooted and re-planted in a precarious row, had lost their leaves.

"Are you saying you want me to?" Johnny said. "Are you asking me to do it?"

Louise looked at him, secretly aghast that she was wearing her mother's old nightgown, that her hair was in braids. She seemed to be crying over her ruined garden. She would have answered, but she was suddenly tongue-tied, her usual ferocity gone.

Frank Mott came out and shook Louise's hand, apologizing for the bother in the middle of the night, suggesting that her boarder might need to be directed toward the AA meetings held every Thursday and Sunday at eight and at ten at the town hall.

That night Louise could barely sleep. She dreamed about her mother's last day on earth. She was small as a bird in her hospital bed, shivering, waiting patiently for the end. She said, "Maybe he'll still be waiting for me." Louise had no idea whom she was referring to; her husband, gone so many years, or God, or perhaps an angel. There had been so much that had been left unspoken between them. Louise didn't know the first thing about her mother, not really, and now it was too late.

She'd had such a restless night, it was nearly ten when she woke. She went downstairs, and while making coffee, she saw something out on the porch. She pushed open the door to find the skeleton of a huge creature laid out, skull and all.

She ran upstairs and shook Brian awake. He followed her, two steps at a time, bleary-eyed. He had been dreaming about being on the cover of *Newsweek* and didn't appreciate being woken. He was also dreaming that he was having sex with every woman he'd met at the Jack Straw Bar and Grill—not one at a time, but all at once, a great, gorgeous, heaving mass of local women.

"Shit," he said when he saw the skeleton.

"Isn't this a good thing?" Louise said. She thought of Johnny in the garden all night, digging and digging, piling up red dirt. She thought of him crouched on her porch in the dark, thoughtfully working the bones like a puzzle. She had a chill and wished she were wearing her robe.

"Good? Are you kidding me? We were looking for prehistoric. This is nothing but a fucking bear. Ursa fucking major."

THERE WAS NO longer any reason for Brian Alter to stay, so he phoned his professor, saying it had all been a hoax and they'd been wasting their time. He'd pack up the bones in a box just to show Harvard that he'd tried his best and maybe still get credit for the whole stupid escapade. But first he got in his Volvo and took off, saying he'd be back later to pick it all up. Desperate for a drink, he headed to the bar at the Hightop Inn, since the Jack Straw Bar and Grill wouldn't have him anymore.

Louise went to examine the skeleton. It was hot, and the air smelled like hay. The skull Johnny had found was huge and sad. It made everything much realer and more pitiful. Louise realized it was a grave they had found, not just a jumbled rubbish heap of bones.

She got dressed in jeans and a T-shirt. She didn't even bother with shoes. She fetched the wheelbarrow and started to work. She wished her mother and aunt had told her the truth about the garden, why it was best left undisturbed. The creature that had been buried here had belonged to someone, been loved. She returned all the bones to the original site, even the bit of bone she carried in her pocket. She was especially careful with the skull. She spent the rest of the day shoveling the whole thing over with dirt and thinking about the way Johnny Mott looked at her.

She was out on her porch in her mother's favorite wicker chair, the old rifle that was usually displayed over the fireplace across her lap, when Brian came back. He was tipsy, so he squinted, not sure whether or not he was imagining the scene before him. It was August first, the day many people in town say that Louise Partridge went crazy and others say she came to her senses.

"What did you do with it?" Brian cried when he saw that the bones were missing.

"This is private property," Louise informed him. "And I will shoot you if I have to."

Brian picked up one of the rocks Louise had removed from the garden and heaved it. It went right through the living room window. The shattered glass was falling when Brian got back in his car and took off, weaving down Hubbard Street. Louise went inside for a dustpan and broom. She'd tell the museum committee that the researcher from Harvard had absconded with the skeleton in the middle of the night. Maybe when things simmered down, she'd admit that what belonged to Blackwell had stayed there.

KING OF THE BEES

THERE WAS SOME QUESTION AS TO WHETHER or not James Mott would be born. When he finally appeared, after eighteen hours of labor, his body was still and blue. There was a haunting silence, and it seemed to those in the delivery room that he wouldn't survive his birth. Then, all at once, he drew in a shuddering breath and revived. There he was, alive and well in the maternity ward at Blackwell Hospital. He never cried, but merely gazed quietly as the doctors congratulated one another, his mother's tears his first glimpse of the world.

He grew to be a big, handsome child, and although he continued to be quiet, he was ardently curious about the life he'd entered so perilously, facing it head-on. He crawled at four months and walked before his first birthday. Other children sat in front of the TV set, but James hurtled into each day. Wherever he went, he managed to find danger. His parents kept a close eye on him, but it was difficult, if not impossible, to keep track of him. When he was two, he disappeared from a family reunion, only to be found in the Eel River. His father was the one who located him. John Mott was the chief of police, as his father before him had been, and perhaps that was why he thought to follow the trail of cracker crumbs James had left behind. When John saw his son floating in the cold muddy water, he dove right in. He couldn't help but think of the Apparition, the little girl whose ghost was said to wander along the riverbanks. It was only a story, nothing more. All the same, John thought, *Not this time. Not mine.*

NO MATTER HOW his father might try to protect him, James continued to be unusually susceptible to harm. When he was six, he stumbled over a yellow jackets' nest during a kindergarten outing. It was a warm September day, the end of bee season, a time when swarms had been known to go wild. John Mott was driving through town when he heard the droning. The other children in the class had scattered safely away, but there was James, smack in the center of a yellow whirlwind, trapped inside the beating, buzzing mayhem of stingers and wings.

John left his car and raced over, tearing off his jacket as he ran, then throwing it over the boy to protect him. James was quiet in his father's arms once the whirlwind had dissipated, even though he'd been stung more than a hundred times. After being rushed to the hospital, he slipped into a coma. His parents waited outside the emergency room until the doctor at last came to tell them their son would either die of a severe allergic re-action or would be forever immune to bee stings.

James went home two days later, the raised welts on his skin the only sign of his misadventure. His parents, however, were deeply affected. After that day, John became the sort of father who was so strict and unyielding that his son had no choice but to rebel. Louise Mott joined forces with her husband, drawing up a list of house rules even she acknowledged were rigid. Num-ber one on the list was *Never Go into the Woods.* Of course James didn't comply. He disappeared the very day his mother's rules were posted on the refrigerator. Louise called for him franti-cally. She raced past the gardens, the ones that were planted, and the old garden she'd let fill with nettles and weeds, not stopping until she reached the end of the fence. There, at the edge of the woods, where the air was darkened and green with floating pol-len, huddled a group of coyotes. James was with them. Louise picked up a stone and flung it, hard, hitting one of the coyotes, scattering the group.

The very next day John Mott drove out to his cousin Mar-tha Starr's place and bought a dog. Martha raised collies, and Blackwell collies were said to possess the ability to watch over anything and anyone. John drove home with the pup asleep on his lap. He was ferocious when it came to protecting his son, and he was only too aware of the punishing ways of the world. He had witnessed too much of the grim turns human nature could take. He'd seen people unwound by fate and desire, those who had made a single bad choice, ruining their lives and the lives of everyone they loved. He'd been privy to men crying in their jail cells, begging for forgiveness, calling for their mothers, each one wishing he could rewind time and start over. John understood that some boys had to be pulled back from the brink. They might curse you, even despise you for doing so, but it took strong measures to ensure that a boy lived long enough to become a man.

JAMES NAMED HIS collie Cody, after his grandfather's dog, and preferred the collie's company to all others. The outside world continued to call to him, and he rambled more as the years went on, going farther afield, defying his parents' expectations and their rules. Tell him one thing, and he'd do the opposite. Say no, and he'd get a glimmer in his eyes. If punished, he would simply climb through his window at night, the dog leaping out behind him. Then he'd disappear at will, up to the woods, or making his way along the highway. He'd be grounded for weeks when found out, but soon enough he'd take off all over again. He fell into a sinkhole in the marshes where the mud was so deep it took five men from the Blackwell fire department to pull him out. One winter he surely would have frozen to death in a sudden snowstorm, if Cody hadn't led him to an abandoned fox den. He'd had so many close calls, he began to wonder if he was meant to be among the living. But if James was willing to accept a dismal future for himself, his father most certainly was not. John refused to give up his watch. He nailed James's bedroom window shut and put a lock on the door. It made no difference. Locks and nails could not keep his son confined. James had already decided that if he couldn't avoid his fate, he might as well enjoy what little time he had.

✎

BY THE TIME James entered high school, he and his father no longer spoke. If one walked into a room, the other walked out. His father still kept watch, but from a distance. That distance grew every day, until the only thing John Mott was watching was his son walking away from him. By then, James was six feet three, handsome, reserved, desperate to get out of Blackwell. One girl after the other fell in love with him, and in his senior year he briefly fell in love back with Brooke Linden. Brooke had a crush on him first. She was waiting for him one night when he climbed out his window, a big grin on her face. She was fun-loving, with a houseful of brothers, and danger didn't scare her. All the same, James broke up with her when he crashed his mother's car. Brooke had been his passenger, and though he might not mind endangering himself, he didn't want to hurt anyone else. Brooke didn't understand when he said he was cursed, although when he walked away, she herself threw out her own string of curses. His back was turned to her, but the words stung.

He tempted fate more than ever after that. He swam in the Eel River during the spring floods, hiked the mountain in bear season, never backed down from a fight at the Jack Straw Bar. He figured that if death was looking for him, he might as well face it head-on. As soon as he graduated he decided to move to New York City. He wanted to get as far away from Blackwell as possible and find a place where danger was an everyday occurrence. He stopped by the police station on his way out of town, his collie waiting in the car.

"What do you want me to say?" John Mott asked when James informed him he was leaving that day without a plan or any goal in mind. "Good-bye and good luck?"

"I don't believe in luck," James told him. "Not in my case."

In New York, James got a job as an orderly; then, after a year of training, he became an EMT. Every time he rode in the back of an ambulance he was reminded of the many close calls he'd had. He was serious and practical, but that wild streak ran deep. He still had an affinity for disaster and longed for the adrenaline rush of accidents. He lived for such moments, as a matter of fact. After he managed to save someone, he felt so alive and euphoric, he had to polish off three or four beers in order to calm down. On those nights, he never managed to get to sleep, and instead he went out walking. He loved New York, how it seemed to have its own heartbeat, how you could be on a crowded street and still be alone. On weekends he took Cody to Central Park, where he liked to hike through the Ramble. In the middle of the city, he was reminded of Hightop Mountain. The way the sun streaked through the trees was so similar, here and in Blackwell. The light was pure and lemon colored, and there were bees nesting in the fallen logs. When James knelt in the leaves and listened to them buzzing, he forgot all the disasters he'd witnessed, the blood and sorrow and death.

JOHN MOTT FELL ill one damp, green spring. His heart condition was unexpected and devastating, too advanced for a cure. James got the call in the middle of the night. He realized that three years had passed since he'd been home. He wondered how that had happened. Time was trickier than he'd imagined it to be. Now when he looked at his dog, he realized that Cody was suddenly old. James's mother had come to New York several times, but his father didn't like cities, or perhaps he was still unable to say good-bye.

James broke the speed limit driving up Highway 91, an edge of panic coursing through him as he crossed the Massachusetts line. He went directly to the Blackwell Hospital. It was late when he got there. He forgot how soft the nights were in Blackwell, how dark the countryside was. He was surprised by how small his hometown hospital seemed compared with the ones where he'd worked in New York City. He left his dog in the car and went inside. John Mott was asleep; there was nothing to do but wait. James went to stand against the window ledge. He felt awkward and much too big. He was used to action, not standing still. He had thought his father would look like a stranger, but he didn't. John Mott opened his eyes. He smiled when he saw James, then closed his eyes again.

When Louise arrived first thing in the morning, James was still there, sitting in a hard-backed chair. They kept a vigil together all that week and watched John Mott die. The fact that he hadn't said good-bye to his father was tearing at James. He wanted to get drunk, run away, jump in the Eel River, but he did none of these things. He only left the hospital to go out and feed Cody, then walk him through the woods beside the parking lot. That's where he was when his father died. When he went back to the room, John Mott was already gone. His mother said, "He loved you best of all," but that only made things worse. James did go out and get drunk that night, at the Jack Straw Bar and Grill. He had the sort of expression on his face that made people avoid him. His old girlfriend, Brooke Linden, was there with a crowd of her friends. She came up and told him she'd heard about his father and wanted to say how sorry she was. John Mott had busted her youngest brother when the boy was a teenager, slinking around town committing petty robberies, something James didn't know.

"Where was I when that happened?" he asked.

"Too self-involved to notice," Brooke replied. "My brother teaches middle school in Lenox now. He'll be at the funeral. Your dad totally turned his life around."

"Really? He was completely absent from mine."

James seemed angry and dangerous, but he wasn't. He was falling apart. He went home with Brooke, who was divorced and had a little boy who was off spending the night at her mother's place. James cried in her bed and told her that he was a monster who should have died a long time ago. He said things he shouldn't have and made a fool of himself.

In the morning, he woke in the dark and took off before Brooke awoke. He'd left Cody at his mother's house, but the arthritic dog had managed to jump out the window, as he used to in the old days, and was waiting for James in Brooke's yard. James bent to pet his dog's head. He felt rescued by the collie, as he had been many times before. They walked home through the fields. It was the time of year when the apple trees were in bloom and bees were everywhere. Blackwell seemed the same as it always had, only emptier, as if someone had drilled a hole in the center of it and siphoned out its heart. James made all the arrangements for his father's funeral. He bought a suit for the occasion. Brooke was among the mourners, along with her brother, Andy, who came to shake James's hand and offer his condolences. John Mott was beloved in Blackwell, and nearly the whole town attended the service. Neighbors James barely remembered came up to him with tears in their eyes. More than three hundred people signed the guest book, too many to have at the house, so the funeral supper was held in the old town hall. When James went outside to get some air, Brooke was leaving.

"You could have said good-bye before you disappeared to New York," she told him. She had her son with her. "This is Arthur." She introduced him to James. "I named him after my grandfather." Her son looked to be about four years old. James shook the little boy's hand. Arthur had something to say, and James bent to hear him.

"People die," Arthur said, sounding sure of himself. He was a quiet boy, prone to getting into trouble without looking for it. At present he had twelve stitches in his scalp from the week before when he'd climbed up a tall ladder set outside the AtoZ Market and fallen on his head.

"So it seems," James responded sadly.

"Then where do they go?" Arthur wanted to know.

"You're asking the wrong person," James admitted.

JAMES SPENT THE summer in Blackwell, helping his mother clear out the cellar and the garage. He felt lost, as if he'd fallen through that hole he imagined in the center of town. Some mornings when he woke up he didn't know what year it was. Some nights he got so drunk he couldn't find his way home.

Brooke started coming over and he found himself looking forward to her visits, and also to Arthur's. Then one day he saw Arthur on the floor, curled up next to old Cody, and he knew. He did the math and couldn't believe he hadn't figured it out before. He asked Brooke why she'd never contacted him. He thought he'd had a right to know that Arthur was his son, but Brooke shrugged. "You didn't seem interested. You were done with me, so I didn't tell you."

CODY DIED NOT long after. He was so old by then that during his last week, James had to carry him outside in the mornings so he could pee. Then the collie stopped eating. James set up a box lined with blankets for his dog when he didn't seem to want to do anything but sleep. He died there, next to James's bed. It was still dark when James lifted the dog's body out to take him into the garden. They had been together since James was ten, and he couldn't remember how it felt to live his life without his dog. He kept thinking he saw the collie from the corner of his eye, even though he knew that was impossible. He thought about Arthur and the question he had asked about where people went and how small his voice had been.

He buried Cody in the southwest corner of the old garden, where it was said only red plants would grow. When he was done, he kept digging. He worked in the garden all week. It was as if once he'd begun, he simply couldn't stop. He tilled the soil, moved rocks, put up a new fence, laid down fertilizer. He had perennials and shrubs delivered and planted each one. He wouldn't have bothered to eat, but his mother brought his meals outside on a tray, fixing him sandwiches and carrot sticks, the way she had when he was a boy. She sat on a metal chair and gazed into the woods. Louise said she'd fallen in love with John Mott when she'd planted this garden, long ago. She'd always imagined the plants turned red because everything she felt had gone into them. She couldn't hide her love away and so there it was for all to see.

James worked in the rain and the heat. He didn't shower and was soon covered with red dirt. He hardly took the time to sleep. Whenever his mother called out that Brooke was on the phone, he said he didn't have time to talk. He was trying to figure out what to do next. He was thinking about his father on the last day he'd seen him before he took off for New York. He wished he had done something for his father, just once in his life, but he didn't know what that might have been, they'd been so far apart. Then one morning he looked up from the row of tomatoes he was putting in and there was Arthur. He'd climbed out his bedroom window and found his way across town. Arthur was standing outside the fence throwing stones into the woods. His mother had told him about the dog.

James went over to him. "Your mom's going to be worried," he said gently.

"I wanted to see where Cody was."

James took the boy into the garden to show him the spot where he'd buried the dog.

"That's where you go when you're dead," Arthur said solemnly.

"Your body goes into the ground."

Arthur thought that over. It wasn't a satisfactory answer. "Your body isn't all of you." He stood there stiffly. "I can hear him breathing," he declared. His voice was breaking, but he sounded convinced.

"I don't think so," James said. "Cody's quiet now."

But there was a sound. It wasn't Cody; it was something entirely different. It was the beehive Arthur had hit while flinging stones. The bees had been disturbed, and now they swarmed toward the garden in a funnel-shaped cloud. James remembered that sound from the time when his father had raced across the meadow toward him and covered him with his jacket. James grabbed Arthur and ran. The swarm followed in a fury, so James kept running, through the fields. He heard ragged breathing, his own and Arthur's. He batted bees away when they tried to land on the child, and he didn't feel a thing when they stung him. When he had no choice and the steep riverbank was before them, James leapt into the Eel River, the boy in his arms. They went into the cold water, then resurfaced, sputtering and safe from harm. James thought about the garden, with soil so red it seemed to have a bloody, beating heart. He thought about where it was people went when they died, and how when he squinted he could see Cody, racing back and forth, barking, how his father seemed to stand right there on the riverbank, turning back the bees, closer than he'd ever been before.

Acknowledgments

WITH GRATITUDE TO John Glusman and to Shaye Areheart.

Many thanks to Elaine Markson for her continuing generosity. Thanks to Gary Johnson and everyone at the Markson Thoma Agency, to Maggie Stern Terris for many kindnesses, and to the editors of the magazines where sections of this book appeared.

WRITTEN WITH LOVE for my family, and for my father, who told me my first story.

The
RED GARDEN

Broadway Books Reader's Guide

ALICE HOFFMAN never fails to enchant us with magical worlds and extraordinary lives. With *The Red Garden*, her thirtieth work of fiction, she transports us to Blackwell, Massachusetts, weaving centuries of intriguing family history with extraordinary legends. From the town's founder—a woman of startling strength and fearlessness—to the many descendants who perpetuate her experience of endurance and wonder, alongside a slew of mysterious visitors (including Johnny Appleseed and Emily Dickinson), the characters inhabiting Blackwell face unique hardships and triumphs, making choices that echo throughout the lives of future residents.

As the Bradys, the Partridges, the Starrs, and the Motts make their home in a region marked by breathtaking beauty as well as brutally harsh winters, hungry bears, and an unpredictable landscape that has the power to take the lives of the most innocent among them, the rites of humanity take on new significance. We meet poets, preachers, actors, fishermen, teachers, many of them harvesting hope—perhaps to find love, or to become a parent, or to ease the memory of faraway trauma. As their fates intertwine, their sensuous storylines blend seamlessly with the natural world around them. And in a corner of the town lies a timeless garden, where sorrows are buried in curious red soil.

Moving, suspenseful, and beautifully wrought, *The Red Garden* is a masterwork of great American storytelling.

Questions for Discussion

1. Hallie Brady's story sets the stage, featuring a woman whose strength exceeds her husband's and whose best source of solace and nourishment is a bear. What does the tale of Bearsville tell us about nature and survival? How do Harry's actions reflect the dilemmas portrayed in the rest of the book?

2. Enhance your reading with a bit of research on the real John "Johnny Appleseed" Chapman. What makes him the ideal savior of the fictional Minette?

3. Though she is not rescued in "The Year There Was No Summer," Amy Starr reappears for future generations. What does her ghost signify to you? Did she liberate Mary by uniting her with Yaron?

4. Like Hoffman's character named Emily, poet Emily Dickinson did not complete her course of study at Mount Holyoke Female Seminary. What does Charles Straw awaken in his young visitor? How does he help her become a "voyager" like him?

5. "The River at Home" captures both the untold suffering and the healing that marked the home front during the Civil War and its aftermath. What ultimately restores Evan and Mattie?

6. In "The Truth About My Mother," how does Blackwell contrast with the modern world? What ultimately ensures that the characters can replace suffering with joy?

7. At the beginning of "The Principles of Devotion," Azurine says Sara taught her that "a woman who could rescue herself was a woman who would never be in need." Do you agree? Are most of the people in your life able to rescue themselves, or do they need others to rescue them? What separates the survivors from the victims in *The Red Garden*?

8. Discuss both Topsys: the brutalized Coney Island elephant (inspired by true, horrific events) and the dog that sustains Sara. Is the special relationship between humans and nonhuman creatures in *The Red Garden* magical or realistic?

9. "The Fisherman's Wife" showcases the Eel River and its hardy inhabitants in a dramatic way. What does this story tell us about fantastic storytelling, as Ben Levy required? What does the wife's tale tell us about hunger in its many forms?

10. Discuss the many types of love that emerge in "Kiss and Tell." Although Hannah has to hide the truth about her romantic feelings, she is able to realize her dream of raising a child. In

what ways does history repeat itself through the story of Blackwell?

11. Blackwell is home to many outcasts seeking a new identity, but the townspeople often fail to identify their own "monsters." How did you respond to the tale of Cal, whom Kate saves, versus Matthew, whose heart she steals? How are evil and injustice born in Blackwell?

12. "Sin" captures the transient figures (family as well as friends) who shape a lifetime. Frank's reunion with Jessie sparks memories but also raises a question: Who were the truly good people in their lives?

13. What does Louise Partridge inherit other than a house? How did you react when Brian, the Harvard researcher she requested, was disappointed to find only bear bones? What stories, emotions, and experiences were planted and harvested in the red garden?

14. James Mott seems cursed, yet he is also a healer. What is the role of fate in lives like his? Was he destined to succeed? Could you relate to the closing scene, in which James is watched over by his father and Cody? Do you feel protected by the spirit of loved ones who have passed away?

15. Which characters were you most drawn to? How would you have fared in their situation? What did you discover about life and history by reading their stories?

16. Discuss other Hoffman works you've read. What themes (perhaps of family, new identities, or the power of magical hope) echo throughout her previous books and *The Red Garden*? What unique vision of the human experience is presented in *The Red Garden*?

An Interview with Alice Hoffman

BROADWAY BOOKS: In an essay for young readers, collected in *33 Things Every Girl Should Know*, you describe the healing power of books, something you experienced during your turbulent childhood. You write, "Often the people who succeed, in spite of the difficulties they may face, have one thing in common. They read.... They have hope because they know that once upon a time there was a boy or a girl, a woman or a man, who managed to survive." Are all of the protagonists in *The Red Garden* survivors, even if they perish physically?

ALICE HOFFMAN: I think I am always writing about survivors. I'm in awe of how people manage to experience great loss and continue on, and how some, like Hallie Brady, the founder of Blackwell, refuse to give up and perish even when faced by the wilderness. On a personal note, as a breast cancer survivor I am even more drawn to characters who manage to survive despite great odds.

There is a sense that the characters in *The Red Garden* manage to "survive" even when they perish if their stories are told and remembered, as is the case with the little drowned girl who becomes the Apparition. Her personal story becomes a shared story. That is the power of history and of storytelling.

BB: *The Red Garden* contains intricate genealogies. Did you create family trees before you began writing this book, or did the intertwining families emerge during the writing process?

AH: I had no idea how intertwined the families would become or how little some of the characters would know of their own heritage. I didn't write the book consecutively, and was often surprised by how interrelated people in Blackwell were. I did a family tree when the book was complete, and discovered that in essence it was a "town tree"—I suppose it was Blackwell's tree of life.

BB: While writing *Here on Earth,* you cared for your beloved sister-in-law and your mother as they faced terminal illness. After the novel was published, you were diagnosed with breast cancer. How have these experiences shaped the way you perceive serious illness, and the way you write about it?

AH: I think that for anyone who experiences a grave, potentially life-threatening illness there is a "before" and an "after." There is a distinct sense that there is a "final chapter" to all stories and for all lives and a sense of how important it is to do what truly matters most, both in fiction and in life.

BB: Most of *The Red Garden* tales are written in the third person. What led you to shift to first person for "The Truth About My Mother"?

AH: Often point of view is not a decision for me—a story or a novel comes with its own voice. In the case of "The Truth About My Mother" the ten-year-old narrator began to tell the story. I heard it in her voice, with details and language she chose. It's a very personal story, and I think the intimacy comes from the voice. Because of this, I became so attached to this character, I included her in the following story, for she seemed someone who was wise beyond her years, and I wanted to follow her into adulthood.

BB: *The Red Garden* is rich with fascinating historical details. What were your favorite research sources?

AH: I loved looking for recipes, plants, clothing—domestic details that would enrich the world of Blackwell throughout the decades. In a way, I built the town and so I needed to research what houses were like during various periods in New England, and the ways in which one house in particular might have changed throughout the years. I also read about eels, bears, Johnny Appleseed, weather patterns, and anything else that would help me understand the town and its history.

BB: Reviewers usually mention the magical realism that permeates your work. Are you comfortable with the term "magical realism"? Does magical living exist only in fiction?

AH: For me literature is magic, and magic is part of the original literary tradition, whether it be mythology, folk tales, fairy tales, ghost stories, the stories of Kafka or Washington Irving—all of it can be found in the greatest literature. I think of "realism" as being "imposed" on fiction—after all, this is not real life, it is art, and art consists of imagination and experience—the recipe for magic. "Magical realism" is a new term for an ancient tradition.

BB: What was it like to grow up on Long Island? Were your childhood neighborhoods anything like Blackwell?

AH: I grew up in a concrete suburb carved out of what had been a potato farm, and like much of the housing built for returning GIs after World War II, every house looked the same, and trees were all newly planted. I yearned to live in a small town, in a Victorian one-of-a-kind house, like the one in *It's a Wonderful Life*—one of my favorite films. When I tell people there was magic everywhere in the neighborhood where I grew up, they find it hard to believe. But it was there, most often to be found in the library.

BB: Ancestry shapes the storyline of *The Red Garden*. Is your family history steeped in lore? Which of your ancestors has intrigued you the most?

AH: History is built out of family stories. My Russian grandmother told me tales of growing up in a tiny village where she could hear the wolves howling all night and where the river froze solid for months until one day it melted all at once. Her stories inspired me, as did her life as an immigrant.

BB: You dedicated this book to Albert Guerard, your mentor at

Stanford. What was the best advice he gave you when you were an aspiring writer?

AH: Albert Guerard was a truly great teacher, writer, and critic, and I was so lucky to have known him and studied with him. He was a great believer in "Voice" and felt that a writer's voice was made up of childhood experiences and readings, dreams, and adult experience. Every writer's voice was unique and original, much like a fingerprint, and if one could tap into one's true voice every story would ring true. He also gave me the freedom to write not what I "knew" and had experienced, but what I felt. Great advice.

BB: Your writing spans a vast array of locales and time periods, from a contemporary *Wuthering Heights* to sisters who may have witchcraft in their genes. How many story ideas do you have at any given moment? What would you like to write about next?

AH: Although I believe every writer has themes that emerge from his or her work, each new book is an adventure for me. My next novel, *The Dovekeepers*, takes place in 70 CE during the fall of Jerusalem and at Masada, the fortress in the Judean desert. It's a complete departure for me in terms of the time period, yet my interest in love and loss, in survivors and in history, is still at the core of my writing life.

About the Author

ALICE HOFFMAN is the bestselling author of more than twenty-five acclaimed novels, including *The Story Sisters, The Third Angel, The Ice Queen, Practical Magic, Here on Earth, The River King,* and *Skylight Confessions.* She has also written two books of short stories, and eight books for children and young adults. Her work has been translated into more than twenty languages and published in more than one hundred foreign editions.

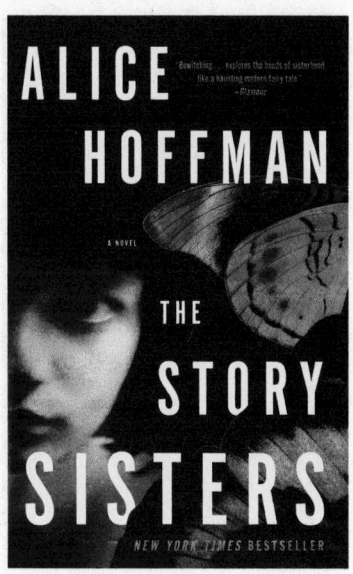

"Hoffman's characters are always moving back and forth, challenging our perceptions, daring us to judge them. Her sentences tremble with allegory. . . . In the end, *The Story Sisters,* for all its magic realism, is about a family navigating through motherhood, sisterhood, daughterhood. It's *Little Women* on mushrooms. (Bookish sisters beware)."

—*New York Times Book Review*

The Story Sisters
A NOVEL
$15.00 (Canada: $17.50)
978-0-307-40596-8

"Like Michael Cunningham's *The Hours,* Hoffman's tale
weaves the stories of women at key moments in their lives
with revelations both stunning and inevitable."

—*Pittsburgh Post-Gazette*

The Third Angel
A NOVEL
$14.95 (Canada: $16.95)
978-0-307-40595-1

Available from Broadway Paperbacks wherever books are sold.